BY

P. H. Newby

THE RETREAT (1953)

A SEASON IN ENGLAND (1952)

THE YOUNG MAY MOON (1951)

AGENTS AND WITNESSES (1947)

A JOURNEY TO THE INTERIOR (1946)

THE

RETREAT

THE
RETREAT

BY

P. H. NEWBY

NEW YORK

ALFRED A. KNOPF

1953

L. C. catalog card number: 52–12202

THIS IS A BORZOI BOOK
PUBLISHED BY ALFRED A. KNOPF, INC.

FIRST AMERICAN EDITION

THE

RETREAT

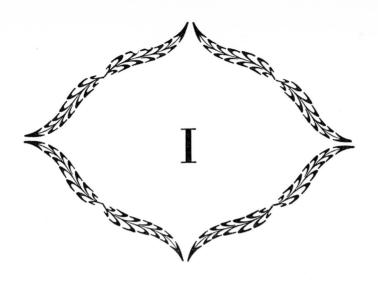

I

Towards the end of May, 1940, the military sub-area of Dieppe ceased to be a medical base. It became a battle-ground. Hospital patients were sent away by ship, by train, and by ambulance; but there was not enough transport for everyone and many patients were told to make their way south on foot. Dieppe itself was their immediate objective.

In this way, F/O Knight of the Nth Fighter Squadron, reasonably fit once more after losing his appendix, found himself walking through the village of Criel-sur-Mer. His only luggage was a small leather suitcase—officers' kit had gone ahead by lorry—and because the

3

sun shone, and because he was on the move once more, he felt happy. For company he had about thirty V.D. patients with greatcoats over their hospital blue. There were medical orderlies staggering along in full marching order, some of them with tins of pears, bottles of Guinness and other oddments they had sensibly plundered from the hospital stores; if their kit-bags were full, they carried the stuff in their hands. An R.A.M.C. warrant-officer tried to establish march discipline, but without success. The men were out on a spree. Some, planning short cuts, dumped equipment and made off in small groups across the fields.

Knight quickly came to the conclusion that a mere R.A.F. officer like himself had no hope of exercising any authority. At that time the R.A.F. was despised. Way ahead was the main road, crowded with refugee traffic from Belgium and the Pas de Calais. Knight decided it was every man for himself. Accordingly he left the by-road he had been following, climbed a gate and made his way to the edge of the cliff. Mail had been distributed before they left the hospital and now he wanted to sit down and read the two letters he had received. They were both written before the German break-through at Sedan.

"*My darling husband,*" he read. The perfection of the expression struck him. What more could possibly be said? Everything coming between those words and the conclusion: "*I am quite well and love you more than I can say, Helen,*" was—as always—so exciting, so disturbing that he could never read her letters in detail. She took pains with them. She had even bought a dictionary to correct her spelling. But the stuff of her letters, the little bits of news, her endearingly hopeful prophecies, her jokes, made her presence so real that he was tormented. There were men who dwelt on every word that their wives wrote. If Knight did that he was shaken for days. The parting was bearable only if the image of Helen was not vividly before him. He skipped sentences and even whole paragraphs out of self-protection. She had been to the theatre with Prudence— her father had quite recovered from that chill—something about an increase in officers' allowances. One thing was clear: this was a very old letter indeed; it was written before she had heard of his appendicitis. Impulsively he raised the letter to his lips; then rolled it into a ball and tossed it over the cliff.

The crowded Dieppe road was a mile away. The sun flashed on the wind-screens of the crawling traffic. Many of the cars were nearly as high again with cases, bedding, and even furniture; a surprising number of them were distinctive with red blankets—why, he could not imagine. There was no chance of begging a lift on one of those overcrowded vehicles. Even if he went down to the road—which, after all, marked the shortest route to Dieppe—the three lines of traffic, all going one way, would make it difficult for walking. There was, too, the chance of strafing. It would be possible to make his way to Dieppe along the cliffs, but the coast was indented, and the twenty miles of the journey would be increased to thirty, or even more. It would, too, probably involve him in climbing, and the two weeks he had spent on his back had not prepared him for anything so strenuous. The best plan would be to cross the main road and see what the country on the other side had to offer.

Suddenly, every car on the road (it seemed) began an indignant, nasal, continental hooting. There was a hold-up. Drivers climbed out and stood on their running-boards. At the cross-roads a farm cart was broadside on to the stream of traffic. A middle-aged Norman in blue overalls had decided his load of pig manure could wait no longer, and indifferent to the abuse, he had driven his grey mare in front of an enormous removal van from Antwerp. He sat on one of the shafts, a cigarette in the corner of his mouth, the reins gathered in his left hand. He laid his right hand on the mare's flank and spoke quietly, urging the beast forward.

Knight saw a British rifleman sitting in the front seat of an overcrowded taxi.

"Going far?" he asked.

The rifleman was exhausted. He spoke without moving his head.

"I hurt me leg."

"What's the news?"

"Jerry's sending tanks into Abbeville."

"Abbeville?"

"Fast, little tanks. I still got my rifle."

"Good for you."

The hold-up did at least make it possible for Knight to cross the road. On the other side was open, undulating country with a belt of woodland in the distance. By this time the farm cart had won free of the refugee traffic and was trundling down a lane in the direction of a small village, just a handful of cottages and a church. It was difficult to say whether the reverberation came from north, south, east, or west. At one moment the sound appeared to travel in from the sea. Knight began to walk quickly. The sight of the cart had given him an idea.

His only doubt had been about his ability to explain himself in French; but now the man had set the mare to a trot. Once they disappeared round the bend in the lane the question was whether or not Knight would ever set eyes on them again. He could not afford to hurry. If the worst came to the worst and he had to walk all the way to Dieppe in his present weakened state he would have to conserve his strength.

But for two ducks on a pond there was no sign of life in the village. On the other side of the church there was a sound as though an unusually heavy barrel were being rolled about a cellar. The door of a café stood invitingly open, and Knight, after a moment's hesitation, entered and placed his suitcase on one of the bare tables. At the very least they could supply him with coffee.

"Hallo, there!" he shouted. "Hallo!"

But the silence seemed only the heavier. Even the distant bombardment had ceased.

"Hallo, there!"

Perhaps the village had been evacuated. He was about to walk into the back room when a black saloon-car drove into the village and halted between the pond and the wall of the churchyard. Half a dozen nuns climbed out, two carrying a large basket. Without so much as a word they seated themselves on the grass and prepared to picnic. The picture was as beautiful as it was unexpected. The landscape had fallen into a pattern of grey stone, blue water, green grass, black gowns, and starched white wings about pale faces.

"*Des allemands!*" breathed a voice at his shoulder.

Knight turned to see a middle-aged woman with a tray pressed flat against her breast. He had enough French to know that she was saying the nuns were Germans and that as he was an English officer he should go and ask for their identity cards. Then he remembered the stories of German paratroopers disguised as nuns. He also remembered that he was unarmed.

"Coffee, *café*" he said. "*Vous êtes seule, madame?*"

"*Allez-y, monsieur. Ceux sont des allemands, je vous dis!*"

There was an ambiguous expression on the woman's face. He even wondered—for it was a naturally merry face—whether she was pulling his leg. One thing seemed certain. He would get no refreshment until he had spoken to the nuns.

He stepped into the sunlight and began to walk towards the picnickers. All six heads were immediately turned in his direction, all six medieval faces watched him without surprise or alarm. A hand holding a tomato was arrested in mid air, a roll lay where it had fallen in the dust. Knight was keenly aware of the woman watching from the room behind.

"Good morning," he said in English after a pause. He saluted the nuns and walked down the road out of the village. No sooner was he sure of being out of sight than he began laughing, a little hysterically. He leaned on a gate and laughed at the dust between his feet. He had funked tackling the nuns not because he feared they were German soldiers; he had funked tackling them because he feared they would turn out to be nuns after all and that they would consider him discourteous. He might so easily have made a fool of himself.

Then he discovered that he had left his case in the café. The impossibility of going back and explaining his conduct to the Frenchwoman was the final absurdity. He marched on with his hands thrust into his trousers pockets.

"You all right, sir?"

He awoke among feathered grasses in full sunlight.

"Eh? What's that? What d'you say?"

"Are you all right?"

Knight sat up. He squinted at the great shape that had now moved between him and the sky and saw that it was the R.A.M.C. warrant-officer. He was wearing his steel helmet and red-cross brassard. Knight yawned.

"Must have dozed off."

"You a patient from the hospital, sir?"

Knight nodded and the warrant-officer began swearing.

"I call it a bloody shame. D'you know how many ambulances went off packed with officers' and sisters' kit? Six of them! I call it a bloody shame telling you to walk when they send officers' kit in ambulances."

"That's all right. You know, I never know what to call you fellows in the army."

"My name's Mace."

"Where are the rest of your men?"

"Making for Dieppe, I hope. They're as raw as you make 'em. Militiamen."

When Knight rose to his feet his first thought was for the two letters, one read, the other unread, he had received that morning. He put a hand into his jacket pocket, and there they were.

"Hallo! Trouble over there!" he said, nodding towards the south. A column of black smoke stood up as firm as a finger.

"They've been giving Dieppe a packet."

"D'you know what I'd like to do?" said Knight, as they walked along the lane. "If I had enough money I'd buy a horse and cart from one of these farmers. As a matter of fact, I was following one of them. But I don't suppose five quid's worth of francs would buy a horse and cart in the present state of the market."

The short sleep had refreshed him. The pain in his side, too, had gone.

"I've got fifty thousand francs in my valise," said Mace. "It's the company imprest account."

"You have? Good for you. We'll have quite a time with that before we're through. There they go!"

The morning was so clear they could pick out the German bomber formation which must have been well over the Channel. Near at hand someone began winding a wooden rattle and a Messerschmidt, its swastikas staring, flipped over the trees and climbed rapidly. The two men lay in the ditch, listening.

"Bugger this for a lark, sir."

"He's not bothering about us."

"What the hell's happening, that's what I can't make out, sir. D'you think we've had it?"

"I'm no general, Mace, but my guess is Jerry's going to get his water cut off if he drives for these Channel ports. D'you see what I mean? My guess is that the British and the French will link up across his line of communications. Perhaps I ought to be a general, after all."

"Well, I hope you're right, sir. But I'd still like to get to Dieppe before Jerry does."

"Let's go and buy that horse and cart out of your imprest account."

They walked in the direction of the column of smoke until it had died down and their shadows were falling on their left. The silence and the serenity of the day were puzzling. They could see and hear nothing of the main stream of refugee traffic because the Dieppe road lay on the other side of an extended line of low hills. But here in the open country there was no work going on in the fields and the two farm-houses they met with were locked up and apparently deserted. Knight tried to milk a cow into Mace's steel helmet, the only container available to them. They had trapped the beast in the corner of a field, but although their hopes ran high when they saw the smooth tightness of the cow's bag, Knight did not have the knack of manipulating the teats. He hurt the beast. It kicked out and as Knight staggered backwards made its escape. They found a pump in a cottage yard and were just about to work it when a tall, thin woman in blue rushed out, her face flaming with indignation.

"What's she say, sir?" said Mace.

"She wants to know why we're retreating."

"I'm not retreating. I'm trying to make myself scarce."

"*Peut-être, madame, vous avez un cheval que vous pourriez nous vendre.*"

"What's going on now, sir?"

Knight had to speak above the torrent of words that his question had provoked.

"I asked if she'd got a horse to sell, but I'm afraid it's no go."

"You're not serious about paying for it out of the imprest account? I'm afraid I couldn't have that, sir. I shall have to hand it over at Dieppe. Besides, one horse wouldn't be much good."

"Have you never seen two men on a horse, Mace?"

The woman suddenly burst into a sobbing that was as violent as her indignation. She stood with her arms rigidly at her sides, the tears flooding from her eyes.

"*Madame,*" said Knight tenderly, "*ce n'est pas la retraite. Nous retournerons.* . . . Poor old girl, she's thoroughly upset. Thinks we're cowards."

Mace stared at her, frowning. He opened his valise and produced a tin of bully beef which he firmly pressed into the woman's hand.

"*Nous retournerons, madame,*" said Knight as they

went out of the gate, "*je vous promis. Ce n'est pas une vraie retraite.*"

"What she wants," said Mace as they walked on, "is a nice holiday at the seaside. That would buck her up in no time. Not that the war isn't troublesome in itself."

"Are you married?"

"Too true. Couple of daughters, both good girls. You married, sir?"

Knight did not answer immediately. Marriage was an inadequate word for the link between Helen and himself. For the lack of a more expressive word he did not know what to say.

"Yes, I've got a wife," he murmured, more to himself than to Mace.

Helen was so much his wife that her absence gave curious drama to the landscape. Normandy was a stage, and every step he took was a step in an over-rehearsed play; the great, romantic play of war as he had studied it in the books and films, the conversation of older men, and the solemn fascination of veterans in the streets on Armistice Day. This march through the hot May afternoon had an old heroism about it; boots had slogged through mud and dust, men had advanced and retreated, singing: *Pack up your troubles.* Now it was his turn. Helen was safe at home. He watched himself by the light of her love, and would have wished his danger all the greater.

"Yes, I'm married," Knight said again. He did not realize it was for the second time.

It was three o'clock in the afternoon by Mace's

watch. With reasonable luck they would be in Dieppe by dusk, but Mace said he happened to know there was no transport out of the town before the following morning. Their best plan would be to spend the night under a haystack. Jerry was sure to knock hell out of the docks as soon as it was dark, and what was the point of running into that?

"What I want is a hot bath," said Knight. "I think I'll make for Dieppe."

Neither of them was hungry, but they each drank a tin of chicken essence Mace had collected from the hospital stores before leaving. For the first time they came on British troops moving north; there were three armoured cars and six truck-loads of infantry with net over their steel helmets. A major in the first armoured car stood up and took their salute gravely, as though he were on ceremonial parade. The men were drowsy and silent, but when Knight and Mace climbed out of the ditch after the convoy had passed, a wit in the last truck caught sight of them and made some remark. Dust hung in the air. Laughter drifted back.

"To tell you the truth, sir, I can't go into Dieppe without the rest of the company. There'd be hell to pay if I was to walk in by myself. You know, there's a water-tower at the side of the road just before you go down the hill into Dieppe. I said I'd be there at nine tonight, and heaven help anybody who wasn't!"

"That's a bit unorthodox, isn't it?"

"I'm not a soldier. I got called up because I was in the St. John's Ambulance. My job's mental nursing.

The ser'nt-major's a soldier but he cleared off with the C.O. in an ambulance. You see what I mean? Bless you Jack, I'm fire-proof!"

"What about your other officers?"

"We're a hospital unit. All our officers are medical specialists. Much too valuable to run any danger, so they were sent off—them and all the sisters—to Le Mans a couple of days ago."

"That's bad."

"Bad? It's bloody disgusting. Of course, when I said I wasn't a soldier I didn't mean to say I hadn't been in the army before. I did my seven years. I did three years in Egypt, and by God! I wish I was there now. Sweet Fanny Adams to do in the afternoon, you know, except sleep and burn the bugs off your bed with a blow-lamp. I wouldn't mind Egypt for the duration. I'm too old for soldiering. I'm forty-five."

"Would you wait here for me a minute?"

"O.K.," said Mace, thinking that Knight wanted to relieve himself. Mace was carrying so much equipment that he had to be cautious in sitting down, and by the time he had settled himself on a heap of gravel, Knight was out of sight. A white butterfly emerged from the hedge and as Mace lazily followed its flight with his eyes his attention was suddenly caught by movement on the slope of a neighbouring hill. It was, to Mace's surprise, Knight himself—he was about a hundred yards away and climbing steadily towards a copse of beeches. Mace was puzzled. Perhaps the fellow had taken it into his head to do a little reconnoitring. But when, after a brief glance backwards, Knight climbed a fence and disappeared among the trees, Mace grunted.

"Bit fancy in his habits, isn't he?" he said, loud enough to be heard on the other side of the hedge. He was sweating more profusely now than at any time since they had started and he loosened the fastening at the throat of his battle dress.

"Ahoy!" he shouted, some minutes later, but there was no reply from the wood. Mace rolled gently sideways down the heap of gravel until he was on his knees. From this position he levered himself to his feet and stood squinting about in the brilliant sunshine.

"Ahoy!" he shouted again, because Knight had been gone at least ten minutes, and Mace was quickly working himself up to a state of mingled anger and fear. Perhaps the fellow did not intend coming back.

Mace was going to shout once more. Then he thought: "No, better not. You never know who's about." It occurred to him that maybe this R.A.F. officer was a fifth columnist. Some of these Germans spoke damn good English. He stood so that a gate took some of the weight of his equipment, wondering whether he ought to go up into the wood to see if the fellow was sending messages. But how could he, a non-combatant with a red cross on his arm, get mixed up in that sort of thing? It would be against the Geneva Conventions. Perhaps the fellow had been taken ill; after all he was supposed to be convalescent. But the immediate question was whether or not to go up into the wood.

"Ah!" said Mace, standing up. Knight had come out into the sunlight once more and was looking round as though to see whether he was under observation. He waved a hand at Mace and plunged down the hill. Yet when he climbed the gate and stood in the roadway with sweat on his face, he did not say a word. Fatigue showed in his pallor: it had the effect of making him appear even younger than his twenty-one or -two years.

"You've been a long time," said Mace, deliberately dropping the "sir."

Knight clapped his cap on his head and gave the warrant-officer a nod, as though to say: "Let's go!" and set off down the road. Mace came up by his side and automatically skipped to get in step.

"D'you see anything from up there?" He repeated the question, but Knight still did not appear to hear; his head stuck forward, he watched the road about six yards ahead. So far as he was concerned, Mace might not have existed.

The sun had westered sufficiently for them to be dogged by shadows bigger than themselves, and they were near enough to the Dieppe road to hear the whine of traffic through the trees. A dozen or so British soldiers had taken their equipment off and were washing their feet in a brook.

"So that's where you are," said Mace.

One of the men jumped up.

"What ho! Quarter!"

They were, all of them, orderlies from the hospital, the very men Mace had been trying to discipline that morning. They clustered round with tiny wisps of vapour rising from their naked feet.

"There's a chap gone up in those bushes with a gun," said one of the men, a nervous cockney. He offered Mace a cigarette with as much seriousness as if it were drill. Mace refused and the cockney offered a cigarette to Knight, who shook his head.

"What the hell d'you mean?" said Mace, flying into a temper. "Now come on, the lot of you! Get your kit on! D'you hear me? What d'you mean, there's a man with a gun up in the woods?"

"Infantry chap," said somebody.

"Queen's," said another. "He was wearing badges. Just an ordinary swaddy. Said the Germans had got an armoured column across the Dieppe road."

"Said it was hopeless to make for Dieppe. He was off to the beach."

"I'll give you all two minutes by my watch to get fell in up here on this road," Mace shouted. "You're going to march into Dieppe if you march through the whole bloody German army."

"It's nonsense about the armoured column," said Knight, speaking for the first time in an hour. "The nearest German on the ground is over thirty miles away." Q.M.S. Mace flushed as though the news came as a personal insult.

"How the hell d'you know that?" All the resentment of Knight that had been gathering force during the last hour now found expression. As the men put their boots on and buckled into their equipment he swung on Knight. "What makes you think you know where Jerry is or where he isn't?"

"Common sense and a knowledge of the country," said Knight calmly. He had recovered some of his earlier jauntiness of manner. "Want to make anything of it?"

"I want to know what you were doing up in that wood for twenty minutes this afternoon."

"Reading a letter from home. Is that all right with you?"

"Fall in!" said Mace furiously to the men who were gathering around. "Come on, let's have three ranks! Jennings, you're marker."

The little party swung along the lane with Mace and Knight at their head. Every shrub, leaf, stick, and stone was sharp in the thin light. The traffic was nearer and deeper toned. Remote but profound concussions shook the air, and there was a scarcely realized yearning in the hearts of all the marching men for the sight of other people. The lane rose so steeply in front of them it appeared to break off against the sky. A rabbit scuttered from behind a bush. Mace started, and swore.

"I was telling you the truth," said Knight. "I was reading a letter from a friend of mine. His wife's had a baby, born dead."

Mace made no reply. He averted his head and tramped on in silence until he suddenly turned and shouted at the men to march like soldiers and not like a lot of jockeys. He was still angry.

Cloud came swiftly out of the west and shortened the day. They were still three miles from Dieppe when a green dusk fell. Traffic on the main road had slackened considerably—indeed many of the vehicles were pulled off the road so that their occupants could sleep —and when Mace's party emerged from their lane they were able to make good progress in two single columns, one on the left side of the road, the other on the right. Miserably out of training as they were, the men plodded along in silence, fatigued to the point where some of them could scarcely put one foot in front of another. Figures, singly and in groups, appeared out of the dank landscape and as quickly made off across the fields in the direction of farm buildings and woods where they might shelter for the night. It was pleasanter for walking because the moist air had settled the dust.

Knight was in the lead of the right-hand column. Twice he had suggested to Mace, who followed him, that they might change places so that Mace could set a more vigorous pace; but Mace said no, they were doing very well. He gave a curious lift to the words as though he intended them to carry unusual meaning— that he wanted to remain where he could keep Knight under observation, for example.

They were now at the point where all routes into Dieppe converged, and every minute or so they would be hailed from the hedge or the step of a cottage; one or other of the men would grunt an answer and the missing orderlies or patients would pick up their equipment and tag on. They passed a board at the limit of the municipality, and straight ahead made out the water-tower; it seemed, like some monstrous fungus, to lean in the darkness. Here was a car-park where families were preparing to settle down for the night; they had removed the mattresses from their cars and lorries and spread them on boards which they had plundered from a neighbouring timber store.

Knight came to a stop. All around was the sound of vehicles being manœuvred, the crying of children, and the low murmur of voices.

"What's up?" asked Mace.

"I'm going down into Dieppe. What are you going to do?" A military policeman in a white helmet and a gas-cape came up shouting: "Medical base personnel keep moving."

"Would you direct me to the nearest hotel, Corporal?" said Knight.

The M.P. came over and peered at him. He saw the wings on his breast. "Christ, beg pardon, sir! I thought somebody was taking the mike."

They were not allowed to enter Dieppe by the main road. They tramped down silent back streets where they could smell salt water long before they could make out the masts and funnels. Guided by military police, a continuous stream of troops followed the railway lines round one of the harbour basins. There was more light here. Across the water they could see cranes, shipping, and the buildings of Dieppe itself outlined against the western sky. A goods engine, the cab rosy with fire, clanked past. When Knight stumbled over a heap of rubble he became aware that Mace was holding him by the skirt of his jacket.

A sentry with a revolver in his right hand flashed a blue light in each man's face before he was allowed to cross the lock gate by the cat-walk; the meaningless examination infuriated Knight, and when the sentry turned the light on him, he swore. He was dizzy with fatigue and lack of nourishment.

"Let me go, will you, Mace?" he said when they had crossed the dock. "Let me go, will you? What the hell's the matter with you? Gone off your head?" He tried to push Mace back, but the man only grunted.

"Keep moving there," said a brisk voice. "What's going on?"

"I want this officer interrogated," said Mace.

"Don't be such a bloody clown," said Knight. "Look here, there must be an R.A.F. mess in Dieppe. I want to get there as quickly as possible."

"I said what's going on?" said the brisk voice again.

"I want this officer interrogated."

"What d'you mean, interrogated?" The man stood so near that Knight could smell the whisky on his breath.

"I'm an Air Force officer, my name is Knight. I've just been discharged from the military hospital at Criel, I've walked all the way—most of it in the company of our friend here—and now I'd be very grateful if you could tell me where the nearest R.A.F. mess is." Knight was quite calm now. He was coping not so much with human beings as with a situation. Everyone was affected by fatigue and nerves, incapable of normal behaviour. "I've got my papers here if you'd like to see them."

"I'm only doing my duty," said Mace. He was more shaken by Knight's quiet statement than he would have been by any display of temper.

Stars glinted overhead but it was impenetrably dark at ground level. All around men were stumbling and swearing. Voices were urging them to catch hold of the valise of the man in front and take it steady.

A blue light smouldered at Knight's feet. Someone had switched on a torch.

"All right, you two, better come over here."

Some minutes later Knight found himself in a sizable wooden hut which had been fitted up as an office. Only then did Mace release his grip. The meagre lighting of the hut—there were large cardboard shades on the electric lamps to deflect the light from the black-out windows—was brilliant after the darkness. Two clerks were at work in the office, both military policemen. One of them was typing, the other speaking into a telephone. "Well, shack me!" he said, and the rest of his sentence was swallowed in laughter.

They could now see that the man who had led them into this hut was a major with a red arm-band bearing the letters D.A.P.M. He removed his steel helmet and revealed a completely bald head; but for all that he could have been no more than thirty. Both Mace and Knight saluted him.

"Now what's the trouble?"

Mace began to speak, but the major cut him short.

"May I see your papers, please?" he said to Knight. "All right, Saunders, I want to hear myself speak."

"Sorry, sir," said the man at the telephone.

"They seem to be all right." The D.A.P.M. handed the documents back to Knight. "Won't you sit down? Here!" He opened a drawer and produced a small metal flask. "Take a swig of that."

Knight found it was whisky. "Thanks."

He had taken barely a mouthful but he suddenly felt as tipsy as though he had been drinking all the evening.

"Now what's your story, Sergeant-major?"

Mace was beginning to wish he had kept his mouth shut. The matter was taking on a different complexion.

"I hope you'll understand I'm only trying to do my duty, sir—"

"Yes, go on!" said the major, not taking his hard little eyes from Knight's face.

"This officer and I have been walking in from Criel together, and he acted queer. What with all this talk about fifth-columnists I thought he ought to be interrogated. Anyway, I thought it was queer, but maybe I'm wrong."

"What did he do?"

"He cleared off for about twenty minutes and I saw him go up a hill into a wood. I timed him by my watch. There was no reason why he should go off like that; and when he came back he wouldn't say what he'd been doing."

"And what had you been doing?" said the D.A.P.M. to Knight. He spoke quietly.

"Reading a letter."

"You mean you climbed up a hill and went into a wood to read a letter?"

"That's right."

"Why?"

"There were personal reasons."

"Have you got the letter?"

"I threw it away. I never keep mail."

"You must admit this is a queer story." The major seated himself on a table. "But I'm ready to admit this is a queer moment in history. You heard the news?"

"What news?"

"They're taking the B.E.F. out at Dunkirk and Calais."

"What's that mean?"

"Search me! These personal reasons of yours. You won't say what they are?"

"Do I have to?"

"No."

"It was a letter from a friend I'd not heard from for some time. I knew it would contain important news. It was so important that I had to be quite by myself when I read it. It might be bad news. When I got into the field I saw there was a wood and it reminded me of a wood back home—there's a beech wood on a hill at the back of the house—and I thought I'd go into this wood and read the letter."

"It took you twenty minutes?"

"It didn't seem like that to me, but if the sergeant-major says so, I'm sure he's right."

"What was the name of the man who wrote the letter?"

"Hesketh."

"Where does he live?"

"Luton."

"You satisfied, Sergeant-major?"

"Yes, sir."

"All right, you can go. Saunders, take the sergeant-major up to the station, will you? You'll find the rest of the Medical Corps chaps up there. That's all right. Good night!"

Mace saluted and marched out without so much as a glance at Knight.

The D.A.P.M. stood up and yawned. "There's a bed in there." He nodded towards a door. "I shan't be needing it tonight. I'll get you some food sent down." He put on his steel helmet and walked out on to the quay as the air-raid siren went.

Shortly after dawn he returned. He entered the cubicle and shook the sleeping man's shoulder. Knight, who had been so exhausted that he had simply laid himself on the top of the bed-clothes and gone to sleep in his uniform, struggled back to consciousness. His eyes opened. But he did not move. He could not move.

"Wakey, wakey, son." The D.A.P.M. folded his arms. "I'd like a bit of shut-eye myself." The boyish figure on the bed looked so defenceless that the D.A.P.M. felt drawn to be of service to him. "Did you have a good night?"

By this time Knight was properly awake. He sat up and swung his feet to the ground. "You won't believe me, but that whisky's given me a hangover!"

"You're not as fit as you might be," said the major. The two men stared at one another. "Jerry dropped some stuff in the night. He got that Salvation Army hut in front of the station; know it? Full of troops. The rest of the lads have been helping themselves to the stores. Good thing. We're all pulling out, did you know that?"

"Out of Dieppe?"

The major nodded. "There's been a beautiful balls-up, if you ask me. You still don't want to tell me what was in that letter, I suppose?"

When Knight rose to his feet he had a momentary dizziness, and the major supported him by the arm.

"If I were you, I'd lay off cross-country walking for a while."

"You been up all night?"

The men felt a curious feminine concern for each other. They could hear shunting on the quay and the wail of a ship's siren, but for the moment that activity belonged to another world. There was catastrophe in the air. The men spoke to each other gently, as though an expectation of imminent violence had stirred kindness as a protest. Knight was perfectly well aware that the D.A.P.M. had dismissed Mace for a fool and did not believe there was any question of treachery. It was his own personal need that demanded a fuller explanation of what had happened in the wood.

"Why did you have to be alone when you read that

letter?" The question was put in a way that implied he, too, received letters that cut deep, and now he wanted to measure Knight's experience against his own.

"Some time ago two friends of mine got married. I knew she was expecting a baby and I knew she was going to have a difficult time. You see, the doctor had warned her."

"This letter was to give you the news?"

It was a privileged conversation. The two men were listening to each other's words but also, it seemed, to echoes of meaning from an area more remote than the cubicle in which they stood.

"The baby was born dead."

"Who wrote to you, the man or the woman?"

"He wrote. She's ill."

"You married?"

"Yes."

The major nodded. He might have been confirming news he already knew instead of hearing it for the first time. He removed his helmet and his bald head gave him an air of ominiscience. He was tipsy with weariness.

"Well, you must have been rather special friends, I suppose. My name is Frost. Do you think you can remember that? We might meet again sometime."

There was a knock on the door and a corporal put his head into the cubicle.

"Town-Major's office on the phone."

The D.A.P.M. straightened up. "Tell 'em I'm coming." He gave Knight a nod. "If you're ready for a move, you and I'll go for a little walk; all right? Sorry there are no facilities for washing or shaving."

Some minutes later the D.A.P.M. joined Knight on the quay and they began walking towards the town. Beyond the *gare maritime* and the fish market windows burned red in the sun. There was a light mist on the water, so that the ships which were loading in the eastern basin seemed to be floating on air. Refugee traffic was streaming across the bridge and just outside the dock-railings trucks full of troops waited for an engine to take them off to Rouen and the south. The two men did not speak until they came to the western basin.

"See that boat?" said Frost, pointing to a cross-channel steamer with crowded decks.

There was a flurry of salutes at the gang-plank. Frost spoke to other officers with brassards and then turned to Knight.

"Right. Up you go, and good luck," he said.

"Am I to go on that boat?" Knight was surprised. It had not occurred to him that he would be able to leave the town so easily.

"You'll have to get a move on. They'll be pulling out in about ten minutes."

Knight hesitated. "Why should you do this for me?"

Frost smiled. "I'm only doing my job. Your hospital discharge papers said you were for evacuation to U.K. Well, this is it."

Instinctively Knight put a hand to his breast pocket where the papers were carried.

"I see," he said. But he knew that more explanation

could be given. Frost knew it too, and for the smallest part of a second the two men smiled at each other, elated with secret knowledge. Then they saluted each other formally, and the Deputy Assistant Provost Marshall for the Dieppe Sub-Area strode back along the quays to his temporary office near the town station.

It was a silent ship. The decks were so crowded it was impossible to form queues for the meal that was being served below. The crowd was quiet enough for Knight, wedged against the rail of the promenade deck, to hear Morse from the radio cabin. In theory the promenade deck was reserved for officers, but in reality all ranks were massed there—men, N.C.O.'s, officers, and even a number of nursing sisters, though so far as Knight could see he was the only R.A.F. man on board. They were not going to England, the rumour went round; they were ordered to St. Nazaire; the Allies were to hold the line of the Seine, and a new medical base area was being established in the Loire valley. A white hospital ship followed them out of the harbour. That, presumably, was making for England. Knight searched the sky but there was not an aircraft in sight.

Nevertheless the anti-aircraft gun in the stern suddenly went into action, and neat puffs of brown were sent high in the clear atmosphere. All on board felt the kick of the gun beneath their feet. The ship's siren gave a number of short, sharp blasts, a bell rang on the bridge, and the vessel changed course so rapidly the following hospital ship appeared to swing out from the land.

"All personnel below decks!" said the loudspeaker. "All personnel below decks!"

They were three miles out, running due south and parallel with the line of hotels and shops that made up the Dieppe front. Knight did not move. Almost imperceptibly the *château* and its rock dipped and rose across the water.

A middle-aged nursing sister with red hair peeping from beneath her steel helmet took his arm. "Come on, sonny. Grandma doesn't like this."

"Why pick on me?"

Already there was room to walk about on the deck, and the sister had merely paused to tie the strings on Knight's lifebelt when all the driving energy of the boat seeped into sound, a column of sound that was based on the bed of the sea itself. Knight tried to force the sister to the deck but bewildered by the suddenness of the onset she fought against him, and both, leaning against the rail for support, were drenched by the explosion of brine. The boat rocked on the edge of a crater. In the wildness of the moment it seemed possible for the vessel to fall to the bottom of the sea. The bomber had already pulled out of its dive. Water smacked against the hull like a hand.

"They're bombing, not gunning," said Knight. He had swallowed so much sea water that he felt hungry and sick in the same moment. "Take it from me, we're better off here than down below."

"I thought you were trying to rape me, sonny," said the sister. She lay on her belly and pressed her cheek to the deck. Drenched figures were lying all over the decks, some swearing, some laughing, but for the most part they were silent, waiting for the next attack. The ack-ack gun at the stern kicked away and the red hair, the flushed cheek and the smell of lilies of the valley were suddenly so close to Knight that he could have kissed her nose without moving. But she left him. First she lost her colour, then she looked indignant, then she rose above him, floating.

"We've been hit," he thought.

He had been turned over. If it had not been for the intense cold, he would have been perfectly comfortable, lying there on his back, gazing up at the sea. Because it was an emergency of some sort, he suspected that it would be foolish to turn his head. By moving his eyes, though, he could take in a great deal. There was a wave arrested at the very moment of breaking into a line of foam. Oil fumes, at the instant of combustion, froze in black and red, at right angles to the horizon. A coil of yellow rope hung in the sunshine like a flower. All the left side of his field of vision was taken up by a mountain of varnished gold that bore a delicate encrustation of elaborately worked metal; the hull of the ship, in fact, with its rust and barnacles streaming.

"Why not?" he asked himself, when the sea slipped like a carpet beneath his feet; and he set off running so lightly across the water he could feel the sharp ridges of the waves through the soles of his shoes. It was a matter of pride that he could make a quick decision and act upon it. He would go to Helen. Although he could not see her she was waiting behind all this brilliance with arms outstretched. The moment had come when he would have to make a supreme effort, and success depended almost entirely on his ability to keep his decision to himself, and so steal away unobserved.

But in this stratagem he failed. Perhaps, unwittingly, he had spoken his intentions aloud; perhaps they had read his secret from his eyes or outstretched hands. But the whole brilliant and detailed picture suddenly started into motion; the green sea yawned with all its salty breath, an under-water explosion produced a magnificent growth of liquid on the surface, flame ran like a frightened animal over the nursing sister's mop of hair, and a sudden thunder was quickly choked into silence. He was detached from the world of matter. He had lost contact. There was neither hard nor soft, and there was no sound of any kind. He opened his eyes and looked up at the golden surface of the sea. Bubbles sped from his mouth and he thought that if he could but follow, they would take him to Helen. He struck out and the morning air cut him like frost.

Physically he felt splendid. Until the bombing he had been stiff from the previous day's exertions. Now, the very violence he put into his swimming restored his circulation; although the waves rolled down upon him from all sides he inhabited a new, more vigorous body which could not be defeated. After an explosion the air sang with metal. A hundred fish jumped, or so it seemed. Fragments of timber, biscuit boxes, lifebelts, a towel, a pipe, bobbed within reaching distance. He was uninjured and quite safe—of this he was never for a moment in doubt. His only anxiety was his inability to travel to Helen as quickly as he would have liked. He thought he would go out of his mind with impatience.

When he was picked up twenty minutes later, clinging to one of the emergency rafts he had fortuitously come across, his first words were: "I've got to get home quickly, you know." Then he said: "Oh, keep me out of that sea," and fainted.

He awoke to find himself swaddled like a baby and swinging in mid air with no obvious means of support. He could neither move his arms nor flex his legs; but he could look out over the wreckage-strewn sea to the distant white cliffs of France. But for this wreckage there was no sign of the bombed ship. He revolved slightly and his field of vision changed. Now he could see Dieppe itself and the numerous small craft that were setting out from harbour on rescue work. To the quiet tinkle of a bell, a destroyer slid into view, a white eye winking furiously from the bridge. Knight felt the effect of a steadying hand. A moment later he was swung over the rail of the hospital ship and laid in his naval stretcher on the deck.

A man in a white smock tried to stuff a cigarette into his mouth, but he spat it out. "Let me out of this thing, will you? I itch like hell. I want to scratch myself, d'you understand? I want to scratch myself."

"Would you give me you number, rank, name, and regiment?" said a voice. A helmeted corporal with a fountain-pen bent over him. They were unbuckling the straps that held him him but they could not work fast enought for Knight.

"I'm all right. There's nothing the matter with me. I'm fine. For God's sake get me out of this thing. I'm itching, I tell you."

"Oh, and I want your religion as well," said the corporal. The men reeked of anaesthetic. Knight was aware that he was surrounded by a great deal of quiet, purposeful activity. Other stretcher-cases were being interrogated and hurried away. It was like being admitted to hospital all over again; and Knight did not wish to be admitted to hospital. He had to get to Helen as quickly as possible.

"7266275 Flying-Officer Richards, John William, of the 17th Fighter Squadron, R.A.F., religion C. of E." he said with deliberation. The war was over and he was already planning his escape. He sat up out of his blankets and found he was naked to the waist.

"Take him to C Ward," said the man in the white smock, trying to push him back on to the stretcher and rewrap him in the blankets. Knight resisted vigorously and contrived to rise to his feet.

"I'm all right, I tell you. If I weren't so damned itchy—"

"Take him to C Ward. You'll do as you're told, Flying-Officer Richards. This is a military hospital-ship and you're under military discipline here. Now don't be a damned fool, there's a good chap." Humiliatingly enough, it was this same man in white who supported Knight when the sun flashed in his eyes and the deck lurched towards him. They draped a blanket round his shoulders.

With a man on each arm Knight walked into the shade, down some stairs, and into what had at one time been the first-class dining-saloon. Now it was C Ward. The sister in charge came up but before she could speak Knight said: "I'm Flying-Officer Richards. I'm sure you're short of beds at a time like this. There's nothing the matter with me. Could you give me some dry clothes? If you put me to bed I'll go crackers."

For a mad moment he thought she was the same nursing sister he had been with before the bombing; but then he saw she was younger and prettier. He was quite sure she would do what he asked.

"Get on to this stretcher and don't argue. You ought to be ashamed of yourself."

"All right, Sister," he said meekly.

From that moment he was busy with plans for the preservation of his anonymity and for escape. He had lost his documents when he had lost his jacket. Even his identity tabs had gone. If he said that his name was Richards there was no one on board who could disprove it. For the authorities 7266275 F/O Richards existed only so long as they could keep him on that stretcher; once out of the place he was no one at all, not even an entry at the Air Ministry. The man who knew himself to be Knight would then be perfectly free.

"The *Dundas* stopped a packet, didn't she?" said the

man in the next stretcher. "Jerry's a gentleman, though. You got to hand it to him. He didn't bomb us, and we was wide open. You can't get away from it, Jerry's a gentleman. They say the bomb went right down the funnel and blew up the boiler room. You're lucky to be alive, mate."

They were using stretchers because there were not enough beds to accommodate all the patients. Looking round, Knight saw that the ward was paved with stretchers, most of them occupied. He saw that he was lying next to a door.

"I got piles," said the man in the next stretcher. "Would you believe it, I been lying in this damn ship since last Thursday. You heard the news? Jerry's in Paris, you know!"

Now that Knight was free to scratch himself he no longer itched. Rather, he no longer itched in a place his hands could reach. The torment was not physical and like a fool he had thrown away the only balm that would have served—Helen's letter. If he had not rolled the letter into a ball and tossed it over the Criel cliff, and if by some grace it had survived when the rest of his papers had not, he would have read it now as he had never read one of Helen's letters before. He would have studied it, memorized it, examined every word. Nothing else could calm him.

"Where you off to, mate? They'll be bringing the grub round in a minute."

Knight slipped from his stretcher and stole through the door into a white corridor. The ship was under way and the floor pulsed with great slowness beneath his feet. There was no one in sight but he found a lavatory and rested there for a while. He wore only the blue hospital pyjamas, not even slippers. He must find clothes from somewhere, and he wanted civilian clothes. He realized, too, that if he was to overcome his feeling of nausea and faintness he would have to find food. He had not eaten since the previous night.

A Medical Corps sergeant looked at him strangely in the corridor, but said nothing. Choosing a door at random, Knight opened it and found himself under observation. Propped up in an ordinary hospital bed was a man of about thirty with corn-coloured hair and moustache. He was playing patience on the back of a large tray.

"Hallo!" said the card player. "You any good at poker?" Knight entered the cabin, shut the door quietly behind him, and looked around. The would-be poker player was alone.

"Army?" said Knight.

The man put down a card with some care and nodded. "Hobbs, Lieutenant, Ox and Bucks., at your service."

"My name's Richards. R.A.F. I was on the *Dundas*."

"That must have been interesting. I heard some noise." Hobbs had a weak but friendly face. "Anything to break the monotony, eh? Nice of you to look in. What shall we play for?" He had been busy picking up the cards and was now shuffling them.

"Your kit," said Knight, nodding at the greatcoat which had been arranged over the back of a chair. If the man had his greatcoat with him the rest of his kit was bound to be near at hand, probably in the built-in wardrobe.

"Here, you're a cool customer. You're naked. I mean, you've got to put up something yourself! Mean to say, I wasn't born yesterday."

"Sorry, thought you wanted a game," said Knight, and he would have left the cabin but Hobbs called him back.

"Haven't I seen you somewhere before, Richards?"

"I don't think so."

"I could swear—now, let me see! Were you at Oxford?"

"No."

"Do shut the door, old chap, and come and sit down. Tell me, though, you must know what a disgusting crime it is for military men to play cards for their kit. Now, I'll be frank with you. I might have looked on the matter differently had you something of your own. But you're a pauper, man, a pauper. Tell you what, we'll play for money. When you lose you can write me out an I.O.U."

"What are you in dock for?"

"T.B."

"That's a long job. You won't need your kit for some time, six months at least."

"What's the game, Richards, my boy?"

The faintness and nausea Knight had been struggling against for the past few minutes now overcame him. He was vaguely aware that hands were lifting him. They were hands that came between Helen and himself, but he was impotent to resist them. Fiends

were ministering to him, understanding only too well
the nature of his obsession and delighting in the ease
with which they were frustrating it. He cried: "Helen,
Helen!" repeatedly but the fiends only laughed. When
he recovered full consciousness he was back in Ward C,
lying on his stretcher, being lectured by the sister.

"All right," he said wearily, "give me something to
eat, will you?"

"You've got to say you're sorry," she said with
exasperating coyness.

"I'm sorry," he said after a painful silence.

After a meal of bread and soup he fell asleep. In the
dream that followed he soared into a realm of happiness from which he had been excluded too long. Although he could not touch her, Helen was there. A
landscape of rock and stream in all the certainty of a
sunny morning faltered under his gaze. The inanimate
world became human. The scenery walked towards
him, in human form, smiling, and he was about to take
his wife in his arms when the sun itself struck out from
behind a cloud. Quite dazzled, he closed his eyes for
the kiss, and she was not there.

The hospital ship arrived at Newhaven at about four
o'clock in the afternoon without further incident.
There would not, normally, have been any attempt at
disembarkation that evening but orderlies appeared
before long with lists in their hands. Knight sat up in
his stretcher, smoking. It was against the rules but this
was an occasion when everyone agreed the rules should
be broken. The sister herself had given him the cigarette.

"7266275 F/O Richards?" said a staff-sergeant. Knight nodded. "Only diagnosed patients are being disembarked to hospital. I'm sorry, sir, that in this emergency there just isn't room for everybody."

"What do you want me to do? Stay here?"

"Officers are to be given rail warrants to their homes."

"Say that again!"

The staff-sergeant grinned. "They're going to send you home, sir. No accommodation."

They led him to the Q.M.'s stores and fitted him out with the uniform of a private soldier; battle dress, side-cap, black boots and the usual underclothing.

"When can I go?" he asked, admiring himself in the glass.

The store was crowded with army officers trying on kit, all of them survivors from the *Dundas*. They looked the better for the experience, Knight thought.

A clerk and an officer sat at an improvised desk in front of the gang-plank. They were making out railway warrants and as each man came up he was asked to identify himself against a typed list and state the name of his home-town. At another table sat another officer with a cash box. He made each man sign a form, and then handed over five one-pound notes for incidental expenses.

"You've got this well organized," said Knight. Then his attention was caught by the crowd of civilians on the dockside, the grey warehouses, the policemen, a red pillar-box, an astonishing number of chimneys, and behind, the green swell of a hill. It was his first sight of England for six months and it came as a shock. He stared so long that the man standing behind in the queue gave him a dig in the ribs.

"I'm sorry," said Knight.

"Name, please," said the clerk.

The early summer evening struck at him with its beauty. Once a sea-gull had caught his eye he could do nothing but follow its flight until it disappeared behind a shed. The splendour of the sunshine exhausted him. He had no defence.

For the third time the clerk asked him his name, and Knight remembered the game he had been playing ever since he had come aboard this ship. "7266275 F/O Richards," he said to the clerk; but when in return he was asked to what station he would like his warrant made out he did not know what to say.

"Oh, Victoria," he said at last. "Give me a ticket to Victoria."

He collected five pounds from the paymaster over a false signature and walked down the gangway in a state of panic. Even at this point might not someone stop him? He was about to enter the country where Helen lived, and the strain had become intolerable. He pushed his way through the crowd and wondered whether he had gone out of his mind. If a meeting with Helen brought but the slightest intensification of his present feelings, he would crack. Perhaps it was an experiment he could not, for the time being, afford to make.

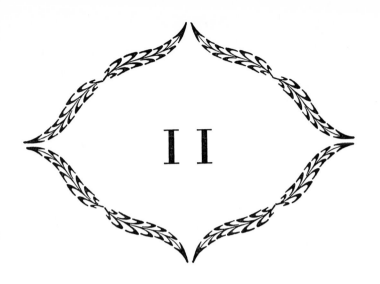

II

FOR two months a party of men had been at work building a hutted camp on the downs between Dunstable and Whipsnade. When the camp was finished it would be occupied by the army, by one of the ministries, by the BBC, by evacuée school-children—nobody knew which of these it would be, and nobody really cared. The situation was magnificent. It was so high. You could see across the northern reaches of the plain of Aylesbury to the limits of Northamptonshire; but the workers were less aware of this prospect of fields and woods than they were of the sky itself. When they had their breaks for tea they often stood in silence, watching the clouds labour out of the west.

At half past five the foreman blew a whistle. The men were ready with their coats on, and at this signal they normally raced for the two lorries which waited in the lane below to carry them into Dunstable. But that particular June evening the men—there were thirty or forty of them—went behind one of the completed huts and formed a rough square on the springy turf. There were several Liverpool Irish in the party and a fight was not an unusual way to finish the day. The fighters enjoyed it, the spectators enjoyed it, and a certain amount of money changed hands. But today the fight was going to be different.

Hesketh removed his overalls and walked to the centre of the ring wearing a stained white shirt and navy blue trousers. He was about thirty-four years of age, and although at first glance he may have appeared slight and his walk something of a dance, there was an air of calculation about him, almost an arrogance, that gave an impression of toughness. As soon as he opened his mouth and began speaking in a thin, high-pitched, educated voice it was clear that he was no ordinary workman. He could swing a sledge with the best of them, so they accepted him as an equal; but always there was a suggestion of mystery. His head had been cropped like a convict's.

Wondering what was afoot the two lorry drivers had climbed up the hill.

"You know we're supposed to be in Dunstable by six," one of them complained to the foreman.

"We'll be with you," said the foreman in a flat northern accent. He was so worried that, to the ac-

companiment of a derisive cheer, he pushed his way
through the crowd and approached the man Hesketh
was waiting to fight. This was a short, dark man in his
late twenties, quite ready, it seemed, to fight in his
overalls. On his face there were little blue scars as
though buckshot were lodged beneath the skin.

"We don't want this sort of trouble, lad. Why don't
you go up to the chap and apologize?"

"I said what I said," replied the man with quiet,
Welsh gravity. "I don't want to fight him. I'm sorry
for him."

"What's the row?" said one of the lorry drivers to a
workman.

The workman exhaled a cloud of cigarette smoke.
"That chap—" He nodded at the Welshman, "said
some'at about that chap's wife." Nodding at Hesketh.
"But I don't really know the rights and the wrongs of
the matter." He began shouting at the foreman. "Hi,
gaffer! Leave the lads alone. They're all right! Anybody meet me with a couple of bob on young Taff,
there?"

"That I will," said a west-country voice. "Couple of
bob it is, Dusty."

"Leave the lads alone!" Several other men began to
shout. Hesketh and the Welshman were standing together and talking quietly. Hesketh appeared to be
trying to reason. He shook his index finger. The Welshman turned and would have walked away proudly,
but Hesketh caught him by the shoulder and struck
him across the face with the back of his hand.

He had caught the fancy of the crowd. For a moment they had thought the fight was off; now he had made a scrap unavoidable. There were no rules, no referees, no rounds. Men fought until one of them decided he had had enough, or, in exceptional cases, the crowd decided for him and stopped the fight.

The two men walked round each other, hands down, not obviously watching for an opening. The Welshman's cheek was still flushed from the blow. The only sound now was the hiss of the grass against the toes of their boots.

The Welshman stopped. "I'm ready to let it go, mate," he said quietly, not looking Hesketh in the eye. For the first time, Hesketh showed anger.

"You're not getting off as lightly as that." He attempted to drive his right fist into the Welshman's face. Taffy ducked and jumped back. Hesketh followed up, trying to catch him by his overalls, trying to stamp on his feet and cripple him; and their heavy boots, now, drummed on the ground. But only their long clean shadows made contact. Most of the men were shouting for Hesketh.

Unexpectedly Taffy turned and began to fight. He was a powerful man but he lacked the art of putting weight into his blows, and he was, moreover, hampered by being so self-conscious. He was neither angry enough, nor fearful enough, to be indifferent to the impression he was making on the gang of workmen. He tried to fight in the way he had seen boxers fight in the news-reels at the cinema; he wagged his left elbow and held his head high. These niceties appeared to exasperate Hesketh all the more, and as they fought, landing crude punches on the other's head, he began to shout insults in that high voice of his.

"That's the stuff, Hesketh lad."

All the same there was something frightening about those cries of insult. They were frightening because they sprang from an intensity of passion which none of the workmen could understand. No normal man fought with this degree of passion merely because his wife had been insulted. The Welshman's nose bled and his red face shone with sweat; Hesketh, in contrast, was as white as the heaps of chalky earth which were dotted about the site.

The Welshman was not trying to hurt Hesketh any more; as well as he knew how, he was pushing Hesketh away.

"Why don't you stand and take your medicine?" Hesketh shouted at him. His face was unmarked. He was as fresh as when they had started.

Hesketh was probably the only man present who did not know what was passing through the Welshman's mind; it was uncontrollable passion that gave Hesketh his ascendancy. They saw him as a wild creature tried beyond endurance. They wanted to laugh but they could not because he was obviously suffering so intensely.

"Then it's true about his wife!" they thought, wonderingly, and wanted to leave it at that. It was enough that a man should have a wife like Hesketh's without having to fight for her. Hesketh appealed as an injured dog would have appealed to them.

But at that moment the Welshman went down.

Stumbling awkwardly over the uneven ground he had dropped his guard and lifted his chin uncertainly. Hesketh saw his opportunity and struck with all his strength—not on the point of the chin, but in the throat. Even so, the Welshman went down because he had lost his balance rather than because the blow had hurt him. Hesketh knew that the blow had made little real impression, and he flung himself on the recumbent man, trying to kneel on his forearms. The Welshman fought back, and the pair rolled over and over on the ground scrapping like cats.

The crowd was bored. This was the way kids fought, all temper and no science. A couple of men stepped forward to separate the fighters with the idea of setting them on their feet again so that the scrap could continue along more orthodox lines. The Welshman was momentarily on top. When he was dragged off, Hesketh remained lying on the ground, his eyes closed, his shirt torn, his trousers putty-coloured with dust.

Silence fell on the crowd. No one moved. Hesketh lay in the bright sunlight like a man sleeping. His attitude was comfortable. It was his air of repose that frightened the Welshman.

"Get him up, why don't you?"

A thin smile appeared on Hesketh's lips, and his eyes opened. "Well, why don't you?" he said.

In reality, he needed no assistance. He rose to his feet, brushed his clothes down, and walked through the silence to the Welshman.

"Thanks," he said, nodding at the man in a friendly

way. He collected his jacket and set off down the hill
towards the lorries. The men were so surprised that for
a while they stared after him; they followed, arguing
who had won the fight. Hesketh was hurt, they decided. Of course, the fellow was deep. There was no
knowing what his game might be. But if he had not
been hurt why did he lie on the ground without moving?

"Reckon you winded him, Taff."

"Do you think he's all right?" asked the Welshman
anxiously.

"You 'ad 'im on the run, son," said the west-coun-
tryman who had just collected a couple of shillings
stake-money. "I know that type. All mouth, no guts!"

"Don't you believe it," said the Welshman.

He was made even more uneasy by Hesketh's attitude when he and the other men arrived at the lorries.
Hesketh had walked ahead so quickly there would
have been ample time for him to climb into the lorry
and secure one of the favoured positions, just behind
the cab. But he preferred to wait, leaning against one
of the wheels. The men began chaffing him. He nodded, grinned; but all the time he kept his eyes on the
Welshman.

"Taff," he said, "you'd do a lot better to be a friend
of mine. I've got something to say to you."

The Welshman detected what he thought was con-
tempt in the voice. "If you haven't had enough,
there's plenty more where that came from!" he
shouted.

Hesketh merely gave him a helping hand into the

lorry and squatted by his side. Although the rest of the crowd had been interested hearers up to that point, it was not possible for anyone but Taffy to hear what Hesketh was saying once the lorry had started. As they rocked along the narrow lane Hesketh began speaking into the Welshman's ear. The men who were watching the Welshman's face could see that he was getting more uneasy and angrier every minute. Hesketh became calmer, more amused.

"Don't think," he was saying, "that I am threatening you at all idly. I mean what I say. I shall kill you. You don't know me. How could you? None of these men know me! So I've got to speak pretty direct. I've got to warn you. If I hear any more loose talk from you about my wife I'll make it my business to kill you. I shall do it in such a way that you won't have any chance to defend yourself. It doesn't matter what happens to me. I should kill you and then go straight to the police. But I don't think all this will be necessary. You'll keep your mouth shut. You're sensible."

The Welshman had lodgings in Dunstable, and was one of the first to leave the lorry. Hesketh, who lived in Luton, was normally one of the last; but on this occasion he jumped out with the Welshman and walked along with him, speaking quietly but with a new air of gaiety that was baffling. Taffy wanted to break free and run. They were walking through a new housing estate and the sunlight was dusty with laughing, racing children.

"My daughter," said Hesketh confidentially, "had the tiniest little hands you've ever seen. You wouldn't think, would you, that tiny hands like that could take hold of a man's heart and squeeze it until it stopped beating?"

"I don't know what you're talking about," said Taff. He walked with his face turned away.

"I'm talking about my daughter," said Hesketh.

"What's this got to do with me?"

"Nothing. I don't want it to have anything to do with you. I've got nothing to do with you. My wife's got nothing to do with you. Leave my daughter alone, too. You married?"

The Welshman did not answer.

"If you're not married and you've got no child of your own, then it's quite true, you don't know what I'm talking about. Go on!" he said. He gave the Welshman a push and released the arm he had, until that moment, been gripping firmly. The two men looked into each other's eyes. The Welshman could have said that Hesketh did not have a daughter, but he was scared where a remark like that might take them. Hesketh could have stopped smiling, but feared what expression might replace the fixed grin his face now wore. After a while, the Welshman shrugged, turned and walked off along the road. Hesketh waited until he was out of sight and then made his way to the nearest bus stop.

The centre of Luton was crowded. The pavements were thronged with shop-assistants, factory-workers and office-workers on their way home. There were long queues for the buses. In one narrow street which led from a factory, the tide of humanity was so great it would have been impossible for a man to make his way against the flow. But tide was the wrong word. Hesketh leaned against a wall to give the pain in his side time to dull; he watched the crowd and the way the sunlight smoked over their heads. It was a human harvest. Ripe bodies swayed in the evening breeze.

When the street had emptied he bought a paper from the news-vendor on the corner, and made his way slowly up the hill to the mid-Victorian terraces. He read the headlines in his newspaper and even paused to read one news item in detail. It was news from the moon. He could not believe that Mr. Churchill's speech had anything to do with him. Hesketh would have liked to believe that he had blood, sweat, and tears yet to offer. But they had been drained off. He was dry. He was an empty husk. When the pain had passed and his head was clear once more it had room for only one question: Where would he find Jane to-night?

Their flat was on the third floor. On the second landing he paused and listened to the silence of the house. A pink cloud was held in the skylight. A cat mewed.

"Jane," he called softly. "Jane, are you there?"

If she were in the flat he wanted to know before he opened the door. "Jane," he called, more loudly, and when there was still no reply he climbed the remaining flight of stairs, and paused outside his own door. "Jane, are you there, my dear? It's me. I've come home. Shall I come in?" He turned the handle and pushed. Strange that the door was not locked. If Jane was out somewhere, surely she would have remembered to lock the door behind her. The flat contained nothing of value, but what they had was valuable to them.

"Jane," he said quietly into the dark little hall. There was no reply. Nothing was disarranged. A book, a pair of gloves, and a china cat rested on a small table. They had been there when he left that morning. In the bedroom everything was neat and tidy. If Jane was in the flat there was only one room left where she could be. "Jane, darling," he said at the door of their living-room. Then he lifted his head and stared.

Oliver Knight, one leg thrown across the other, was sitting in an arm-chair facing the door. He was wearing a neat grey suit and glittering black shoes. As Hesketh came into the room he removed the cigarette from his lips to smile. He waved a hand.

"Come on in, why don't you. Make yourself at home. Cut yourself a slice of cake. Put your feet on the mantelpiece."

"Oliver! How did you get in?"

"I'm alive and well. Wouldn't it have been nicer to say something about that? I came in through the door. How else do you think I came in?"

"Oliver!" Hesketh could only stare.

"There's such a thing as a master key, and your landlady on the ground floor has got one. I've been here two hours, reading." A book lay open on the floor and he indicated it with his foot. "I must say your open-air life suits you. You look well. You look all ruddy and strong. Where's Jane?"

Hesketh walked across the room smiling. He seized Oliver's left wrist and pulled him to his feet.

"Oh, Oliver! Oliver! Let me look at you! You're just the same. You haven't changed. You don't know what this means to me. You're just the same as when I saw you last. I thought everything was different. But you're just the same. Let me look at you." He made Knight stand in the centre of the floor and he walked round and round him admiringly. "You've no idea how good it is to see you." He put an arm round Knight's shoulders and the two men stared at the book on the carpet.

"Why are your hands bleeding?" said Knight.

The skin on Hesketh's knuckles was broken. He had not noticed until now. It was all that he had to show for his fight with the Welshman; no doubt they had bled for a little while after the skin had been broken, but Hesketh was sure they were not bleeding when he read the newspaper. He could scarcely have failed to notice. It was as though the sight of Knight, after an interval of nearly a year, had caused his blood to leap, to break out. Hesketh was so excited he had to go into the bathroom to be alone for a while. He bathed his hands.

"There is blood," he thought exultantly. "I was wrong. I am alive."

"Where's Jane?" said Knight, at the door.

Hesketh wiped his hands. "I don't know."

"You don't know!"

"Oh, she's somewhere about the place, I suppose."

"You suppose!"

"Can I get you something to eat, some tea or something?"

The two men were standing side by side, looking out of the sitting-room window. The house was on higher ground than the rest of the town. Chimneys smoked below them. The valley was blue and gold under its industrial haze. Westward a line of trees was intensely black.

"When I say I don't know where Jane is," said Hesketh deliberately, "I mean that she is probably somewhere about Luton. Probably. Perhaps she's gone to London. I don't know. When I come home from work, sometimes she's here, sometimes she isn't. Sometimes she comes in very late. She never gets up in the morning when I do. Sometimes she stays in bed all day. If I had her in the room with me now I still shouldn't know where she was. We sleep together. In the night I lie awake and listen to her breathing. She sleeps very heavily. I don't know where she is. In the evenings I spend my time walking about the streets looking for her. When I find her she isn't there—"

"You talk as though she'd gone off her head."

"Perhaps she has. No one will tell me."

"Perhaps she has?" Knight repeated the words incredulously.

"Not that I need any telling."

"You mean she's ill?"

Hesketh nodded.

"What treatment is she getting?"

"She goes to the doctor, on and off."

It was a year ago, when Knight was still at Cranwell,

that he had received the letter from Jane in which she had announced her intention of marrying Hesketh. There had been another letter from his mother full of girlishly enthusiastic comment on the news. It was incomprehensible. The news was hardly unexpected but when it came he was numbed. He wanted to cry out in protest. Hesketh was such a fool. But Jane was so right in everything she did; she went to church regularly and she had a wisdom of her own which made people nod their heads in agreement when she spoke; even then, with her letter in his hand, Knight found that he was nodding his head. If that was what Jane wanted, then it must be right. He had not been able to attend the wedding. The last time he had seen her was a frosty autumn morning in Worcester. They met outside the market and watched men wheeling crates of apples past a bank of white chrysanthemums. Not once did they mention Hesketh. They had said very little, but it was a meeting for themselves, alone. Before they parted, she did a surprising thing. She kissed him. Then he saw her walking quickly in the direction of the cathedral, so sure of herself, so happy, so carelessly cruel to him. Knight stood looking down on Luton and the smell of those white chrysanthemums seemed to fill the room.

"That cup of tea," he said. "I wouldn't say no."

They stood in the kitchen to drink it.

"What have you had your hair cut like that for?" he asked Hesketh.

Hesketh passed a hand over his cropped skull. "I thought I'd like it. Never did like long hair. There's a lot of dust on my job. Long hair would get dirty. Looks more workmanlike, too, I think."

"Wouldn't surprise me if it got on Jane's nerves. Didn't she ever say anything? You look like a criminal."

"I am a criminal."

Knight put his cup down and looked at Hesketh. "That's better. Why are you a criminal?"

Hesketh's face was transformed. He cut the air savagely with his hand. It was an indictment. He was judge, prosecutor, and prisoner, all rolled into one, and the verdict was guilty. "It's my fault. Why was I born?"

"I could give you a coarse answer."

"You've changed, Oliver. I was wrong to say you were just the same. I was so glad to see you. You must forgive me. It was a shock to come on you like that. We'd been without news of you so long."

Half an hour later they went out to look for Jane. It was already dusk and there were lovers in the doorways. A squad of soldiers carrying white kit-bags marched up to the station, followed by a warrant-officer with a red lamp. It was as though the black-out had not only obscured the lights, but muted sounds as well. The air was close.

They drew a blank at the café on the outskirts of the town which stayed open all night to cater for lorry drivers. Hesketh said Jane was often to be found there playing the penny-in-the-slot machines. A man busy pushing plates of baked beans through a hole in the wall said no, he had not seen Mrs. Hesketh all the evening, and he gave Knight a wink. By this time it was so dark they could see the searchlights over London.

"How often do you have to look for her like this?"

"Oh, not more than now and again," said Hesketh. For some reason he had taken it into his head to play his disaster down, and he sounded grotesque.

They went into a public house and Hesketh spoke to the man behind the bar, but without result. Knight would have liked to stay for a drink, but Hesketh wanted to press on.

"There's a Church Army place in the middle of the town. We're sure to find her there."

But Jane was not there. "I wish you'd go back to the flat," said Hesketh. "I'd rather look for her myself."

The air-raid siren, when it sounded, turned their eyes to the sky. They listened intently, as though the siren were delivering a complicated musical theme which they had to grasp completely if they were to understand what was to follow. There were but few clouds. Stars were scattered about the pallid darkness. When silence fell there was a furtive movement in the town. There were hurried footsteps, whispers, a sense of urgency.

"You don't think she's back in the flat by this time?"

"Maybe," said Hesketh.

But they made no move. In the direction of London was a cone of searchlights. Knight was the first to pick out the throb of the lone raider. By now the town was ringed by searchlights, and the square before them was milky in their reflection. Knight tried to think himself into the skin of the German pilot; a bit jittery, perhaps, uncertain of his position, anxious to do the right thing, a little in love with and a little hateful of the dark country which lay below. So far as Knight could judge, the bomber was immediately over the town, but still the searchlights could not find it. It occurred to him that those long fingers were feeling for the enemy with the same kind of apprehension that he and Hesketh were looking for Jane.

They were walking along a side street when they heard the bomb in the air. A Bofors gun near the station was firing blind. The clattering tram-like rush of the bomb was at them, and them alone. The two men lay in the road, their hands over their ears, their mouths gaping a little. The road bucked, the air tore like calico, and the heavy concussion came to them from streets away, perhaps farther off than that. They had been in error. The bomb was not for them. It was for Jane. The bomber wound itself up, like some remote aerial clock, and the searchlights hissed in the silence that followed.

"You all right?" said Knight when they had picked themselves up. They began hurrying in the direction of the explosion.

It was some time before the town recovered from its stupor. An ambulance shot past, jangling its bell.

"Now then," said a sudden voice out of the darkness, "if you're not firemen, demolition men, rescue men, doctors, nurses or just plain lunatics, I want you. Come on now." They could make out the air-raid warden's steel hat as he stood in their path, with arms extended.

"I'm looking for my wife," said Hesketh.

"I don't mind about lunatics," said the warden, "they're a burden on the rates. Come into my parlour and let me look at you. Looking for your wife? Very suspicious. Now, if you were wives looking for— Hey!" The warden made a grab at Hesketh who was trying to make off.

But it was Knight who caught Hesketh's arm. "She's here!"

"Jane? Where?"

"I heard her voice."

Guided by the warden's hand, Knight led the way down the steps. He made a right-hand turn, parted a curtain of blankets, and opened a door into the shelter. By the light of two hurricane lamps he could see crowded benches and hear, very telling, very clear, very insistent, the voice that had penetrated to the street outside. Yet now that he could see Jane, her voice faded under the general hubbub. Perhaps a moment ago she had been the only one to speak. Perhaps it was the general silence that had made her audible. Or could he have heard her through any noise, her clear voice striking the one note to make him ring, like a wine glass, in sympathy?

Nothing that Hesketh had said was any preparation for what he saw. Her beauty made him hesitate. She shone like a nocturnal flower. He had never thought of Jane as being beautiful in any conventional sense, but whether it was the effect of the lamp or whether he had transfigured her with the joy of his discovery, she now had a sweet, serene grace of countenance. She was to

be loved. He turned his head away, then looked back
again, startled. She was stitting on a bench and leaning slightly forward to hold the hand of a small boy.
The line of her face was finer than Knight had remembered it. Her hair was done differently, too. It was
spun like dark silk over her head. Gazing at her, not
moving, not speaking, he was calm for the first time
in weeks. "She looks about eighteen," he thought.

Hesketh rushed up to her and began speaking excitedly. She turned her head and looked at him with a
smile. She put out a hand and patted him on the knee.

"Hallo, Jane," said Knight.

The *All Clear* was sounding and there was a general
movement to go. Sleeping children were picked up.
There was laughter.

"Hallo, Oliver," said Jane, allowing her eyes to rest
upon him for no more than a second. She showed no
surprise. Until that moment she could not have known
whether he was alive or dead. He had not written.
Yet her greeting was one she might have given a friend
she saw every day.

"But don't you understand, John," she said to the
child, "I want to take you home, and if you don't tell
me where you live, I shan't be able to."

"I don't live anywhere special," said the boy. He
was about eight years of age, dressed in a torn green
jersey, flannel shorts, and sandals. There was a furtive
expression on his dirty face. "Sometimes I lives with
me Dad, sometimes I lives with me Mam, sometimes I
lives with me Gran."

"Where does your mother live?" said Jane.

"That's all right, missis, I'll look after young Johnny there." It was the warden. He held his steel hat in his hands as a butler would hold a tray. "Kids playing about the streets at all hours. Got to collar 'em, you know, when the old buzzer goes. Got to do the job. He's not afraid of anybody, are you, son?"

"If you'll tell me where his mother lives, I'll take him home," said Jane.

"No, you see it's all in the job—"

"I'll take the boy home," said Jane with such decision that the warden looked startled.

"Just round the corner." And he gave the address with an injured air.

Outside there was a breeze in the night and the stars were sharpened. Jane held the boy by the hand. She gave him all her attention. As they walked along she spoke to him quietly. Had he any brothers or sisters? Unexpectedly she asked him whether he had ever seen the sea, and the boy said yes, he had seen the sea tons and tons of times.

The house turned out to be one in a poor terrace. The boy proved too quick for them. Jane had no sooner knocked on the door than he tore his hand free and darted away into the darkness.

"Who is it?" came a woman's voice from the other side of the door.

"Let's go home, Jane dear," said Hesketh.

It would have been a waste of effort trying to catch the boy. It was dark; he knew the district and they did not.

"Yes?" said the voice of an anxious woman. The

door was only partly open. No light shone from behind; John's mother was to remain no more than a voice.

"I was bringing your little boy, John, home. But he ran away. He's gone up there," said Jane.

"He always does that," said the anxious voice, and the door closed as silently as it had opened.

"Let's go home, darling," said Hesketh and took her by the arm.

Jane had shown such firmness in bringing the child home herself that Knight expected her to knock on the door again. She would want to satisfy herself that the boy had somewhere to go. She would only have to speak, for John's mother to hear. They could hear the woman breathing noisily on the other side of the door.

"Yes, let's go home," said Jane. She put the incident completely out of her mind. She had made her gesture and it had met with no success. "Poor little boy," she said, but there was detachment in her voice. She might have been speaking about some unfortunate child in history, a young prince who had disappeared mysteriously in the night, and whose bones were discovered centuries afterwards under a paving-stone.

It was closing time for the public houses and the streets were full of soldiers, some of them singing. An engine clanked over the railway bridge and the glow from its firebox was the brightest part of the night. As they climbed the hill towards the flat, Jane spoke to Knight. Her head was turned in his direction and he could smell her sweet breath; it was as though she had been drinking milk. "I sleep well these nights, Oliver. I sleep like a log. I've never been happier. I'm quite calm in my mind. No dreams. I just get into bed and float into deep, deep sleep. Slumber. 'Tis the voice of the sluggard. Tell me about Helen. How is she?"

"I haven't seen her since I came back," said Knight.

"Well, you'll see her soon, won't you, Oliver? And you'll give her my love."

There was no exclamation. She did not want to know why he had not seen Helen since returning from France. Her quiet acceptance of his remark made Knight want to stop and embrace her out of gratitude. But they kept on, all three of them, walking quietly; and as she walked Jane yawned loudly now and again, laughed, and said: "Oh dear, I shan't need any rocking."

None of them had any thought for food. While Jane prepared herself for bed Hesketh and Knight remained in the sitting-room, for the most part in silence. The house was so quiet that they could hear the slither of her garments on the other side of the door.

"Jane, dear," said Hesketh. He tapped on the door and held his head slightly forward. "Are you in bed?"

There was no reply, and Hesketh returned to Knight. "She musn't be excited, you understand. I try to accept the whole situation calmly. After all, we're human beings together."

"That's what I call an optimistic statement," said Knight. "What else do you believe in?"

Hesketh was tapping on Jane's door as if he were not married to her. He looked at Knight and as though coming to an important decision, put his hand on the door-knob and turned it gently. When the door was opened he moved with the silence of a cat.

"Oliver!" he whispered. He was standing in the doorway with a soft light behind him. He beckoned. "Come and look at her."

Knight hesitated. He was aware of some incongruity he could not bring himself to consider. A strange pattern was being presented, but no matter how quickly his eye moved, the pattern never fell within his field of vision. He did not want to enter Jane's bedroom, but he went, and the two men stood at the foot of the bed, looking down at her.

Although she had been in bed no more than a few minutes she was already profoundly asleep. Once more Knight was struck by her beauty. In the light of the bedside lamp she seemed almost visionary; a spot of light glistened on the closed eyelid of her left eye and he stared at it fascinated.

The two men listened to the measured breathing.

"You see how strange she is," Hesketh whispered.

"What do you mean, strange?"

Hesketh glanced at him. "You know—I told you. She's not *here*, if you see what I mean."

"Don't talk rubbish."

They went back into the other room and closed the door behind them.

"But Oliver, she's not herself."

"I don't understand you."

"What are you looking at me like that for? She *isn't* herself. She's ill. She needs care and love and—"

"Jane's all right. You're the one who's gone nuts, if you ask me."

Hesketh rubbed the palm of his hand over his cropped head. He looked at Knight doubtfully.

"She's all right," said Knight vehemently. "What are you getting yourself in such a stew for? Why don't you stop worrying? Jane's fine. She knows what she's doing. I understand Jane. Jane's fine, I tell you. Now, will you believe me?" He looked round. "Where am I going to sleep?"

Although the rest of the night passed off quietly and no warning was sounded to disturb the sleep of those who were capable of sleep, there were two occasions when Knight rose from the settee which served him as an improvised bed. He walked silently up and down the room with naked feet. He was impatient for the moment when he and Jane would be alone. Through the curtainless windows—he had taken down the black-out screens—he caught glimpses of town and country-side drifting in moonlight. "Listen to me, Jane," he was saying to the woman in the next room, "listen to me! Tell me what it means! Tell me why I am here!"

Yet when Hesketh came to him with a cup of tea at half past six he was so soundly asleep that Hesketh had to shake him by the shoulder.

"I've got to go to work in half an hour's time," said Hesketh. "It's wonderful that you're with us again, Oliver. We shall have so much to talk about. You must have a lot to tell us. I've not even asked about Helen. You must forgive me. I was so confused last night. I get so wrapped up. Talk to Jane, Oliver. Don't say anything about the baby. We never mention it." It was all said in a whisper.

He was already dressed. As Knight sipped his tea, Hesketh stood in the middle of the room spooning up porridge from a soup-plate. There was no sign of Jane, and no sound from the bedroom. The questions that most men would have put, the explanations that most men would have given, clearly never occurred to Hesketh; and Knight, as on so many occasions in the past, experienced the mingled exasperation and affection which had always coloured their relationship. Hesketh did not even want to know how long he planned to stay.

Knight went to the bathroom and buried his face in cold water.

"I shall be away all day. For once I shall know Jane's all right. She'll be with you. Talk to her. I shall have to leave you to get your own breakfast. She's still asleep."

"Why don't you wake her up?"

"I always let her have her sleep out if I can. When she wakes up, see that she gets her breakfast all right."

Knight had slept in his underclothes. Now he dressed and shaved with Hesketh's razor. He adjusted his tie with elaborate care and then, to Hesketh's horror, walked into the bedroom, leaned over the foot of the bed and called Jane's name over and over again, but with the same gentleness one might use to wake a child. Jane lay in exactly the same position as when he had seen her last.

"Jane," he said when she had opened her eyes and

was staring at the ceiling, "the sun is shining and we're going out for a long walk today. D'you hear me? Why don't you say something?"

"All right," she murmured, quite unsurprised.

"Where are you going?" said Hesketh while they waited in the other room for Jane to dress. "You mustn't tire her. She's still weak."

"There's nothing the matter with her," said Knight.

Hesketh shook his head as though he did not agree but could not argue.

"Listen," said Knight, approaching very close and speaking so quietly that Jane could not hear through the open door, "what would you do if Jane disappeared?"

"Disappeared?"

"What would you do if you came home one evening and you couldn't find her? And you went on looking and you never found her?"

"People don't disappear like that."

"Of course they do."

"She might disappear for a time, but I should find her in the end."

"How long would you go on looking? A month, a year? What would you live on?" At the expression on Hesketh's face Knight felt pity, yet the reassurance he wanted to give was incapable of expression in words. Jane and he would soon be alone. The moment was so near that Knight wanted to postpone it, merely out of compassion for Hesketh. After Hesketh had kissed Jane, Knight accompanied him to the bus stop and listened patiently to most detailed instructions on the subjects he might discuss with Jane and the subjects he might not; there were firm orders about not making her walk too much.

"You worry too much," said Knight.

"See you about six," said Hesketh. Before the bus came along he reverted to what Knight had said about Jane disappearing. "In a matter like this I'm not like other men. You've known Jane longer than I have, you know what a wonderful person she is. From any common-sense point of view she made a mistake in marrying me. There's such a thing as luck and I haven't got it. Everything I believe in is wrapped up in Jane. I've no other beliefs. If she disappeared I should have nothing to believe in. Nothing. I should be a machine. I shouldn't know the difference between right and wrong. Why should what has happened have happened to us? What have we done wrong? Why did it have to be us and not you? D'you know, I had a fight yesterday? Things are turning to violence. I can't do anything except by violence. But I let the other man beat me. Now, what do you make of that?"

"Don't worry about Jane. She'll be all right."

"See that she has a good breakfast, there's a good fellow," said Hesketh, climbing up into the bus. He nodded and smiled; he waved his hand, and was borne off, sitting very erect.

"Now!" Knight took a deep breath.

At first he climbed the hill slowly. A cat appeared on a wall, arching its back. He paused to fondle the animal. Deciding that he had wasted more time than he could afford, he began to walk more briskly. He awakened to the animation of the town. A factory hooter was sounding, an engine was whistling at a signal, housewives were beating mats on the pavement, and a group of girls were chattering their way through the sunshine. It occurred to Knight that this return from the bus stop was taking rather a long time and he even wondered whether he had made a mistake and passed the house. He had forgotten the number. Then he looked up and saw Jane's face at a window. He waved and ran eagerly up the stairs.

"Jane!" he called as he entered the flat. There was no sign of her. He looked into the bedroom and she was not there. "Jane!" he called once more.

"Yes, Oliver?" she said from the kitchen.

He was silent with relief. "Oh! there you are," he said after a while, very casually. "I thought I'd lost you, for the moment," he said. "I thought you'd run off somewhere."

"I might have done." She spoke without interest. Knight watched her. She was buttering toast. Occasionally a spot of butter would be left on one of her fingers and she would remove it with the point of her knife. It was one of Helen's mannerisms, too. But it was all that the two women had in common; Jane was dark and serious, Helen was fair—a good-humoured young lady some people would have considered frivolous. Jane was like himself; Helen was like his mother, and possibly that was why he loved her so much.

After a while Jane's silence began to bother him. He had finished up the porridge, eaten some toast, and drunk a cup of tea when he said: "Do you wish I hadn't come to see you?"

"I'm very glad you came, Oliver. I'm always glad to see you. Why should you say that? We're old friends."

"That's all right then."

It was Knight who did the washing-up. When he joined her once more she was wearing her coat and was on the point of going out through the door. If he had not walked out of the kitchen at that moment, he felt, she would have gone without him.

"What do you do with yourself all the time, Jane?" he asked as they made their way down into the town. "I wonder you don't start teaching again. I'm sure they'd be glad of you."

"Oh, I walk about when the weather's fine," she said, "and talk to people. I've got a lot of friends here. There are a lot of nice people in Luton."

"Is that where you're taking me now, to see some of these people?"

"I thought you were taking *me* somewhere."

"Right you are, Mrs. Hesketh!" he said ironically.

It was the first time he had ever addressed her by that name, and he would not have done so then had the sun not glinted on her wedding ring. They had arrived at a bus stop, and she was raising her hand. The bus was full and it swept past, ignoring her signal. As another bus, travelling in the opposite direction, appeared round the corner, Jane crossed the road to hail that. She was half-way across the road before Knight realized what was happening.

"Don't you care which way you go?" he asked when they had taken their seats on the top deck.

"No," she said, "all ways are pleasant."

"You nearly left me behind."

Twenty minutes later the bus came to its terminus in a village with a grey church, a couple of pubs, some cream-washed cottages, and a row of council houses. Hedges, with an occasional elm tree, radiated through meadows where cattle grazed or the grass was being cut for hay. Soldiers came out of a Nissen hut and stared after them as they made their way up a gently rising lane. The sun was hot, and so far as this was possible, they walked in the shade.

"Jane, for God's sake, speak to me!" he said abruptly. The ground rose no higher. From that point hedges and fields sloped away into a heat haze. A battery of greenhouses glittered like a lake.

"Speak to you, Oliver? Of course I'll speak to you. What would you like me to say?"

"You must have realized I was a deserter."

"It hadn't occurred to me, and in any case I don't believe it."

"Jane!" The pressure of his hand upon her wrist was so great that she cried out. He apologized. "It's perfectly true. I am a deserter. I've got no papers, I've got no identity card, no ration book. Officially I'm dead. A ship was bombed and when they picked me out of the water something had cracked in my mind. All I could think of was getting to Helen as quickly as possible. I thought the war was over. After what had happened it seemed perfectly obvious that the war was over. They kept interfering with me and I wanted to be left alone. I gave them a wrong name."

"What do you want me to say?"

"What do I—?" He looked at her with a flushed, bewildered face. Yet her question had been perfectly reasonable. What had he expected her to do but make the obvious observation that he had better stop being a fool and report to the nearest R.A.F. unit?

"I haven't explained it very well, Jane. I'm trying to get to Helen."

"No, Oliver, you're not explaining it very well. It doesn't matter."

"But it matters a great deal. Now listen carefully. A few days ago I was travelling in a train dressed exactly as I am now. You'll remember my speaking of the Nixons? I always kept a certain amount of kit at their place in Wembley. They had some of my civilian clothes there. You see, I used to go up to town on leave and change into these clothes at their house. Well, I went to Wembley, picked up these clothes— I didn't say much to her—and, as I said, I was travelling in a train. There were only two other people in the compartment; two men, one big, the other small. The big man was pulling the little man's leg. He kept laughing and saying that when Jerry landed the little man would be for it. He said that this little man was just the sort who made the Germans angry, and they'd do all sorts of terrible things to him. It was a joke, and the little man knew it was a joke, but he looked as frightened as hell. The more frightened he looked the more the big man laughed. I just sat and listened. It was all a bit of a shock. For the first time I realized the war wasn't over. The big man would never have joked if he had really thought there was a likelihood of the Germans making a landing. You don't talk like that whan a war is over; that's the way you talk when it's only just begun. I knew then that I'd cracked."

"I don't think there's anything the matter with you, Oliver," said Jane. "I don't think you've cracked. You're perfectly all right. I've never seen you looking so well."

The calm way she said this caused Knight to examine her curiously. "Is that all you've got to say to me?"

"Oliver," she said, moving against him so abruptly that he had to take her in his arms to prevent himself from falling, "Take me away with you. Look after me for a while."

III

THE Air Commodore was disturbed. There was another possible error in Records, and the only consolation he could, for the moment, think of sprang from his assessment of the present situation. He had considered the state of the world in that June of 1940; he had decided the situation was disturbed. It was abnormal. Mistakes were only to be expected. The recent retirement from the Continent had interrupted the smooth flow of unit casualty returns; posting orders had gone astray; military hospitals were failing to notify admission and discharge of R.A.F. personnel; worst of all, from the administrative point of view, a

number of officers and men reported dead had subsequently turned up again. One was glad to know they
were all right, of course, but there was no denying it
made one feel an awful ass!

"There has been a whole day since you received our
telegram, Mrs. Knight," he said. "Why didn't you get
in touch with us immediately?"

"I don't want to bore you," she said. "It's two days
since I got Oliver's wire saying he was all right. Naturally I was expecting him home any moment. The
wire was sent from Newhaven. Then yesterday your
wire came: 'missing, believed drowned.' I wasn't too
worried. I suppose I thought I was too young to be a
widow."

Mrs. Knight was so young and pretty that the Air
Commodore would have liked to say something gallant, but he was held in check by her steady gaze and
the suggestion of a smile about her lips.

"And then you're always reading the papers about
people being reported dead and then they turn up
again," she said, staring at him.

The Air Commodore frowned. "Naturally the press
gives publicity to these quite exceptional cases."

"I was expecting Oliver every moment after I got
his wire. He said he was on his way home. But now
that two days have gone by . . . !"

On the desk in front of him the Air Commodore had
the telegram Mrs. Knight had received from the Air
Ministry, the telegram she had received from her husband, and a file of papers relating to the missing man.
He felt well disposed towards the young woman but he

could not help wondering whether she was too pretty to be trusted with information which had not yet been released to the press. He doubted the discretion of pretty women.

"I want you to tell me where he is," she said.

The Air Commodore spoke cautiously. "Now let me see. We know that your husband was admitted to a certain military hospital in a certain part of France on May 16th. We know that he was operated upon for appendicitis. We know that he was discharged. It's a trail we're following. This is where the trail becomes confused. According to information in our possession, your husband embarked on a certain boat for England. This boat was involved in an incident. And the unfortunate fact is—or so it appeared—that your husband is not officially listed among the survivors. I hope you'll agree that on the face of it we were justified in sending that telegram to you."

"I'm sure your methods are admirable," she said.

"Well, they have to be, don't they? Names and numbers—yes, they may be that on paper. But we keep reminding ourselves that they represent human beings. You see what I mean? The fact remains, however, that you subsequently received a telegram purporting to come from your husband, and handed in at Newhaven post office. There is no chance, I suppose," and here the Air Commodore hesitated, "that someone was playing rather a cruel joke?"

"Only Oliver could have sent that wire."

"Then if he's all right," said the Air Commodore explosively, as though the astonishing facts of the situation had burst upon him for the first time, "why the devil hasn't he been to see you?"

"That is precisely what I'd hoped you would be able to tell me."

"Aha! Mrs. Knight." He was on the point of saying that even the Officer in Charge of Officers' Records himself could not have answered such a question without knowing much more about the intimate married life of F/O Knight and his wife than in fact he did. But he thought better of it. "A Regular officer," he said. "It's hard to imagine him behaving like this without good reason." He looked at Mrs. Knight carefully, seeking to convey that if he had been in F/O Knight's shoes she would never have had a moment's anxiety about his conduct.

"Good God!" he said suddenly. He rose to his feet and walked round his desk to stand immediately in front of her. "I think I've got it!"

Helen Knight's eyebrows rose in astonishment.

"I think I've got it!" He turned and pressed a buzzer on his desk. The door opened and a W.A.A.F. corporal appeared.

"The list of *Dundas* survivors, please, Corporal," said the Air Commodore. By the time this was placed in his hands he had resumed his position behind the desk, his eyes gleaming with excitement. He ran a pencil down the names, grunting: "Hm! There we are. Hm! Well that's not so difficult as it seemed. But who'd have thought it? A Regular officer. Your husband was at Cranwell, Mrs. Knight?"

"So I believe."

"Now this here is a list of people picked up out of the sea after a certain incident, you follow? There's one thing about this list that's foxed us. There's a chap down here who doesn't exist. See? There he is! No, I'd better not show you the list, perhaps. Security and all that nonsense, you know. But I'll tell you the name of this mysterious figure: 7266275 Flying-Officer Richards, John William. No such officer. It's a wrong entry. I've got a feeling in my bones that Flying-Officer Richards is really Flying-Officer Knight. My dear, your husband hasn't come straight home to you. Can you think of anyone else he might have gone to first? His mother, for example?"

"Naturally I've tried every place I could think of. He hasn't been to his mother. She's as worried as I am. I honestly don't see what you're getting at."

"You don't? Now, think carefully."

She shook her head. She knew that she was beginning to colour, and she cursed herself.

"Let me see now. Within, say, twenty-four hours, I shall know for certain if your husband is Flying-Officer Richards. But I still shan't know why he gave a false name. Perhaps I'm jumping to conclusions. We mustn't do that. Your husband has an excellent record. Do you know if he's got any private anxieties?"

"No. He's got the usual public ones, I suppose."

Mrs. Knight puzzled the Air Commodore. One would have expected the wife of a missing officer to show more emotion.

"I'd better be running along, then," she said.

"You're staying in London? May I have your address?"

"I'd better give you a ring when I've got an address. My bag's in the left-luggage at Paddington."

The Air Commodore accompanied her as far as the lift, talking urgently and making gestures.

"Please keep in touch with me. If your husband turns up send me a telegram immediately. Immediately, you understand?"

Outside in the sunshine she remembered the way he had scurried back to his office, and she too began to hurry. The race was on! At that moment the Air Commodore was undoubtedly going through the routine of declaring Oliver a deserter; photographs would be circulated, the police alerted. For her part, Helen was determined to reach Oliver before any military policeman. But how? "Don't panic," she instructed herself. "Keep calm!"

The pavements were so crowded that she stepped into the roadway in order to make quicker progress. She tried to resist a compulsion to look into the face of every passer-by. During the next half-hour she saw Oliver a dozen times. Once he hurried straight towards her and she tried to collect herself for the enthusiasm of his greeting; but at the last moment the man was transformed into a stranger. She saw Oliver step on to a bus. She saw him dart down a side street. She saw him talking to a policeman.

Near Trafalgar Square she found a telephone kiosk and dialled a familiar number. For what seemed an unendurably long time she listened to the ringing of the Wembley telephone; and then she was talking to Molly Nixon.

"But what a pleasant surprise, Helen!"

"Have you seen anything of Oliver?"

"Not since he was here. Why? Is there anything the matter?"

"Oh! do answer me, Molly. Have you seen Oliver recently?"

"But how strange you are, my dear. I am answering you. I saw Oliver yesterday when he came in to pick up his stuff, but I haven't seen him since. Is there anything the matter?"

"Yesterday! Listen, Molly. If anyone—*anyone*—asks you if you've seen him you must say no. I'm coming to see you. I'll be with you just as soon as I can get there. Remember! Not a word to *anyone*."

"But Helen—"

Ever since Oliver had gone to France, Helen had thought peril lived in the air. The danger he ran was of being shot down, of crashing, of a parachute failing to open. When he went into hospital she was glad because for the time he was in bed he was safe. She had never thought of Oliver in the water. Now she saw him lying in the sea, and her imagination translated him. He was a man made remote by salt water. She would not know how to speak to him. Perhaps he would not know how to speak to her.

It was in the house of Molly and Dan Nixon that Helen had met Oliver for the first time. Dan had some civilian job on Oliver's station. The Nixons were extravagantly hospitable people and they had thrown a succession of parties in the weeks preceding the outbreak of war, possibly to relieve the tension, but more probably because they liked parties. So far as Helen knew, the Nixons were the only friends Oliver had in London. If the fact had occurred to Helen before, she would have wasted no time in getting in touch with them; but Molly Nixon was a handsome, motherly, childless, pink-faced woman who was about twenty-five years of age, and what was more, came from the same part of the country as Oliver. Helen was jealous of her, and had not until that moment thought of approaching her for news.

The two women kissed each other affectionately. Molly, in the middle of her cleaning, was wearing one of her husband's cloth caps to keep the dust out of her hair. "She's putting on weight," Helen thought, with gratification.

"How Dan would have liked to see you. He's been sent up to Scotland, though, and here's poor me all on my ownyo! I reckon Dan was a bit smitten with you. He is a dear! I'm all by myself. But I don't do so bad, you know. They say the war's over. Good thing, too, I reckon. My word, you do look nice in that costume. That cost a pretty penny, I know."

"Molly, I've got to find Oliver."

The woman gave Helen a close, smiling scrutiny, "Come in here, dear, and tell me all about it. Men are the very devil, aren't they?"

Helen was indignant. "It's nothing like that."

"Well, whatever it is, tell me all about it."

"I've been to the Air Ministry."

"So-ho!"

"As far as they're concerned Oliver is missing. And as far as I'm concerned Oliver is missing. But you say he came here."

"So-ho!"

"Well, did he?"

"Helen dear, he came in like a thunderbolt and he was all dressed up as a comic tommy. Let me see now. It was yesterday morning. He didn't say much, didn't even give me a kiss. He just picked up some of his stuff out of that suitcase and was out again as though somebody had tied a cracker to his tail. It was all for you, I thought. Lucky little Helen! He just couldn't wait to get at you."

"Did he say he was coming to Reading?"

"Of course." Molly began to chuckle. "Don't look so harassed, girl. I'll make you a cup of tea. So he didn't turn up? If you like, I'll show you the soldier's suit he left behind."

"But where could he have gone to?"

"Secret Service," said Molly shortly. "That's what it is, take it from me. Of course they wouldn't crack on at the Air Ministry. Oliver always was a highly intelligent chap. He's been picked out for the Secret Service. They wouldn't tell you, would they? I mean, it wouldn't be secret if they did."

"No, Molly. It's nothing like that. Are you sure you don't know where he's gone?"

Molly brought her a cup of tea. "You don't think he's got another woman, do you? It wouldn't surprise me at all to learn that my beloved Dan has a wife and three kids in Purley or one of those places. Oliver's so young, though, isn't he? Take it from me, Helen, it's Secret Service."

"Do you mind if I look at his belongings?"

"Or perhaps he's gone to see Hesketh," said Molly some ten minutes later when Helen had finished her fruitless examination of her husband's suitcase.

"Hesketh?" Helen almost added: "Who's he?" But the expression on her face was enough to reveal her ignorance.

"Surely you know Hesketh? Hasn't Oliver spoken to you about him?"

"Oh, Hesketh!" said Helen, wondering how she could extract information about this mysterious person without confessing that Molly knew more about her husband's affairs than she did herself. "What makes you think he's gone there?"

"Come off it, Nell! You've never heard of Hesketh, have you? Why should you? There's no reason why you should. You and Oliver got married so quickly you didn't have time to find out a great deal about each other. There's nothing wrong. Don't look so intense, dear. Hesketh's an old pal of the family. Very rum, dear. Very desperate, odd, romantic! Hesketh and Oliver were at college, or somewhere together, and then Hesketh ran amuck, or went to the bad. He might know."

"Where does he live?"

"They, dear. There's a Mrs."

"Well, where do they both live?"

"It's funny you should ask me that; because if you'd asked me last week I couldn't have answered you. He knew us, Hesketh did. Came here once. Not very nice, dear. Shows his gums when he smiles. Then when the Dunkirk flap was on he wrote for news of Oliver. Luton, I think the place was."

"Have you got the address?"

"Why don't you go home, dear? Oliver's treating you very badly. That young man wants a lesson, he does. Catch me chasing after Dan."

"I suppose my curiosity has been aroused," said Helen lightly.

Molly did not remember Hesketh's address and she had to search among the confusion of papers on her husband's desk before she found his letter. Helen had not seen a letter written in red ink before. In neat, clerk's writing Hesketh had phrased his query with some elegance of language. He took advantage of the brief acquaintance with the Nixons to further trespass upon their time, etc. It amounted to no more than a request for any news they had of Oliver.

"Do you know Hesketh's address?" Helen asked.

"You've got it there in front of your nose," said Molly.

"I know that. But do you remember the address?"

"Can't say that I do."

"Good! Then if anyone comes asking for it, you just won't know, will you?" Helen put the letter into her bag and made for the door.

Molly looked after her with some astonishment. "But surely you trust me?"

"Of course I trust you. My idea is that the Air Ministry thinks Oliver's a deserter. They are bound to make inquiries. I couldn't bear to put you under the strain of telling a lie for my sake. Good-bye-ee!" She kissed her hand.

From the post office on Paddington station she sent a wire to her mother saying she was going to Luton and would telephone later; then she collected her suitcase and made for St. Pancras. She built little hope on the mysterious Hesketh. It was unlikely that a man who had to approach the Nixons for news of Oliver would have any clue to his present where-abouts. But she could not afford to neglect the pos-sibility. If Molly had lost the letter, if she had remem-bered no more of this man Hesketh than his living at Luton, Helen would still have gone there. She was in temper to walk the streets of Luton asking the passers-by if they happened to know a man by the name of Hesketh.

It was late afternoon when she arrived. She was struck by the slenderness of the thread by which she had been drawn into this dusty industrial sunshine. She had never been to Luton before, and the very strangeness of the streets seemed to argue that Oliver was not here. How much wiser she would have been to remain at home! Perhaps by this time he had arrived. There were any number of simple explanations to account for his taking two days to travel the eighty or so miles which separated Newhaven from Reading. She ought to have been calm and patient. The truth remained that the telegram from the Air Ministry had frightened her.

The pavement was hot through the soles of her shoes. The steel framework of a deflated gas-holder trembled in the currents of air that rose from a flat expanse of factory roofing. The town was dead with heat. An old man slept in a bus shelter. Cars left tire-marks in the softened road-surface. In a café where Helen went for a meal, her first food since breakfast, the waitress was listless, and an electric fan droned soporifically. No, said the waitress, she did not know that address, she was a stranger in Luton herself, Hackney was her home. Helen was refreshed by the tea. She went into the cloak-room and stood for some moments watching the water rush out of the tap. It was a cooling, consoling sight. She dipped her handkerchief in the basin and wiped the heat off her face. With the help of her make-up she now felt a little more prepared for whatever Luton was going to provide.

It would have been wiser to leave her suitcase at the station; or to have taken a taxi. But if Oliver was not in Luton she wanted to postpone the disappointment of discovering that fact as long as possible; and if he was in the town she would look all the more pathetic lugging a suitcase along, and she suspected she might have to appeal to him in this way. "No, I won't, though!" she thought. "If he's all right I shall lose my temper!"

A policeman directed her. She left her suitcase in the hall and climbed the bare stairs to the third-floor flat. There was no reply to her ring, and she looked at the card on the door again to make sure she was not mistaken. "Mr. & Mrs. Hesketh," it said, in neat red-ink lettering.

"Hallo!" said an old-woman's voice from the hall below. Helen looked down the staircase well and said "hallo" in her turn.

"Hallo!" said the old woman again. "Who's that?"

"Do you know if Mr. Hesketh is in?"

There were firm footsteps on the stairs, and a plump, foreign-looking man of about forty, his face masked in sweat, appeared before her. He wore vest, grey slacks and carpet-slippers. Black hair stood out from his chest.

"Are you the doctor?" he said in his hoarse, trembling voice. The light was poor on this third-floor landing. "I'm sorry," he said, peering at her. "I thought you were the lady doctor. I was going to say she's gone out. They've all gone out."

"I'm looking for Mr. Hesketh."

"That's what I say. There's nobody at home. Mister won't be back afore six. If you're a friend I'll let you in to wait."

She would have liked to cross-examine the man but the kind of questions that occurred to her would have sounded officious. "Has a stranger called on Mr. Hesketh in the past twenty-four hours?" No, she could not put the question.

"Lady doctor? Is there somebody ill? The Heskeths are friends of my husband's."

It was an unfortunate remark. She saw that in some way it had undermined her claim to know the Heskeths. Perhaps this man, whoever he was, would now turn her away.

"You see," said the man, "I'm on the night shift these days and the wife's been taken queer. I thought you might be the lady doctor, then you could take a look at her. I suppose you wouldn't like to come and take a look anyway?" He prepared to retire.

"I'd be grateful if you'd do as you said and let me into the flat."

"Well, if there's anything missing," he said, not offensively, "I shall remember your face, and what's more I shall have your bag which is downstairs. You see, I've got to protect myself. You only need the one key to open all the flats in this building. No umbrage, I hope, miss?" He delivered the unusual word "umbrage" with some relish, admitted her to the flat, and noisily locked her in.

It came as a shock to realize that she was a prisoner, but she understood the man's motives. "No," she thought, "I won't take umbrage."

It did not appear to be a room that had ever known Oliver. Delicacy prevented her from examining it in any detail; it was bad enough to be an intruder without violating the privacy of people she did not know. The room lacked character. It proclaimed itself a "furnished room" which, together with a bedroom and the usual offices, could be rented for the week or month. Two arm-chairs, a settee, a carpet, a huge chromium-plated electric fire with dust obscuring its glitter—of all these things she was less aware than of the airlessness; all the afternoon the sun had been beating on the closed windows. The atmosphere was so oppressive she felt she might faint unless she admitted some fresh air.

She had scarcely opened the large, old-fashioned sash-window before she heard him running. There had been a cry in the street, too; of that she was obscurely aware. Boots clattered on the stairs. Amplified by the well, the noise was tremendous. The man with the old woman's voice was calling out, but the newcomer, whoever he was, did not pause. Helen could measure his progress both by the increasing volume of sound and by the difference in pace when the man was walking along one of the landings. At the second landing she sank into one of the chairs opposite the door. As he came up the third flight of stairs she rose to her feet once more.

He was there! Hesketh (of his identity there was no possibility of doubt) rattled the key in the door. He flung it open triumphantly and stood there with his hands raised in a melodramatic gesture. "We're on the move!" he cried. "The Heskeths fold their tents!" Then, catching sight of her, he broke off and looked about the room as though doubting whether he had entered the right flat.

"I feel I owe you an apology," said Helen into the silence.

The silence went on and on. Neither moved. Without having formed any previous picture in her mind of the man Hesketh, Helen was nevertheless taken aback by what she saw. His cropped skull made him look like a convict. His stained blue overalls spoke the workman. A certain delicacy of features and an "educated" quality of voice argued the man who had come down in the world. He escaped the ordinary classifications; and perhaps it was this that caused Helen to act cautiously. Perhaps she was afraid of him. Any normal man who had hurried on such a hot afternoon would have been sweating profusely; but Hesketh was dry like a dead leaf.

"I feel I owe you an apology, Mr. Hesketh," said Helen once more. As though released from a trance he closed the door behind him; he searched the room with his eyes. He made a gesture towards the window. By this time he was breathing more normally. He expelled the air from his lungs through pursed lips.

"Did you just open the window?"

Helen nodded.

"I thought you were my wife. I saw you there. You must forgive my—" —and he smiled in a self-deprecating way— "I don't normally burst in on people like this."

"You are Mr. Hesketh?"

"At your service."

"Molly Nixon gave me your address. I came out specially to see you. I'm Helen Knight."

"Helen Knight?" He did not understand.

"Oliver's wife."

"Oliver's wife!" It was a drawn-out shout of delight. Hesketh's face was illuminated. All the exuberance which, at his first sight of her, had been damped down, now found expression once more. "Oh, Helen, may I call you Helen? How wonderful!" He darted up to her, seized one hand and kissed it vehemently, explosively. If only he had dared he would have kissed her on the cheek. His excitement was contagious and Helen found herself laughing. "Oh, Helen!" he said rapturously. "I've heard so much about you. And we've never met! Just think of that! We've never met! We've had to introduce ourselves to one another. How Oliver would laugh! Why are you standing there? Why don't you sit down, for heaven's sake?"

She could not understand his happiness. He asked no explanation for her presence. His assumption was that she knew all about him, was deeply concerned for his welfare, and could not wait to know the latest developments in his never-ending struggle against sorrow.

"I've got the sack," he said.

"But isn't that bad?" She heard the amusement in her voice and thought despairingly: "Oh Oliver! Where are you?"

"Bad? It's splendid. I'd had quite enough of it. I made myself quite impossible. I insulted the foreman. He had to sack me. Now we're free. We can go away from this damnable town and live where nobody knows anything about us. You see," he said more seriously, "I had to make them give me the sack. If I'd handed in my notice I should have had to stay on till the end of the week. Where are Jane and Oliver?"

"Is Oliver here?" she said, trying to speak calmly.

"Of course Oliver's here, and Jane's here, we're all here! Life is going to be wonderful again." He looked into the bedroom, he looked into the kitchen, he looked into the bathroom. "They said they were going out for a walk. They'll be back any minute. I must change my clothes. Oh, how beautiful you are, Helen. I always knew Oliver would marry a beautiful girl. You must both be terribly happy."

When Hesketh had washed and changed into a grey flannel suit he came into the room where Helen had been waiting. His sleekness made him look smaller. He was unnaturally quick in his movements, unnaturally alert, unnaturally deferential.

"What, aren't they back yet?" he said in surprise, and Helen did not answer because he was not really addressing himself to her. He looked at her like a startled mouse; but his mind and his amazement were centred on his absent wife.

"How is Oliver?" She intended her question to sound ironical.

"Of course! You haven't seen him. He said that. Well, he will have a surprise, won't he?"

"Did he tell you why he hadn't come home?"

"Home? Oh, you mean your home. Do you mean to tell me that Oliver came to see us before coming home to you? Now isn't that just like him! But he doesn't mean anything, my dear. I've known him a long time now. I've known him a longer time than you. He's terribly impetuous and thoughtless. Single-minded, too. Artistic temperament. You've no idea what a surprise it was to Jane and me when we heard he was married. Never thought Oliver was the marrying kind."

"Jane?"

"Of course, you don't know Jane. Do you mean to say," Hesketh went on incredulously, "that Oliver has never told you about Jane and me?"

"Never."

"But what's the boy been thinking of? Jane's my wife. I was at college with Oliver. He's my best friend. If it hadn't been for Oliver I should never have met Jane. It's a most interesting story. Did he never tell you?"

"How long do you think they'll be?" She could not possibly stay alone with him any longer. Nothing had any consequence unless it related directly to himself. He went on talking, talking, talking; about Jane, and himself, and Oliver; telling her of the days before she had met Oliver until she wanted to put her fingers to her ears. The man seemed to have only one object: to establish that he and Jane existed as vitally important people in Oliver's life. Helen felt she must be looking crimson with anger.

"Is there a hotel in Luton?" she demanded.

"Of course. There are lots of them."

"Which is the best one?"

Hesketh said he was not familiar with the hotels of the town. He would rather not say which was the best. What did she want to know for anyway? Helen must understand, quite clearly, that so long as Oliver was in Luton they were both to be guests in the flat. He would be most injured if they went to a hotel. When Helen still maintained a silence, Hesketh began to recite the names of the hotels in plaintive tone. Helen picked on the first he mentioned.

"I shall go there. When my husband comes in you can tell him where I am. I shall go to bed at ten o'clock. He's not to disturb me after that. I shall leave for London at ten in the morning. You can give him my time-table. You understand?"

"But—but—oh dear, do forgive me. I've forgotten your name."

"Mrs. Knight," she said, almost sick with fury.

"No, I mean your first name."

She was through the door and descending the first flight of stairs before he realized that she was angry. He pursued her to the second landing. He pursued her to the first landing. "My dear, you mustn't get upset because I forget your name. I'm an awful fool. D'you hear me? I'm a fool. I'm a fool, I said. Do please tell me what your first name is. You've simply no idea of the terrible life I am having. Or you'd have pity on me." He caught her up in the hall. "Do you believe in reincarnation? I sometimes think I must have been some terrible monster in a previous existence. And now I've got to expiate everything. I've got to suffer. Do let me carry your case for you."

They went down the hill so quickly together that passers-by stopped and stared. A dog jumped out of a gateway and took a bite at Hesketh's trousers, but he did not notice.

"My name is Helen. I don't care tuppence whether you remember it or not. It's quite irrelevant. Where's this hotel you're taking me to?"

It was a large commercial hotel in liver-coloured brick down a side street. Hesketh said he had once stayed there himself when he first came to Luton looking for a job, and that although the saloon-bar was noisy, the manageress was friendly, and the prices reasonable. The manageress, as it turned out, was suspicious. She came out from behind her desk, and ignoring all Hesketh's claims of acquaintanceship, examined Helen and her luggage closely, and asked if she might see her identity card.

"I can give you a single room, madam," she said firmly.

"Let me carry your bag up," said Hesketh.

"There's a boy to do that," said the manageress. "And I'll come up myself to show the room. If you'll kindly wait here," she added, looking at Hesketh insolently.

"Don't forget to tell my husband what I told you to tell him," said Helen. "I shan't be coming down again."

Once alone in her room she took off her shoes and stretched out on the bed with her eyes closed. If only she could cry she would feel better; but the tears would not come. It seemed incredible that Oliver had treated her so badly. She wondered what kind of woman this Mrs. Hesketh was, and why Oliver should apparently prefer her company to his wife's. She wanted to hate Oliver but the hate, like the tears, would not come.

She was much too frightened. Then, in spite of the laughter from the saloon-bar, she fell asleep.

She was awakened by the ringing of the bedside telephone. For a while she lay looking at a ceiling made golden by a declining sun. It required an effort to realize where she was; with her realization came the conviction that she was about to speak to her husband for the first time in months.

But it was Hesketh, speaking from a public call-box.

"I wondered whether you'd like to go to the pictures."

"Have they come back?"

"No. I thought we'd kill time by going to the pictures. You won't want to sit about in that hotel by yourself all the evening. I want to make sure that you've forgiven me. Why can't we go to the pictures? We all need cheering up."

She looked at her watch. It was seven o'clock.

"No, thank you. It was good of you to telephone." And she put down the receiver. She rose from the bed, sponged her face, dressed, and sat in front of a mirror with the lipstick poised. What if this man told Oliver where she was, and Oliver did not come? She grimaced at her reflection, and tried hard not to be sorry for herself.

Hesketh was waiting at the reception-desk when she went down for dinner. There was no opportunity for escape.

"I can't understand it," he said. "They've still not come back. If Jane had been alone I could have expected it. But Oliver would surely see she wouldn't wander off."

"I'm rapidly losing interest in this situation," said Helen.

"It's all right for you. You don't have to live on your nerves like I do."

"You know nothing whatsoever about me." How could she get rid of this dreadful man? If she walked into the dining-room he would be sure to follow. He might even insist on sitting down at her table.

"That's true enough, Helen. But you know nothing about Jane and me, either."

"To be perfectly frank, I don't want to."

Hesketh's jaw dropped. "I'm sorry Helen. I didn't know I was annoying you."

"If I weren't so hungry I probably shouldn't be so rude. So if you'll forgive me——"

Hesketh stood at the door of the dining-room with an expression of such puzzled concern on his face that Helen, who had caught a glimpse of it in passing, felt a pang of compunction. If she was right in her suspicion, this silly little man was going to suffer as much as she. Lifting her eyes to a wall mirror she saw by its reflection that he was still standing at the door. In the altered perspective of the mirror he was sharply but minutely defined, his smooth skull glistening like a bead.

Helen suddenly realized that the two men at the next table were discussing Hesketh. The tables were placed so close together that she could not have avoided hearing even if she had wished to do so.

"His wife's as mad as you make 'em. They're strangers. Evacuées, I suppose you'd call 'em. Can't help feeling sorry for 'em. She goes mooning about the place as though her feet weren't quite touching the ground, if you see what I mean. No sense of time or place. He has to spend hours looking for her sometimes. Attractive woman, too."

The speaker, a severe-looking man in a well-cut suit, leaned forward, and the rest of his remarks were inaudible to Helen. The other man at the table, equally severe and equally well dressed, grunted heavily over the confidential information he had just received, and pointedly changed the conversation. Looking into the mirror once more Helen saw that Hesketh had gone.

Right up until the end of the meal Helen thought the miracle would happen and Oliver would appear. But he did not come. The evening had become so strange she felt the need of a reassuring voice, and went to telephone her mother.

"No," she said in reply to the expected question. "But he's here, and I hope to be seeing him tonight."

"A telegram came this afternoon."

"Who from?"

"Why, from Oliver, of course. His mother's been on the phone too, asking for news."

"What does the telegram say?"

" 'Please forgive delay. Trying to reach you as soon as possible. Fondest love. Oliver.' "

Helen was silent for so long that her mother asked anxiously: "Are you there, Helen?"

"Will you read it again."

Her mother repeated the message.

"Where was it handed in?"

"Luton. That's where you are, isn't it?"

"What time was it handed in?"

"Let me see now. Nine o'clock. But it's taken ages to get here. What does it all mean, Helen? Why do you sound so mysterious?"

"Now don't you worry, Mummy. As soon as I've seen Oliver I'll give you another ring. But I won't ring after ten, so don't wait up."

She went to her room and produced note-paper out of her case. She carefully wrote down Oliver's telegram while she could be sure of remembering it accurately, and then, with pencil in hand, sat studying it as though she suspected a hidden meaning which with patience it could be persuaded to yield up. It was exasperatingly vague. She even wondered whether Molly had been entirely wrong in her suggestion that Oliver was busy on some special work; it was not impossible. The Air Ministry's telegram and Oliver's own two telegrams only made it highly improbable. She groped for possible explanations. Was it fancy or were the words of this second telegram not so much a statement as an appeal? She had a curiously vivid picture of Oliver in a flying-helmet gesticulating for help out of a cloud.

That summer evening he was out and about in the town. She could not, after all, remain in her room, working herself up once more to an impossible pitch of resentment. He would not come. She knew that. Jane would not let him. It was impossible to be jealous of

Jane as she might have been jealous of an ordinary woman, not after overhearing that conversation at dinner. But Helen could think of her as a witch whose enchantment had to be broken.

The bedroom was stuffy and there seemed to be no more air in the streets. Bats flickered between the houses and shops and it was odd to see them in such a place. If she walked slowly, soldiers tried to speak to her. She began to hurry. The sky held bright clouds, but the valley in which the town lay was filling with shadow. The shadows reached out from street to street. Cigarettes glowed in doorways. When the traffic noises subsided, as they did from time to time, heavy boots could be heard tramping on remote, hollow pavements.

Without planning to do so she had arrived at the Victorian terrace where Hesketh had his flat. As though expecting her, he came down the steps to meet her. She did not pause. She did not speak and she did not expect him to speak. The thinning light gave delicacy to the houses; they drifted by, they were unreal, people neither entered nor left those cavernous doorways. Hesketh coughed twice. They went on climbing the hill. The stale air of the town gave way to a fresh country breeze.

Helen stopped. "Is it possible that Oliver and your wife have gone away together?"

"Gone away?" The thought had obviously never occurred to him. Even now he resisted it, and spoke irrelevantly. He had been waiting on the steps because it had seemed the best place to wait. At any moment Jane and Oliver would appear. Even now they might be climbing the stairs to the flat.

"You know your wife and I don't. I only know Oliver. At least, I know him a little. Don't you understand? Do you think they've gone away together?"

"Where to?"

"What does it matter? Do you think they've gone away together?"

"You don't understand, Helen. They haven't gone away. They are here, in the town. I shouldn't be surprised if they've gone to the pictures. I hope I didn't say anything wrong when I suggested we might go to the pictures. I thought it was a sensible thing to do."

"Is there anything the matter with your wife?"

"She's not well."

"What's the matter with her?"

"She's a little unwell, that's all. She'll get better."

"I'm going back to the hotel."

When they reached the flat, Hesketh suggested that he might run upstairs and see if they were there. She could hear him climbing the stairs, she could hear him walking along the landings, she could even—the night was so quiet—hear him unlock the door of his flat and walk in.

"Well?" she said when he rejoined her.

"They really are terribly late. It's wrong of Oliver to keep her out so late. I'm getting a bit worried."

Helen had already taken a few steps down the hill, but at Hesketh's words she stopped and came back to him. "Don't you understand," she said curiously, "that your wife has left you?"

"No, no, no, that's impossible."

"They're not coming back," she said.

Now that Hesketh did at last understand what she was driving at, his calmness surprised her. He would take her back to the hotel, and they would have another talk in the morning. She was not to upset herself. She must get a good night's rest. There was absolutely no excuse for imagining that Jane and Oliver would do anything wrong.

IV

KNIGHT marvelled at Jane's bitter humour.

"If you were to go off somewhere," he said, "what would *he* do?"

They were sitting on the top deck of a country bus; meadows, hedges, lanes, cottages, unravelled in the sunshine.

"Kill himself."

"Yes," Knight nodded, "he'd do that." It astonished him that he and Jane should be so callous.

"Tickets, please," said the conductress.

"All the way," said Knight. "Two all the way."

"All the way? To Aylesbury?"

"If that's where you're going."

Jane opened her handbag and in spite of Knight's protests insisted on paying for the tickets with a ten-shilling note. When she received her change she pressed it into his hand. She made him hold his two hands together and emptied the contents of her purse into them; notes, silver, coppers, perhaps ten pounds or so in all. Coins slipped through his fingers and rolled about their feet. Notes fluttered to the floor. Knight knelt to retrieve all this money, and Jane showered more coins upon him. She found a book of stamps in one of her pockets and threw it down. She would take none of it back. Knight must keep it for her. He was to look after her.

"When we get back to Luton I'll give it to your husband, madam."

"He would only try to give it back to me. Keep it. Besides we're not going back to Luton."

"But if you were really going away at the very least you'd have packed a few belongings. You've only got what you're wearing."

"Oh God!" she said. "I wish we could put the clock back. I wish we were back where we were two years ago."

Knight decided that as soon as they arrived at Aylesbury he would telephone Helen. He would telephone the Air Ministry, too. But about this plan he said nothing to Jane, wanting to prolong as much as possible the serenity which had settled on them both. For the most part they sat in silence. The upper deck of the bus was as warm as a greenhouse, and they drifted along the country lanes, stopping at this village to pick up one passenger, and at that village to set him down again, only half awake, dreaming, smiling to themselves, wishing that the journey would go on for ever.

On the outskirts of the town there was a control point manned by two armed military-policemen and a civilian-policeman. All vehicles were being stopped and the occupants scrutinized. At Tring an exceptionally fat man in his late fifties had climbed to the upper deck of the bus and seated himself immediately behind Jane and Knight, where he smoked a pipe and chuckled at some private joke. When a military-policeman came upstairs he found only Knight, Jane, and this fat man; and what was more, the fat man baying with laughter and offering to come quietly.

"I'm a Jerry parachutist," he said.

The M.P. came up to the front of the bus and stared at the trio.

"What's the trouble?" said Knight.

"No trouble," said the M.P. in an imitation American accent, "it's what I'm paid for and it's also a pleasure."

Fortunately he had such a high opinion of his powers of observation that he asked no questions and demanded no documents. He ignored Jane and the fat man. He scrutinized Knight in a way that advertised his rare ability to pick out Germans, deserters, and other undesirable people without descending to the cruder method of interrogation. He nodded, gave a mock salute, and retired.

"Jerry parachutists," said the fat man. "There was

a plane flying low last night, over 'Alton it was, and of course everybody says parachutists."

Whoever the police might have been looking for, Knight was under no illusions about the narrowness of his escape. He had no wish to be picked up in that way. At a moment of his own choosing he would certainly report at the Air Ministry in person—he dismissed his recently formed intention of telephoning—he would go up to London and walk into the Air Ministry and say: "Here I am! Knight! You thought I was dead, didn't you?" But it would have to wait until he had seen Helen.

"I could do with something to eat," said Jane.

They did not wait for the bus to carry them into the centre of the town. Knight had an idea it would be safer to make a more devious approach, and dropping off at some traffic lights at one end of the long High Street, they walked along a side street, crossed the deserted cattle-market, and entered a shop-lined square through an archway. Neither he nor Jane had been in Aylesbury before, but there was no mistaking the route they ought to follow. The town was set on a hill and they walked up it.

Knight pointed out a restaurant. "We'll get something to eat over there. Then d'you know what I'm going to do? I'm going to put you on a bus back to Luton."

They walked across the square but Jane made no answer.

"You understand I'm not coming back to Luton?" said Knight.

Jane did not say a word. There were stone—or were they iron?—lions crouching in the square, and she paused to pat the paw of one of the creatures and smile at the absurd expression on its face.

"It'll be a pleasant run back for you," said Knight, "all by yourself."

But his words appeared to make no impression upon her. Once in the restaurant, however, she absented herself for a while and when she returned he saw that she *might* have been crying. There was a pink softness, almost a warmth, on her face. Her eyes were brilliant.

"You mustn't be so hard on Martin."

"Martin?" Knight looked up. "How odd to hear him called Martin. I never think of him except as Hesketh. I'm not hard on him."

"He's always been good and kind."

"But you hate him."

"No," she said slowly, "I don't—hate him."

In spite of having said she was hungry Jane ate little. She was too restless. Knight paid the bill and they went out into the sunshine once more. At the bus station they consulted a time-table and discovered there was not another bus back to Luton for three-quarters of an hour. Neither of them had a watch but they could see the gold face of the church clock over the roofs of the houses.

"Let's go and have a look at the church," Knight suggested.

He could never enter a church without thinking of Jane. Within a few hours of meeting her for the first time—it was the Christmas of 1937—she had carried him off to the village church where he had helped her set up a Nativity scene for the children. He was an unbeliever then and he was an unbeliever now, but Jane's belief had impressed him. He had loved her, but her true ascendancy over him had been established by her faith; innocent and optimistic as he was, he saw that her faith conferred an experience of the world and a calm lack of optimism that aroused his envy. She knew that there would be war when he had thought there would be peace. She was never cynical. She was wise.

They walked in the cool shadow of a cobbled lane. Churchyard grasses were seeding on the graves. A party of schoolgirls in white straw hats, carrying tennis rackets, were taking a short cut; and as they went past, their round eyes looking out of their fair round faces had the calm speculation of sleepy kittens. Inside the church Knight discovered an Elizabethan tomb with the stone figure of a kneeling woman. He called Jane over and read out the inscription:

"Goode frend, stick not to strew with crimson floures
This marble tombe wherein her cinders rest,
For sure her ghost lives with the heavenly powers,
And guerdon hath of virtuous life possest."

In front of the kneeling woman, in an ordinary jam jar, was a single red poppy.

"Let's go into the sun," said Jane. It was the first time she had made a suggestion of any kind, and Knight thought she shivered. It was cool in the church only in contrast to the heat outside, and whatever chill

Jane was experiencing could only be psychological.

"Somebody believes in keeping up an old custom."

"Who is Lady Lee to anybody now? I wouldn't put a red flower on her tomb."

"You think she should be forgotten?"

"We ought to forget ourselves." For the first time Jane was taking the initiative. By the time Knight had caught her up once more she was walking quickly, impatiently, down the churchyard path. "Why did you bring me here?" she said angrily. "It was a rotten thing to do. Haven't I got a right to forget, if I want to?"

Knight tried to take her by the arm.

"You're as bad as Martin," she went on. "You want to keep dragging me back into the past. I've forgotten all about it. I've forgotten who I am. I've forgotten the child, she was never conceived. I never felt her quicken. She was not born. I don't want love and tenderness and understanding. I don't want taking care of. All right, Oliver," she said more calmly, "you've done you duty. You've been to see me. Go away now and leave me alone." She was dry-eyed. They stood in a courtyard whispering and the whispers rustled back from the red eighteenth-century walls.

"You've a right to do whatever you want to," he said.

"Yes, everybody's got a right to do just what they want to. You do what you want. I'll do what I want. Only for God's sake let us leave each other alone. Let's get away from this place."

They came to a street where there were shops, and walked on the side where the sun shone. "I'm not going back to Luton," she said.

"Then what are you going to do?"

"You were right," she said after a pause. "I do hate Martin. It's because every time I look at him I keep remembering. How can you ask me that question: what am I going to do? You know very well what I'm going to do. Whatever it is, we're going to do it together."

Half an hour later they were in a bus bound for Oxford. If Hesketh had been there to challange him, Knight would have had only the one answer to give: "Jane and I are lost in the wood and we are trying to find our way. We can scarcely see and we are afraid of feeling. And as we press on the trees are closing up behind us and barring our retreat. There is no retreat. We must go on and on."

"When I was a child I thought God would help me in all my troubles," said Jane.

In a wheat field beyond Thame lay a scarlet banner of poppies. They stared at it mutely and Knight, automatically testing his power to judge distances, had a guess at the length of the field before counting the number of telegraph-posts by way of check. It was not the field itself so much as the extent of the poppies he wanted to estimate. And this was difficult. There was a curious recess in the middle of the field and the poppies appeared to pour into the recess like scarlet water running out of a bath. This complicated the perspective. The heat, too, was playing tricks. What had at first appeared a banner or carpet was now hoist at one corner; it was an enormous wing of colour. Then it was an ellipse. Then it was a pit into which they would, bus and all, tumble. Knight jerked his attention to the woodland on the other side of the road. His senses were playing tricks. Perhaps he was going dotty.

"Where are you taking me to?" said Jane.

"God knows! I must write to Helen. Will you remind me to write to Helen at the very first opportunity?"

Poor kid! Unless she had put it down to the vagaries of the service she must be quite bewildered by his behaviour. For that matter he was bewildered himself. He suddenly screwed round in his seat to take one more look at the field of poppies, but it was already out of sight. Yet was it? He could see a field of yellowing wheat, and what was more he could discern the curious depression which he had noticed at the heart of the poppies. He wanted to ask Jane whether she had noticed the poppies but was restrained—quite irrationally—by the fear she sould say yes. "That field?" he would say, pointing at the one he now saw; and she would say: "Yes, that one. But there are none there now, are there?" And he would have to say: "No, we have only seen one poppy and that was on a tomb in a church. There are no other poppies. No one else is trying to make us remember."

So he kept silent. They rode past the dilapidated cottages, and the council houses, and the smart pubs. Wheatley spire pricked above the elm trees. The woods thinned, the hills became bald and green, a lake winked in the sun, a group of soldiers stood at a road junction staring; eventually they saw a waste of red houses with spires and towers beyond; and they rolled down a leafy tunnel towards Magdalen Bridge and Oxford.

"*My darling wife:*" (he wrote in Oxford Public Library)

"Well, it's good to be back in England once more, and to know that I stand on the same bit of land as you. I always had a grudge against that English Channel because it divided us. You'll never forgive me for not putting in an appearance before this, but as a matter of fact I've run into some old friends of mine who've had some bad luck and I'm just lending a hand to get things sorted out. Won't go into details. It's all a bit of a bore, really. How's Whiskers behaving himself? Don't feed him meat. If you have any nasty letters from the Air Ministry, for heaven's sake just put them in the fire and think no more about them. I'm all right, you understand, darling. There's nothing to worry about. The only trouble with me is that I love you so much it's hard to believe— being the pessimist I am—that you really exist and that you're not some sort of vision I once had. I can't say I miss the old appendix.

With all my love,
Oliver

P.S. I'll be with you before the end of the week."

. . .

As an explanatory note it was miserably inadequate. For some moments he sat staring at the letter-card. Even if he had wanted to write any more there was no room left. He took it over to Jane who was sitting at a table reading a magazine.

"What's this?" she asked. Characteristically she had asked no question when he had bought the letter-card at the post office, nor when he had borrowed the fountain-pen she carried in her handbag.

"It's a note to Helen."

"You want me to read it?"

She read quickly, then laid the card flat on the table and covered it with her open hand. They conversed in whispers. Even so, readers at other tables looked up disapprovingly. Long, powdery beams of sunlight traversed the room.

"Who's Whiskers?"

"The cat."

They sat looking at each other.

"It's a cruel letter. Why did you show it to me? Is it a good marriage, Oliver?"

"Yes, it's a very good marriage," he said. "We've only had a fortnight together. It's a good marriage from my point of view. She is everything I want in a wife. I love her so much I'm frightened to go to her. Does that make sense?"

"No."

"Could you write a better letter?"

"I think so."

Knight tore the letter card into small pieces and threw them into a waste-paper-basket. He told Jane to remain where she was while he went across the road to the post office and bought another. When he returned he took Jane to a table isolated in the far corner of the reading-room, produced the fountain-pen, poised it over the letter-card and said: "Well?"

"I can't tell you what to write."

Knight looked at her. "Than write yourself. Write in your own name."

"No," said Jane. She rose to her feet. "No, no, no."

Knight knew that it was here, in Oxford, that a choice would have to be made. For another hour there remained the possibility of choice. Then he and Jane would be at the railway station with a decision to make. It was a matter of choosing between two platforms. From one platform the trains ran to Reading and to Helen; from the other they ran to Worcester and beyond; to the hillocky, western border of the Severn valley where he and Jane had first met.

The pavements were so crowded that progress was difficult and they walked in the road, dodging the traffic. The sun discharged light and heat in their faces. Cars hooting, bicycle bells ringing, men and women shouting, music from a radio shop—it was as though the summer afternoon were a room too small to hold all this noise. Knight bought a newspaper and glanced at the headlines. It was reported that details of the German plan to invade Britain had been secured; there was a map with named landing-places and black arrows thrusting to isolate London. Reading, he saw, was a primary objective.

"Jane," he said when they reached the station. "I'm

going to take you to Worcester. Mother will be very pleased to have you and look after you for a bit. I'm going to Reading in the morning. This has gone on long enough."

Words were necessary only for the man in the ticket office, for the ticket collector, for the elderly lady travelling alone who needed reassurances that she was on the right train. Jane and Knight had nothing for each other that words could express. From the window they could see to a more distant horizon than at any time since they had set out for Luton. Three-quarters of what they saw was sky. Coniferous windbreaks, so remote that they were motionless, were the tiniest of sepia brush-strokes across a silver hill. The bare, free, summery, wind-scoured Cotswolds made frank gestures of welcome. Jane and Knight were a man and a woman with a history of feeling for each other safely behind them. Now and again they turned their eyes from the landscape and looked at one another, smiling.

After the sky and the long lines of the Cotswolds the Severn valley was a different country. Evesham was a frontier town. Hedges, orchards, trees relaxed in the evening light. The air was mild. The Malvern range stood against the western brightness. They were returning to a landscape which they had once shared. When Worcester threw out its suburbs to meet them the train carried Jane and Knight into the years before the war; they stood on the long, curving platform of Shrub Hill, momentarily recovered from the dream of catastrophe. It needed only a few words from Jane to jerk them back into the present.

"I can't go to your mother's house."

"I'm not giving you any choice."

"She wouldn't understand."

Knight called a taxi. Until they were safely seated in the taxi and Knight was confident Jane could not escape, he kept a tight grip on her arm. As they made their way through the narrow, crowded streets near the station he allowed his fingers to rest lightly across her wrist. In his eagerness to take in the sights and sounds of the city where he had spent so much of his childhood he forgot that they were making for a house where they were not expected, and where their arrival would cause surprise, delight certainly, and possibly bewilderment. The leather upholstery of the taxi was damp; it gave out a stable-and-harness smell, exciting him. He leaned forward to obtain a better view of the old houses in the Shambles. There was the cathedral. There was the brown river itself, being churned up by a tug and a line of barges.

"What do you mean, she wouldn't understand?" he asked as the taxi carried them into the suburb where his mother and stepfather lived. Were they not coming home? What more in the way of explanation could be asked of them?

The house itself gave no signals. The large, stone-framed windows looked blankly on to the rose garden. At the very top of the house the blinds of two miniature windows had been drawn, and they looked out like sightless eyes. The outer door was closed. Perhaps there was no one at home.

"What do you mean, she wouldn't understand?" He

picked a yellow rose and handed it to her absent-mindedly. She held the stem so that the flower hung head-downwards. She did not look at it. She did not smell it.

"Your mother is watching us." The air was so still there was no need to speak above a whisper.

Knight looked up at the first-floor window. Catching the last sunlight, the round face floated like a pink mask against the dark interior of the room. Still holding her yellow rose Jane gazed up the street, patient under observation. Instinctively Knight took her arm. He would have called up to his mother if only he could have been sure she would hear on the other side of that sealed window. "What's the matter with her?" he thought. "Why is she so still?" He smiled. He raised a hand. It occurred to him that he had not seen his mother since the wedding nine months ago.

It seemed a long time before she came down the stairs, opened the door and kissed him. She was silent with excitement. He gripped her tightly with his left arm and she stood with her head against his chest as though to listen to the beating of his heart. He could not help noticing the streaks of grey in her hair; she had been absurdly proud of her brown hair. Now only the brown curls she carefully preserved over her forehead were quite free of grey hairs. He wondered whether she had dyed them. A middle-aged widow who married again would naturally have to be careful of appearances. She put an arm round his waist.

"Oliver!" she said faintly. "Where's your uniform?" Then she produced a handkerchief from the sleeve of her knitted brown jumper and blew her nose loudly. "Oliver, two men have been here making inquiries about you."

"What sort of men?"

"Plain-clothes policemen. That's what they said they were. They told me that if you came I was to ask you to telephone them."

"Aren't you going to ask us in, Mother?"

She could grapple with only one thought at a time. "They were polite, I must say that for them. Oh Jane, darling, don't break that poor rose up." For Jane was slowly picking the rose to pieces and dropping the petals one by one on the step. Jane lifted her head sharply.

"I'm sorry. I didn't realize what I was doing."

The older woman embraced her impetuously and tearfully.

"Oliver, Jane," she said when they had gained the drawing-room, "for heaven's sake tell me what is the matter. Helen's been telephoning me, I've been telephoning her. To make matters worse I found myself speaking to her mother, and you know I can never understand a word she says. She talks so fast and she does take you up so if you ask her to say it again."

"It's nice to know I'm not forgotten." Knight looked round the room. The furnishings were discreetly expensive. Carpets, furniture, pictures indicated money—far more money than his own father had been able to provide; and, to be honest, the handsome room revealed a good taste to which his father never had any pretensions; neither had his mother, for that matter. Knight looked at her and smiled. This was not her house. It belonged to Black. If Black was as regular in his habits as he used to be, at any moment he would walk in, smelling of his leather-warehouse.

His mother was excited by the word "forgotten." All her attention was given to him. Her eyes did not leave his face. They made passionate appeals for reassurance.

"Oh, I don't mean that you would forget me. Did those men want to pick me up as a deserter?"

"A deserter? They said they wanted you to telephone, that's all. They were nice young men, Oliver. They wouldn't have called you a deserter. You're not a deserter. You haven't done anything wrong."

"Well, I've brought Jane to you."

"I've left my husband, Mrs. Black."

"Yes," said Knight, turning sharply and looking into his mother's face. "She's left Hesketh."

At the very moment when they wanted to look into her eyes she turned her head away. For the first time they were talking about themselves to a third person. Knight loved his mother as a son; Jane loved her as an old friend. They wanted to look into this loved face to judge by the expression there the kindest verdict that could possibly be passed upon them. They needed guidance on the role they would have to play.

"Then you must go back to him, Jane," said Mrs. Black. Her words were a reminder of a circumstance Knight had forgotten. She loved him in the way most mothers loved their sons; she had, too, a warm regard for Jane. But for Hesketh himself she had a strange, incalculable affection which—how could Knight ever have forgotten it?—had been manifest at their first meeting and had never faltered. Hesketh and Mrs. Knight—as she had been then—understood one another. Had they been more of an age they might have been lovers. As it was, the marriage with Jane had been partly due to her manœuvring.

"What has Martin done that you should treat him like this?"

"Jane is ill, Mother. You don't understand."

"And what about Helen? Does she know you are here? I'm trying to be sensible. I keep looking at you, Oliver, and thinking: 'Thank God he is alive.' It's a surprise and—and a shock, seeing you again like this. I was standing up there in the window, and you looked like ghosts in the garden. Why do you say I don't understand? I know Jane is not well, poor child. Martin has written me many letters, and I've written many letters to him. I know what the poor boy has suffered."

It was hard to tell whether it was excitement or anger. Her face had gone pale; then colour flooded back. The powder, where it had been dabbed on too thickly, stood out on one side of her nose. Strong feeling made her look younger. "I can't believe you know what you're talking about, either of you. Come into the kitchen and let me get you something to eat."

They were, all three of them, ravenously hungry. Mrs. Black put on a white apron and cut ham sandwiches which they took from her hand and ate standing. The kitchen door stood open to the lawn and the willow tree, and Knight went out for a while to smell the evening. The thin chiming from the cathedral hung about in the bushes. A tug hooting on the river spoke of the salt water from which it had come. No place to rest, it seemed to say. Under the sleepy twittering of birds in the willow tree he could, knowing himself to be invisible, look up the garden to the kitchen where a light now burned; he could see his mother and Jane standing close together, yet not speaking. There was a summer-house. Inside the summer-house he could no longer see the kitchen; he was quite alone with himself. There was nothing to prevent his climbing the wall and dropping down into the lane which he knew lay on the other side. But why should he wish to escape? It had nothing whatsoever to do with the policemen who had called to make inquiries about him. The urge astonished him. He had experienced a similar urge nine months before on the morning of his marriage. He remembered being told that all men wanted to escape just before they were married.

"Oliver!" It was Jane's voice. She was in the garden, looking for him. He made no reply. "Oliver!" He could hear her feet brushing over the grass. Her shoes tapped on the path. It was wrong that Jane should have to come searching for him in the garden. If anyone came at all it should have been his mother. "Oliver!" said Jane once more, so close that he could hear her breathing.

"I'm in here, Jane."

"Your mother's sent Martin a telegram. She's been

dictating it over the telephone. It means that he'll be here in the morning."

But when Jane and Knight re-entered the house they found that Mrs. Black was not alone. Black had arrived. They could hear his exclamatory voice in the hall. He was asking questions. He was listening to answers. He was grunting. He was asking another question.

"I'll not leave you," said Knight to Jane.

"Oliver!" Black came forward, his arms extended, his face radiant. Since Knight had seen him last he had begun to grow a beard and the thin brown growth made him look more like the conventional portraits of Shakespeare than ever. "My God! It's good to see you," he said explosively. There was no doubting the sincerity of his welcome. He threw an arm round Knight's shoulders and hugged him, quite determined to welcome the warrior home again in the way convention told him warriors should be welcomed home. He did not understand what his wife had been telling him. He smiled at Jane and put out his free hand to close his fingers affectionately on her wrist, but he did not understand why she should be there. He drew his stepson to the sideboard and poured out a whisky.

"What'll you girls have?" he shouted. He poured out another whisky for himself. His wife had told him men had been at the house making inquiries about Oliver but he did not know what it meant and did not want to know.

"Have another," he said, and Knight nodded, holding out his glass. He had not touched any alcohol for so long that a very little of it intoxicated. His mother and Jane drank sherry. He saw the flush on Jane's cheek and how bright her eyes were. He went over to her and whispered in her ear.

"I'll not leave you."

"Oh yes," she said.

"I'll not leave you. Mother, you had no right to send that telegram to Hesketh."

"Oh yes," said Jane, rising to her feet. She placed her glass on the table and they all watched her closely. "She has every right. This is your mother's house. I didn't want to come. I can't see Martin. Oh, can't I be left alone? I must," she said putting her hands to her head, "have some peace of mind."

"Peace of mind?" said Black. It might have been an expression he had never heard before.

"Jane, dear," said his wife, "you know how fond of you I've always been. You won't have any peace of mind away from your husband. You know how devoted he is to you. I'm sure you could never have had a more patient and understanding husband."

"I don't want patience and understanding." Jane would have run out of the room if Knight had not caught her; and it was to him she spoke, with her face not more than three inches from his. "He keeps pouring his patience and understanding over me, and I can't bear it. I've done dreadful things to him, and he's patient with me."

"What is all this?" Black groaned. He put some more sherry into Jane's glass. Marriage suited him; he had put on weight, he was jovial, he was self-confident;

he was an altogether more engaging man than the bridegroom Knight remembered. At that very moment, in the act of pouring out sherry and asking for the situation to be explained to him he was, in fact, thoroughly enjoying himself. Perhaps business life in Worcester was humdrum. He welcomed excitement even if he could not be bothered to understand the reason for it. His eye caught his stepson's and he winked.

"Would you lend me some money?" said Knight.

Black straightened and became serious at once. "Yes. How much do you want?" There was great meaning in these words. No nonsense about me! you'll notice I don't ask you what you want the money for. You are my stepson. I am good to you for your mother's sake. I try to treat you like my own son. I have complete trust in you.

"A hundred pounds," said Knight.

Eyebrows shot up but it was part of Black's idea of a game not to exclaim on the size of the amount.

"I'd like it in one-pound notes," said Knight.

"And you'd like this straight away? I don't think I've got so much money in ready cash." He motioned his wife back. "Now, my dear, don't excite yourself. I understand Oliver. Oliver understands me. After all it will be his one day. I have no other heir."

"What do you want this money for, Oliver?" she demanded.

He stepped across the room, caught her two hands together, and raised them to his lips. They stood looking into one another's eyes, he smiling, she staring with a touch of fear. He saw how her left nostril, slightly dilated, was trembling; it was a familiar trick. His memory of it went back to earliest childhood when with the eager, passionate, detailed curiosity of a child he had studied her face for the slightest variation of mood. It meant a heightened expectancy of good or bad. Looking at her now he thought how incredible it was that she should be his mother; that there had ever been any other relationship between them but the one established that very moment: he knowing what the next step would be, and dominant; she loving and fearful.

"It's a secret," he said.

He accompanied his stepfather to the small room on the first floor which was known as the study; in reality it contained two easy chairs, a glass-fronted cabinet with fishing-rods and a sporting rifle, a portable wireless set, a green baize table only suitable for playing cards, and on the wall an elaborate pipe-rack and a frame of tropical butterflies. There were no books, no writing material. There was, however, a small safe on the floor in the corner. The safe was so full that when Black opened it, documents, sealed envelopes, and bundles of papers tumbled out on to the floor. He extricated a cash box, made sure that it was open, and handed it over to Knight with the words: "Help yourself, old chap."

Knight counted the money. "Twenty-six pounds eleven shillings and threepence."

"What say you take the twenty-five quid and I'll make you out a cheque for the rest, eh?"

"No, I couldn't use a cheque."

"I suppose you know what you're doing, Oliver?"

"Twenty-five pounds will be enough for the time being." He stuffed the notes into an outside pocket. "Jane and I can't stay here tonight."

Black let out a whistle. "Your mother won't like that, old chap."

"You're being very decent to me. But then you always have been very decent. You mustn't think I'm taking it all as a matter of course."

Black brushed these thanks aside. "You're going to upset your mother frightfully, you know. What the hell are you up to, eh? Now, one man to another. I know Jane. Nice girl. I know you. Nice young fellow. I mean, is there anything between you? You're not in love with her?"

For the first time since he had been picked up out of the Channel, Knight gave a direct answer to a direct question. The evasion and the deception of the past few days was a burden he could no longer carry.

"Yes," he said, knowing that it was the truth, but that it was only a part of the truth. It was not a final answer, but it was positive; it gave him something to act upon, and no sooner had the word passed his lips than he felt liberated from a prison.

Jane was alone in the drawing-room. She lay in an arm-chair with her eyes closed, surrendering herself by an act of will to the will of others, waiting for the event, acquiescent in circumstances.

Mrs. Black had retired to her room; the crisis had frozen her. Oliver's excited face, his demand for

money, the obvious impropriety of his wandering
about the country with Jane, the mysterious questions
that had been put to her by the plain-clothes policemen—all this implied a greater trouble than she had
the courage to face. In the privacy of her room she
could deceive herself. It was a happy room. The chair
she sat in revived the quietness of other hours and
allowed her mind to wander pleasantly; the mirror
reflected a scene familiar from days before the outbreak of war; it reflected comfort and reassurance. The
sight of the twin beds caused her to think of her first
husband, Oliver's father, and to wonder whether the
boy hated her second marriage as certain friends said
he must. He had been so sweet about it. But one never
knew.

"Mother," said the gentle voice on the other side of
the door, and she did not stir. The door was not locked.
There was nothing to prevent his walking in. "Are you
there, Mother?" It was not a real question. He knew
she was there, and she detected the assurance. The
twin beds prevented her from answering. Their presence in the room gave the boy an unfair advantage.
She very well remembered the delight on his face when
she had told him she intended marrying again. She
had never doubted his approval. How well his stepfather had treated him, too!

Knight waited for some time in silence. When he
was assured his mother had no intention of answering
him, or of opening the door, he called out—with
gaiety, it seemed to him: "I'll be seeing you, then.
God bless!" Again he waited. Again there was no re-

ply. He was standing so near to the door that it needed but a slight lift of his head to bring his lips in contact with it.

"I don't like you going off like this," said Black. "It isn't natural. It's as though you don't trust us. Your mother and I only want you to be happy."

He followed the pair out through the front door and into the summer evening. As yet it was early for the black-out regulations to be in force, and there were lights in the house opposite. Through a break in the trees they could see a pin-prick of light on the slopes of the Malverns seven miles away. Black's car was parked in front of the house, and he offered to run them anywhere they chose. He could not be more accommodating.

Once Jane and Knight were safely in the back seat it seemed natural to him that he should drive westward, away from the town, towards the countryside of hills and trees which rolled like a dark wave before the sunset. The level beams illuminated the interior of the car, and Black pulled down a blue panel over the wind-screen so that he would not be dazzled. They had the road to themselves. Far ahead they could see it shining across a hill.

"Where are you taking us?" said Knight.

Fast driving always elated Black. He felt indulgent towards his two passengers. "However mad you are you've got to have a roof over your heads. I thought I'd drop you at the cottage. We still go out there for week-ends. There's everything you'll need."

"The cottage!" Jane exclaimed. "You're taking us

to the cottage?" She sat forward. Quite clearly the news surprised, even shocked her. "But everyone in the village knows us. The children will remember if nobody else does."

But Black would not or could not hear.

"It's only for tonight, Jane," said Knight. "We might as well spend the night in the cottage as anywhere else. In the morning we can be away. What if the people in the village do recognize us? We've done nothing wrong. You're Miss Oliphant, the school-teacher who went off to be married." He understood her feelings perfectly. It was not the possibility of scandal that Jane was afraid of; the return to the cottage was a return to the past. Here they had met, before Jane even knew of Hesketh's existence. And a return to the past was what neither of them wanted. The scene of past happiness would mock them, and they wanted to escape as much from that kind of mockery as from their immediate pursuers.

Black switched off the engine. They were parked in front of the cottage. The familiar white gate gleamed in the dusk. The foliage of the fruit trees, grey with the half-dark, hissed in the breeze. No one moved. Black looked straight ahead down the hill which led to the bridge and the village. After a while he lit a cigarette.

"I suppose you two know what you're doing," he said, without turning round. "Eh? What's that?" But they had not replied. "Well, we've had our little spin. Shall we go home now?"

"What do you mean?" said Knight.

"Back to Worcester."

"Oh no!" said Jane.

Black shrugged. "What am I going to say to your mother when I get back, Oliver?"

They climbed out of the car and Black led the way through the white gateway and along the path. The garden was neglected. Dimly on either hand they were aware of tangled growth; heavy darknesses lay beneath the unpruned trees; there was the sweet, sappy reek of too many plants fighting for a share of light. They did not close the front door behind them. Jane found candlestick and matches in the familiar recess at the bottom of the stairs and went up to the room which had once been her own. Black put a match to the twin wicks of the oil lamp in the living-room.

"Well, Oliver," he said as they looked at the two ridges of blue flame, "this is a funny how-d'you-do, and no mistake about it, eh?" He turned up the wicks and the two men looked about them in the yellow light. "You'll find there are plenty of stores laid in. Your mother and I are often over here. If Worcester comes in for some bombing we thought of moving in. You won't do anything to make your mother unhappy, Oliver?"

"What are you up to, Jane?" Knight called from the foot of the stairs. He felt uneasy if she was out of his sight for more than a few minutes. He came back to Black. "Do you want me to give you a receipt for that twenty-five quid?"

"No, I don't want a receipt, Oliver. Does this mean I'm going to be called as a witness in divorce proceedings?"

"Divorce?"

"I take it for granted you know what you're doing."

From Knight's point of view, Black was raising a totally irrelevant issue. To talk of divorce implied that the forces of life could be regulated, the spirits exorcised, and sanity restored by a playing about with the relations between individuals. A more drastic cure was needed.

"The last thing I wanted to do was to embarrass you," Knight said ironically.

"What am I going to say to your mother?"

"Just let her ask the questions. You'll think of something."

"You want me to go?"

"Yes."

"Will you be here if I run over tomorrow?"

"No."

Black suggested that they ought to walk all round the cottage to make sure that no light showed from the outside. The moon had risen and at the back of the cottage, where there were no trees, there was light enough to tell the time. The unmistakable, rank smell of a fox hung in the air and they went to explore the deserted chicken-house. A rat ran out between them. Black at once broke out into bitter denunciation of the county health authorities; he did not know how many times he had reported the presence of rats on the premises. But what had they done about it? Nothing! He had put down poison. He had set traps. But with what result? You saw for yourself!

"That fox has been here within the last hour."

"Oh, a fox!" said Black impatiently. He did not mind foxes.

They walked round the cottage and out into the road, Knight leading the way. Was the man never going? It had been a mistake to allow him to bring them to the cottage. It had been a mistake to come to Worcester in the first place.

"God knows," said Black, "I only want to be of some use to to you. If only I were as young as you are, I'd feel a lot better. When you get to my age you're helpless. What can I do? They won't even have me in the Home Guard because of my leg. Damn it all, it isn't as if I didn't know how to use a gun. I had four years of the last lot, remember!"

"You mean I'm a coward."

"Come back with me now, Oliver." Black was persuasive. He whispered: "Just think what your father would say if he were here. I've always told you I wanted you to regard me as your father. Jane will be all right by herself for tonight."

"Remember," said Knight, "if anybody wants to know where we are you don't know anything about it. You haven't seen us since we left the house. Don't even tell Mother. Anyway, we shall be gone in the morning."

He remained in the roadway until the sound of Black's car had died out eastward in the night. For some reason his head was filled with thoughts of the fox. He even climbed on to a stone wall in the vain hope of catching a glimpse of the animal in the moonlight. After all, it could not be so very far away. He spent some minutes in the garden trying to follow the tracks of the animal by his sense of smell. He tried to think himself into the fox's skin. Why should it visit this particular garden? The thought of the fox elated him, and when he went into the cottage to find Jane in the living-room he could talk of nothing else. She looked at him as though she could not understand a word he was saying.

"Martin will be here in the morning," she remarked quietly.

Since her marriage Mrs. Black had spent money on the cottage, the only property left her by her first husband. A bathroom had been installed. The water was heated from gas contained in a portable cylinder. It was Jane who explained this. While the two men were talking she had been taking a bath, and now she was dressed in some of Mrs. Black's clothing which she had found in one of the bedrooms: a blue silk dressing-gown, blue slippers, and so far as Knight could judge, nothing else.

"How close it is! We want a thunderstorm to clear the air. I'm going to bed now." She sat stiffly in one of the arm-chairs staring at the lamp as though hypnotised.

"However quickly he came he could not be here before tomorrow afternoon. We shall be gone by then."

As Jane still made no move to go to her room, Knight wondered whether it was ready to receive her. Perhaps the bed was not made. But when he climbed the stairs and entered the room he saw by the light of the candle she had left burning that the counterpane had been removed and the sheets turned down. Only Jane could have done this. The twin beds in the other room were undoubtedly as his mother had left them, severe as tables under their blue counterpanes.

"Can I get you anything to eat or drink?" he said on returning to the living-room. Jane, who had not moved, opened her eyes.

"No," she said. He was unable to meet her calm gaze.

They could hear the church clock, two miles away, striking the hour. The sense of the intimacy in the room was so great that, unable to bear it, Knight walked into the garden once more and stared across the rolling countryside, dreamy under the moon, towards Wales. The smell of fox was stronger than ever. Was it possible that the animal had returned during the last few minutes? Knight had the feeling it was watching him from the shadows. It was strange. There were no longer any chickens to attract the fox, there were no chickens for miles. Yet if the fox had indeed returned to the garden—and of this Knight now felt sure—it could only be for food. He listened. The night which he had thought quiet was full of noises. Foliage trembled, water dripped on stone, a field of grass ripe enough for hay hissed like a snake. Something metallic winked in the moon, and there was a slate-pencil squeak from the chicken-house. Rats! Knight threw a stone and it struck a tin can.

"Jane!" He stood in the open doorway calling to her. There was no reply, so he called again. Even now his mind was busy with the fox. The animal's presence was so real to him that he was convinced he could see its pointed mask and bright eyes merely by turning his head. But he did not turn his head. He walked into the cottage and found Jane in the chair where he had left her, her head back, her lips parted, fast asleep. At the sight of her he was weary himself. Kneeling, he laid his head in her lap. Her thighs, naked beneath the thin silk, warmed his cheek; he lifted one of her hands and rested it on his head, covering his right ear. Still she did not wake. He took a fold of the silk between his lips and pulled it as delicately as if he were drawing a cobweb though a keyhole. In a moment he was standing up, carrying Jane in his arms as though she were a child, and marvelling at her lightness. Her eyes remained closed.

It was difficult to carry her upstairs because of the narrowness of the stairs. Anxious not to wake her, he climbed up sideways, with painful slowness. The pace of her breathing had, it seemed to him, changed and he wondered whether she was awake.

"Jane," he said softly.

But she made no reply. He could scarcely hear her breathing. Surely she was awake? There was no light on the stairs, and he could not see whether her eyes were open or shut. For that matter it was not easy even when he had carried her into the bedroom, because by

the flickering light of the candle there could be no
certainty. He laid her on the bed and sat gazing into
her face, the feel of her body still warm in his arms.

"What's that?" she said abruptly. The tone revealed
that she had been awake for some time.

Knight snuffed the candle and drew the curtain.
The window was open and the smell of night rose from
the moon-soaked garden and the fields beyond. They
had heard a scream. In the madness of the moment he
had thought, so near and so loud was the screaming,
that it came from Jane herself. He had wondered what
he was doing to cause her so much pain. The white
night, as he looked at it, expressed the scare vividly.
The pallid swell of a bare meadow was a landscape
from a dream. He was steadied by the stink from the
snuffed wick of the candle.

They heard the scream again. It was frightening. It
had crossed the meadow, and now pierced the night
from, surely, the other side of that wall! Murder was
being done within a stone's throw. Yet it was not
ordinary fear that kept Knight rigid within the bedroom. Violence was being committed, it seemed to his
tired mind, in which both he and Jane were partici-
pators. They were not innocent.

The fox moved like a shadow along the wall, its
brush like a plume in the moonlight. The animal came
and went so quickly that Knight could not be sure of
having seen it. One moment there was an impression
of violent stealth along the granite teeth of the wall;
then were was only the granite itself, glinting its tiny
mirrors when he moved his head.

"It was a vixen," he said.

"A vixen?"

"Yes. It was a vixen on heat." He laughed with relief. The sweat cooled on his face and body. "It was nothing, just a vixen. It's a terrible noise for an animal to make." He was well aware that Jane had been far less scared than he. He drew the curtain and fumbled for the matches. "Black and I smelt a fox in the garden when we came. Well, it wasn't a fox, it was a vixen."

"Don't light the candle," she said.

"It's out of season. It's a row you hear in the winter and spring, normally. The vixen's either mad or sick. There was a mad vixen near Bibury when I was a kid. You could hear it most nights. That was early summer too. They went out with guns but they never found her." He felt shaky. They could still hear the beast screaming. He could not have lit the candle even if he had wished. The matches were not to be found. He sat on the bed and putting out a hand found that it came to rest on a wrist.

"How can an animal be mad?"

"Jane," he said, "what are we going to do?"

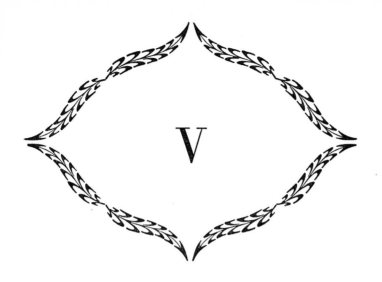

V

"WHAT do we do now?" Helen looked about her in the morning sunshine. "Creep in on them through the undergrowth?"

She and Hesketh had been the only passengers to alight. Eastward the curving track flashed brilliantly, wavering in the heat.

"You see that road climbing up the hill? You can't see the cottage. That's the road to it but the cottage is over the hump. It's beyond all those trees."

The hill was on the other side of a river, so shallow at this time of the year that its course was ribbed by long islands of white pebbles. Half way across the bridge Helen and Hesketh took refuge in a V-shaped recess while a convoy of ambulances passed. They stared down at the brown water until they had the illusion the bridge was forging upstream.

"I'm sorry," said Helen, "but I just can't face this, you know."

"According to Black, they won't be there."

After the last ambulance had passed, Helen retraced her steps to the village side of the river. When Hesketh caught her up she said: "I've got to remember my dignity. At a time like this a girl should be with her mother. I don't want to scratch their eyes out. But if they came up to me now I wouldn't know what else to do with them. I couldn't think of anything to say."

"We might as well go up to the cottage now we've come all this way. Then we'll go back to Worcester." Hesketh's pallor was arresting. It glowed through the tan, silvering it like the skin of an onion. The effect was mask-like. "This is no time to think of dignity."

"I was only joking."

"This is no time for joking."

Although it was little past ten o'clock the sun was so hot that they went and stood in the shade of a tree. Ever since Hesketh had received Mrs. Black's telegram the previous morning his manner had been touched with fanaticism. He listened politely to whatever Mr. and Mrs. Black had to say to him but he gave the impression that his mind was made up. He had decided on a certain course of action, and nothing would prevent him from carrying it out. Except for affirming that Helen and he must go to the cottage together and alone—he would not let Black take them there in the car—he gave no indication of what his course of action would be. Helen had become afraid of him. The greater her fear the gayer she became. She sat on the grass while Hesketh, his feet planted wide apart, stared up into the tree and repeatedly passed his right hand over his cropped head.

"Wait here. Don't go away," he said abruptly. After a few paces he returned and looked down upon her, smiling. "Helen, dear. If I'm not here by twelve o'clock I want you to go straight back to Worcester." He spoke gently. "You understand? In all probability I shall be with you again in less than an hour. If they told Black they were leaving yesterday I expect they meant it."

This time he did not so much as look back. Force of habit made him pause on the bridge. In the slack water behind one of the buttresses two brown-backed fish lurked in near-invisibility. The cooler air over the water made him conscious of the arid, skin-cracking, heat of his body. Before setting himself to the long hill he would have liked to bathe his face.

He believed that Jane and Knight were still at the cottage, for no better reason than an inability to conceive where else they could go: and as he neared the cottage his anxiety was at this late stage that they might escape him. He might have been stalking the shyest of wild creatures. The road itself would certainly be under observation but by climbing over a stile and crossing a meadow he calculated that he could arrive at a point immediately opposite the cottage. The recently cut grass was spread in broad bands across the meadow, and the stubble was springy beneath his feet. Fifty yards away, on the north side of a hedge, rabbits bolted into a patch of grass not yet cut. May blossom still sweetened these hedges. The higher he rose the more he could see of the surrounding countryside, and wherever there was a moving object, man, beast, or even a car-wind-screen flashing along a distant lane, his eyes would turn upon it accusingly. He walked over the brow of the hill and saw the slate roof of the cottage through a brier hedge cloudy with dogroses. But where was the gate or stile?

He walked ten, twenty yards in one direction, and then finding no break in the hedge hurried back again. He walked even farther along the hedge in the other direction but still he was disappointed. The grass was so long here that it conserved moisture near the ground, and the toes of his shoes glistened. He tried to force his way into the hedge but the briers cut at his hands and face. That he should be so near his destination and yet held up by a hedge was intolerable. His impatience exacerbated, he looked about for some thinning of the leaves, or at least a bush free of thorns or briers. When finally he burst through the hedge into the roadway beyond, his jacket was torn across the back from collar to waist; he put a handkerchief to his forehead and it came away scarlet.

It seemed strange to Hesketh that Jane and Knight were not waiting for him in the roadway. They must have been expecting him. Had they not heard him fighting through the hedge? They must have heard

him. But the road was empty, and the morning silent
with birdsong. Hesketh pushed open the gate and
walked in the cool shadow of the fruit trees through
the neglected garden. The front door stood open.
Plainly Black had been wrong and he was right: they
were still at the cottage, and the thought of his own
shrewdness elated him. For a while he was so pleased
with himself that had Jane and Knight appeared in
the doorway he would have run forward delighted as a
child.

But they did not appear, and when Hesketh stepped
over the threshold he was frowning with expectancy.
There was no one at home. As soon as he entered the
living-room he could sense that the cottage was deserted. Nevertheless he walked from room to room
calling for Jane. He could not bring himself to climb
the stairs. He stood at their foot calling: "Jane, are
you there, Jane? Jane?" feeling it was not for the first
time that he stood just where he was, uttering those
very words. The moment was too familiar. The cottage
itself took part in the ritual; the front door creaked on
its hinges, the fly buzzed in the window, a curtain
stirred. He knew without going upstairs that the beds
were made up as though they had not been slept in.

On the kitchen table were the remains of breakfast
for two. A bowl of clean water stood in the sink, and
Hesketh was surprised to find the water still warm
when he dipped a hand into it. If Jane and Knight
had left, it could only have been a matter of minutes
ago. And the open door meant, surely, that they were
somewhere near. Hesketh removed his jacket and

washed the blood off his hands and face. Even as he looked at his face in the glass the angry scratch which began over his right eyebrow and ended somewhere near the top of his left ear broadened and glistened. There seemed to be no way of stopping the bleeding. Temporary though it might be, the scratch amounted to a real disfigurement, and he was vain about his personal appearance. When Jane saw him in a few minutes' time she would say: "Oh, your face is bleeding," and probably she would smile. He would not dare to tell her how he had received the scratch. She would think him ridiculous. His inability to arrest the bleeding made him want to leave the cottage immediately. Why had he been such a fool as to force his way though a brier hedge?

"Jane! Oliver!" He stood at the back door shouting their names angrily. How could they, his wife and his best friend, treat him so badly? When he now emerged into the back garden he was carrying a walking-stick with a heavy iron ferrule. He walked past the derelict chicken-run using the stick to decapitate dandelions and tall white daisies.

He stood with the stick in mid air. An animal had appeared with the abruptness of hallucination on the stone wall at the end of the garden. Hesketh did not move. The animal did not move. In the full sun it looked like a small dun-coloured dog with a feathery tail and a crocodile grin. The animal was gone before Hesketh had time to realize it was a fox. He ran to the wall and looked over. There was no sign of it. Seeding grasses, not much darker than the fox's coat, silvered in the sun. Surely a fox with a coat that colour was a freak? Surely foxes were only out and about during the night? Hesketh sprang over the wall and began beating about in the long grass with his stick but the fox had obviously got clean away. The land was not farmed. It was rough pasture broken by patches of yellow gorse. When Hesketh stood by one of these patches he could hear the pods popping in the sun. Over there were more shrubs—the beginning of a spinney, perhaps. No knowing which way the fox had gone, of course, but Hesketh followed a path, looking about him sharply. A fox! He had never seen one in its natural state before, and the encounter filled him with wonder. He retained a most vivid impression of its unwinking boldness. What would he have done with the fox if he had managed to catch it? Suppose he had crippled it with a blow of his stick. Could he have killed it? No, it was quite impossible. If he had aimed a blow at the fox and broken its leg, say, how the creature would have fought! It would have asked no quarter. It would have been without self-pity. Hesketh looked at the blaze of gorse, wide-eyed with amazement, like a child. He did not know why he should be so happy.

Then he saw Jane and Knight. They were about thirty yards away walking in his direction. Because they were picking their steps so carefully they had certainly not seen him. Hesketh wanted to shout: "Hey! You two! Have you seen a fox? I nearly touched him." But at that moment he remembered why he was there with a heavy stick in his hand, he could feel the mask of blood that had dried on his forehead, and with something of the fox's art he disappeared quickly from view, stepping behind a hillock of gorse, and lying full length on his face.

They were laughing. Hesketh, who had closed his eyes with the logic of a child to make his invisibility more effective, now awoke to his foolishness and saw an ant walking along a blade of grass. Other blades of grass towered above him. A dandelion parachute settled on the back of his hand. Beyond all this brightness was the dark heart of the gorse; he could see under the skirt of blossom and spiked leaves to the dark centre of the bush. Jane was laughing quietly on the other side—a low, happy laugh which he had feared never to hear again. Knight himself chuckled. No words were spoken. The pair had paused in their walk, and for a moment Hesketh thought they might have spied him lying absurdly in the grass, and were laughing at that. But the laughter came from too deep a source. It was their conversation. Hesketh felt their happiness as keenly as he had experienced the wildness of the fox. Jane was humming, though it would not have been possible to make out the tune; she made her own music like a bee in the grass.

"Look," said Knight. "Can you do that?"

Whatever Knight did Hesketh could not have seen it but Jane said excitedly: "Let me try!" and the pair went on down the path towards the cottage.

When he felt it was safe Hesketh sat up and watched their heads disappear from view. If he shouted after them presumably they would turn; if they heard his running footsteps presumably they would wait. But would they? He had the feeling that even if they had met him face to face they would not have seen him but passed him like a phantom. Using the stick for support, Hesketh rose to his feet and looked about him in the resplendent morning, moved to the point of tears.

The sun beat down with such strength that be began to take off his jacket. His hands clutched the front of his shirt. The jacket? He had removed it in the cottage in order to wash; he had draped it over a chair and forgotten to put it on again. Jane could not fail to notice it immediately—she never failed to notice such details—and she would certainly know it for his. Hesketh threw his stick away in exasperation; as it sailed through the air the iron ferrule flashed in the sun. If it had been at all possible Hesketh would have rushed to the cottage by some devious route and rescued the coat before Jane and Knight saw it. They must not know he was in the neighbourhood. They must for the time being at least forget him. What matter, so long as Jane was happy? It had been a revelation to find her capable of so much happiness. And now that happiness was threatened because of his carelessness. He actually groaned aloud. By violently rubbing his forehead he had opened the wound again and the blood tickled across the skin. He had the absurd idea of rushing after them saying: "It doesn't matter! Nothing matters! Only be happy, Jane, for God's sake be happy!"

It would never do. He walked away downhill, taking long strides, occasionally jumping a low bush.

Until he remembered Helen he had no clear idea of where he was going, no thought but one of putting as much ground between the cottage and himself as possible; but when he did remember the girl waiting for him in the village he came to an abrupt halt. He looked about him more calmly. "All right!" he thought. He climbed a wall, trudged steadily down the road, crossed the bridge, and found the girl waiting for him in precisely the spot where he had left her, under the tree. At that moment the church clock struck eleven.

"Black was right," he said. "They'd gone."

"Gone?" Her eyes were huge. The tip of her tongue flicked between her lips. She stood up slowly and moved away from him, staring all the time. "Oh!" she said breathlessly. He wondered why she was so frightened. The life of the village went on all around them. An old lady drove by in a smart trap, the sun winking on the harness-ornaments and paintwork. But Helen and Hesketh were cut off from that world.

"The place was deserted," he said. "I had a good look round. I didn't go upstairs. I should think they did just what they said they'd do. We'd better go back to Worcester. Perhaps there'll be some more news there."

"You're lying," she said. "What have you done?"

He saw now that it was impossible to deceive her.

"I scrambled through a hedge and got pretty well cut about, as you see."

"What have you done? I shouldn't have let you go by yourself. Where's your coat? Go away! Don't touch me! Don't come near me!" She did not raise her voice but she was shaken with emotion.

"They'd gone," he said angrily. "Don't you understand? There's no need to work yourself into such a state. They've gone." He clung to the lie even though he was quite aware she knew he was lying.

Suddenly she was in control of herself. Her colour returned.

"What have you done?" she demanded.

"Everything's all right. There's no need to lose your head."

"Where's your coat?"

Before Hesketh realized what was happening she had passed him and was hurrying towards the bridge. For the first time villagers began to notice that something unusual was taking place. Two women with shopping-baskets looked after the girl. She had reached the middle of the bridge before Hesketh caught her up. A passing lorry forced them both into a stone recess.

"I saw them," said Hesketh.

"Then why did you lie to me?"

"We shan't do any good." He was so angry that he scarcely knew what he was doing or saying. "I love Jane, d'you understand me? Nothing would ever stop me loving her. Nothing is too good for her. I would do anything for her." He caught hold of Helen's wrist so violently that she cried out in pain. "I saw them, d'you understand me? I must go away and think. We must do what is best."

"Let me go," she said.

"We're going back to Worcester."

He could see that she was still persuaded some violence had been committed in the cottage. The
scratches on his face, the loss of his jacket, indicated a
struggle. He was even prepared to let her believe this if
it would frighten her into returning to Worcester with
him.

"I want to go to Oliver," she said almost piteously.
"I want to see my husband."

"Do you believe me when I say that Jane's happiness is the main thing in my life? It's true! What else is
there for me? And after Jane the most important person to me is Oliver."

"Let me go!"

"I'm sorry." He had not realized he was still holding her by the wrist. But once released she did not dart
off as he had expected. She stared about her at the
river, at the village, at the low hills rising in the sunshine as though she were looking at them for the first
time. "I left my coat in the cottage. I took it off to
wash. Then I forgot it when I went out to look for
them. They were laughing."

She did not understand.

"First of all I saw a fox. Yes, they were laughing."
"Laughing?"

This was a word that made a difference. Helen repeated it and for the first time since Hesketh had overtaken her on the bridge, looked him full in the eyes.

"What were they laughing about?"

"They were just laughing. I dodged behind a bush."

She looked at the long scratch on his forehead, so

obviously what he said it was—a scratch from a brier or thorn and not the result of any blow.

"So they were laughing, were they?"

"I promise you, Helen, that if you go back to Worcester now, you won't regret it. Won't you trust me?"

"I don't trust you. Why should I? You saw a fox?"

"He was running along a wall, in broad daylight, too. But he just disappeared and it was soon after that I saw Jane and Oliver. I heard them laughing." He repeated the word because he could see it had made a profound impression upon Helen. This one word had stopped her from climbing the hill to the cottage.

The decision was made without further talk. They walked off the bridge and made their way up towards the station where Hesketh discovered that his ticket and his money were in his jacket pocket. Helen bought a ticket for him.

"They'll see your coat?"

"Yes, they'll know I've been there," said Hesketh soberly.

But during the half an hour or so they had to wait before the next train it was not Helen he had to restrain from rushing up to the cottage; he wanted to go himself. If only he could hear Jane laughing that would be enough. He would steal away again. Or, better still, he would remain quite unknown to them on guard; if danger threatened he would run in and warn them.

"We mustn't tell anyone," he said.

Helen looked at him. It was the hottest time of the day, and the fact that Hesketh was without his jacket would certainly not excite comment. The sky was glazed with heat. Roses flamed on the bushes in the station-master's garden.

"We mustn't tell them at Worcester, I mean, that Jane and Oliver are still here."

"Are you out of your mind?"

"Mrs. Black can be stupid, you know. She might easily tell the police. You wouldn't want that, would you?"

"I don't care what happens," she said with a ferocity that startled him. She was exhausted by the heat and dazed by Hesketh's unpredictability. If it was true what he said, that his wife and Oliver were at the cottage, why in God's name had he come away without speaking to them? Could she possibly believe him? He had nothing in common with the man she had accompanied from Luton. It was as though a wand had been waved over him. He even smiled.

They were followed into the compartment by a heavily built man who placed a two-barrelled sporting-gun on the rack before turning to reveal black eyebrows and powerfully creased cheeks. He was all hard, hairy masculinity. He wore stained whipcord breeches and steel-shod brown boots. He gave a friendly nod.

"Strangers in these parts. You're not a German troop, are you?" he said drily, looking at Hesketh's shaven head.

"I'm not a German troop." And this was the man who had said it was no time for joking, Helen thought.

"Because if you were a German troop I should shoot you," said the farmer. He lifted his eyebrows to indicate the gun above his head.

"Rabbits?" said Hesketh.

"Foxes," said the man, and Helen started. The farmer noticed. "They're vermin, aren't they? I lost two geese last night. No hunting in war-time. Well, we shoot them. Anything wrong with that?"

There was an edge of humor to everything the man said. He squinted about him, his knees well apart, and his hands planted upon them. Probably his humor was a form of shyness but it gave double meaning to his words. He was talking of foxes but the tone of his voice made implications.

"It's damned difficult to shoot a fox," he said. "You've got to get up early."

"I've seen a fox at midday," said Hesketh.

"Maybe," said the man disbelievingly. "You've got to be up before light."

"I saw a fox not more than an hour ago."

"Dudley Zoo?"

Hesketh explained where he had seen the fox, and the man knew the place but he still did not believe that Hesketh had seen a fox there.

"What did you do?"

"The fox was gone before I could do anything."

"It didn't raise its hat to you, or say good morning, or ask for a light, I suppose." The man lay back in his corner coughing with laughter. "The next time you go out in the midday sun you take damn good care a fox doesn't shoot you. I expect it was one of them disguised German paratroopers." At the next station the man got out, taking his gun with him.

"I wouldn't worry too much," he said before shutting the door. "Seeing a fox at twelve o'clock, well, that's not too terrible. It's when the fox starts talking, that's the time to worry."

Hesketh spoke with some bitterness of the stupidity of shooting foxes; they were such wary beasts it was almost impossible to kill them outright, he had heard. Hunting with hounds was kinder. He became very boring on the subject, and in Helen's heat-dazed mind there arose a confusion between foxes and Jane Hesketh. She had never seen the woman, and it became easy to imagine her face to be a pointed, cruel mask. As Hesketh continued it seemed that the confusion was less hers than his; one moment he was speaking about the ease with which foxes could be exterminated if they weren't preserved for hunting, and then he was saying they were beautiful, that if you set out to kill a fox and found one at your mercy—helpless in a trap, say, or seen over the sights of a gun—you would have to let it go because it was wild and you envied its freedom. You envied without being jealous. You hunted and hunted and then you fell in love with what you hunted. For the first time that day Helen began to cry. Hesketh did not notice. He had closed his eyes, and when they arrived at Worcester he was fast asleep in his corner, with a smile on his face.

Her suitcase was at her mother-in-law's. Otherwise Helen would have been tempted to catch the next train home without leaving the station. If she had been more determined or more humiliated, she might have abandoned her belongings in her anxiety to be home; as it was, Helen was too tidy-minded to feel she could leave without saying good-bye to Mrs. Black. She assumed that her marriage was finished; she did not know just how one went about divorcing one's husband, but presumably the first step was to go to one's solicitor. Before this happened she wanted to make Oliver's mother believe that she had not been hurt; she did not want the Blacks to think she was hard, but she could not bear to think they might be sorry for her; she wished to play a more amusing role.

Worcester was thronged with soldiers. Everywhere one looked there was khaki. The pavements were so crowded that groups of soldiers drifted along the roads, dodging the traffic. Redcaps went about chivvying them. Helen heard one of them tell a soldier to put his cap on but the soldier merely gave a friendly nod and passed on with his hands in his pockets. A complicated organization had broken down. Troops did not normally debouch into a town in this way. The wrong instructions had been given. An officer leaned out of a staff car and called to one of the military-policemen. "Get them all back to barracks immediately," he shouted.

Helen and Hesketh found it impossible to board a bus, and they had to walk. A crimson-faced corporal was leaning against a wall with a half-emptied glass of beer in his hand. When Hesketh stopped and asked him what was happening the corporal stared at Helen and said: "Invasion's begun, mate."

"Who's invading what?"

"We're invading Worcester," said the corporal, laughing.

In contrast with the centre of the city the wharves were almost deserted. A barge was unloading cattle cake, and two girls walked briskly in the direction of the cathedral. Hesketh said the corporal had made him jump with his invasion talk; but the Germans would never land in England. Their landing-craft would be destroyed, their bombers would be shot down. What Napoleon had been unable to achieve was certainly impossible for Hitler.

"Oh, please!" she implored him.

"Eh?"

As they crossed the bridge Helen wondered what her feelings would be when Oliver returned to flying duties; as inevitably he would, with or without a court-martial. The Air Force was far too short of trained pilots to dismiss him from the service if it could possibly be helped. What then? Would he be a hero, and would he be injured, and would she visit him in hospital, and would they be reconciled? No, she would never forgive him.

"I didn't mean to annoy you," said Hesketh, imperturbably.

"Are you going to divorce your wife?"

He was shocked. "Good God, no! You don't understand. She's ill. She's not herself."

"And Oliver?"

As they walked on, Hesketh made despairing gestures. Perhaps none of them had long to live. One never knew in war-time. Circumstances were so different. People behaved differently.

At the corner of the road in which the Blacks' house was situated Hesketh stopped and made Helen withdraw behind a screen of rhododendrons. She had not been given time to see what had disturbed him, but by the way he stood there in silence, one hand laid restrainingly on her arm, his head on one side, listening, it was plain that caution was necessary. Hesketh did not need to speak. His manner was eloquent in it-itself. "I promised you a new development," he appeared to be saying, "but this is not it." He waited so long without speaking that Helen asked him what the matter was.

"I'm wondering what to tell them."

"Who?"

"The family."

"The truth, I suppose." She was exasperated. "I don't know what you mean."

By discreetly pulling aside one of the branches it was possible to see down the road without being observed from the house. Helen saw that an open car, very large and old-fashioned, was parked in front of it.

"There's somebody else arrived," said Hesketh.

"Well?"

"Listen, Helen. They weren't at the cottage. You understand me? When Oliver told Black they were leaving the following day, he spoke the truth. Oliver always speaks the truth. Once he's made his mind up he never changes it. He's not like the rest of us. There —was—nobody—there." He looked at her unwinkingly, and something of her fear of him returned. It was impossible to know what was passing through his mind. That morning while she had waited for him in the village, the belief that Hesketh was capable of murder had numbed her. Now she even wondered whether she had misinterpreted the change that had come over him; the man who had walked down the hill with blood running from a scratch across his forehead might have been satisfied because he had achieved what he had come for.

"Let's go to the house."

"Do you agree they had left the cottage?"

She looked at him steadily. "You saw them both there. Did you do any harm to them?"

Hesketh was impatient. The scratch across his forehead no longer bled, and it was quite black in the sun.

"If you thought I might, why on earth did you let me go to the cottage alone?" Hesketh lifted his head sharply as though listening to a distant shout. "You don't know what you're saying," he said quietly. "Helen dear, I promise you I did nothing wrong."

The car might be old but it was certainly powerful. Heat quivered over the radiator. Whoever its owner might be he had driven fast and probably for a considerable distance. The carefully preserved bodywork was coated with dust. As the engine cooled, the bonnet ticked like a clock. Black's car was not to be seen, and Helen assumed he was away at work.

Mrs. Black opened the door herself. Obviously she had not expected Helen and Hesketh to return so soon, and now that they were here she looked for the others.

"Well?" she said. In spite of her question there was "Don't tell me. I don't want to hear" in her manner. Instead of waiting for an answer she drew a handkerchief from her sleeve and, sneezing violently, clapped it to her face. "This dreadful hay fever," she said.

Once inside the hall, Hesketh, in a penetrating whisper, said: "Who's come?" Because of her sneezing the woman was incapable of answering. Indeed she probably did not even hear his question. But Hesketh persisted. Helen took her mother-in-law's arm and guided her to a chair. The sneezing-fit rendered Mrs. Black quite helpless. When finally she lowered her handkerchief, her face was flushed and her eyes were streaming.

"It's all nerves," she said. "Did you see them?"

"Everything's quite all right," said Hesketh reassuringly. "Now don't you worry about anything. Is there something I can get you? Whose car is that outside?"

"Oliver's commanding-officer has come. He's only been here a few minutes."

Hesketh spoke briskly. "Helen, I think you ought to take Mrs. Black to her room for a while. No, no," he said with a warmth that was intended to sound gallant, but which did not conceal his anxiety to get the two women out of the way, "there must be something to relieve your sneezing. Have you ever tried smelling-salts?"

"For God's sake answer my question," said Mrs. Black. "Did you see Jane and Oliver?"

"No," Hesketh answered after a momentary hesitation. "They'd gone. The cottage was empty."

Mrs. Black rose to her feet. The sneezing-fit had passed. She put on a cat-like dignity of manner which, while confessing that her pink face and streaming eyes made her quite unpresentable, nevertheless submitted that the present occasion was too important for such trifling considerations.

"In that case come in and meet Wing-Commander McKendrick."

"Will you let me handle this, Helen?" Hesketh asked softly.

Helen could not speak. She shook her head.

McKendrick rose to his feet when they entered the room and came forward with a pleased expression on his dark, somewhat forbidding face. He was a man of about forty. Although clean-shaven there was a film of hair on each cheekbone, and this, coupled with the enormous eyebrows and heavy, blunt nose made his smart uniform look like fancy dress. It was a face that yearned to be bearded. He was a Victorian preacher born too late. He knew who Helen was without being introduced. Hesketh was given the merest glance and a nod.

"Have you seen your husband, Mrs. Knight?"

"No."

"Pity. I've just come down from the Air Ministry. This is a bit of a how-d'you-do, isn't it?" He had a deep, baying voice that was almost comical. But there was no nonsense about the man. On Helen he made an immediate impression of hard masculinity—not unsympathetic, but knowledgeable and efficient. Hesketh tried to speak but McKendrick would not listen to him.

"Your husband's a valuable man. He's a very good officer. I like him, you understand? He's a trained fighter-pilot. Frankly, we don't give a damn what he's been up to. We need him too badly. You haven't seen your husband since he came back?"

"No."

"If I could see him now, d'you know what I'd do? I'd give him a fortnight's leave. We need him back on duty—we need him desperately—but he's no good to us unless he's in a sensible frame of mind."

This was not the kind of talk the Air Commodore at the Air Ministry had given Helen; she warmed to Mc-Kendrick immediately, and sensing her feeling, his manner softened. By the way he looked at Mrs. Black and at Hesketh it was plain that he wanted to talk to Helen alone.

"I understand you've been over to see your husband this morning."

"It didn't work out quite like that. . . . You mean you'd take Oliver back and no questions asked?"

"Make no bones about it, Mrs. Knight. It's no closely guarded secret we're going to need every fighter-pilot we've got during the next few months." It bothered him that he could think of no courteous way of asking Mrs. Black and this other fellow to withdraw, and he coloured slightly. Helen could not prevent a note of bitterness from creeping into her voice.

"I don't see what all this has to do with me."

"You must forgive me for intruding, Mrs. Knight. You make me feel infernally rude and indelicate, and so on. But as things are, we simply can't afford luxuries; I can't afford, you see, to let any domestic trouble deprive the country of a valuable chap. We're up against it. There's no need for me to make a patriotic speech. We've got to make sacrifices, personal sacrifices. I've just got to see your husband as soon as possible. I've had the sleuths called off. They'd do more harm than good. But I've got to see him for myself."

Helen did not know what to say. She did not understand this talk about sacrifices; what sort of sacrifice did McKendrick expect her to make when so far as she could see she had nothing left to sacrifice?

"I'm sorry to be such a disappointment to you," she said. "I don't feel very heroic or patriotic this morning."

"You're hungry, that's what's the matter with you," said Mrs. Black. "You'll feel better after lunch. You'll have lunch with us, of course, Mr. McKendrick? My husband ought to be back at any moment now."

"Did you see your husband this morning, Mrs. Knight?"

"No." So far she had been able to speak the truth. But in a moment she knew she would have to deceive him.

"They'd gone," said Hesketh.

Aircraft flew so low over the house that the noise for some moments prevented conversation. A small metal bowl on the mantelpiece suddenly picked up the vibration, and rang out like a bell. McKendrick was staring at Hesketh. He simply did not know what to make of a chap who took the flight of his wife so calmly. He looked at Hesketh's cropped skull and his thoughts were revealed as clearly as though he had uttered them: "Well, here's a queer fish, damn me if it isn't!"

"You see the delicate position I'm in. I hope you won't think I'm impertinent, sir, but what do you propose doing now?"

"I've no plans," said Hesketh briefly.

"I shall go home," said Helen, although the question had not been addressed to her.

"That's Reading, isn't it?" said McKendrick. He had briefed himself thoroughly at the Air Ministry. "I'm going back to town. Will you let me drop you at your home?"

"Why not?" she thought. There was no point in remaining. It would have been wiser not to come in the first place. Yet McKendrick's decision to return to town so promptly surprised her. Half an hour in Worcester had been sufficient, apparently, to convince him that he was wasting his time.

Mrs. Black had another sneezing-fit. She went to the open window and leaned out gasping for breath. When she recovered and turned her flushed face upon them, she said: "But you can't go off without some lunch, Mr. McKendrick. If only you'll wait a while, I'm sure Oliver will walk in. I've got a feeling he'll walk in at any moment. It isn't like him to upset me like this. He must be worrying about me."

"Where do you think they'll make for?" For all

McKendrick's hesitancy the question could not be anything but offensive.

"I hope to God you don't find him," said Hesketh.

"Why?"

"Oliver is an old friend of mine. I don't want him to die young."

McKendrick picked up his cap and looked questioningly at Helen.

"I left town at nine and reached here at twelve. With a bit of luck I ought to be back at five. Are you ready?"

Without a word Helen went upstairs to collect her belongings. Weeping internally, she took a firm grip on a hairbrush and stared at the aloof face which looked back at her from the mirror. She watched for the tears to come; but they did not come. Producing lipstick, she looked from the hand that held it to the reflection in the glass; as though the ordinary evidence of her senses could not convince her that the hand trembled and only the mirror had authority. She remembered how Oliver had once tried to kiss her reflection in a mirror. "Oh God! make me hate him. Don't let me go on loving him," she thought.

"I'm ready," she said to McKendrick when she had reached the hall with her case in her hand.

"Helen, you can't go off like this. Mr. McKendrick, be sensible. Lunch is on the table." Mrs. Black stood between them and the door. In order to leave the house they would have to push past her, and she gave the impression that if necessary she would resist them. It seemed absurd for her to attach so much importance to their staying for lunch. Helen wondered whether she would ever see her mother-in-law again. What reason would there ever be for their coming together?

In spite of McKendrick's impatience to be off, his natural courtesy prevented him from insisting.

"Well, Mrs. Black, you're certainly treating me far better than I deserve. I thought Mrs. Knight and I might have a snack on the road." He hung his hat on the hall stand and followed the women into the dining-room.

They had already started the meal before Helen noticed Hesketh's absence. Mrs. Black dropped a fork in consternation.

"But he was here a moment ago. He was standing there looking down the garden."

The normal assumption would be that Hesketh's absence was without significance, that he would walk into the dining-room at any moment, but the occasion was not normal, and Mrs. Black sent her housekeeper to look for him.

He was not to be found.

"Poor darling! It's been such a shock for him," said Mrs. Black. "I don't suppose he knows what he's doing. It would be dreadful if he did some harm to himself. Oh dear! Why did I think of that? Yes, I know it's trying for you, too, Helen, but poor Martin is such a fool, the poor dear! No, it's no good. I can't eat a thing. But please don't mind me. Go on, both of you." She left the room and they could hear her sneezing and calling: "Martin! Martin!" first of all upstairs and then out in the garden.

Helen found that McKendrick was studying her from the other side of the table, and she blushed.

"You got a father, Mrs. Knight?" he asked.

"Yes."

She noticed that he had eaten scarcely anything. He was wildly impatient to be off.

"Please don't think me unimaginative and—"

"Of course not," she said quickly. She had no appetite either, and her eyes meeting McKendrick's, an understanding was established. They rose and would have walked straight out of the house, climbed into the car, and driven away if only they could have found Mrs. Black.

"There she is," said McKendrick from the front door.

Mrs. Black was walking with steady solemnity back from the road junction. She had no protection from the sun. One hand was held up to shade her eyes, the other held a handkerchief to her nose. Her white linen dress was in its brightness the point where all lines of perspective—the kerb, the iron railings, the neat grass verge—appeared to meet; its whiteness was not cool but intensely hot. The noon had an incandescent heart. McKendrick and Helen walked a few yards to meet her.

"There's not a sign of him."

"I know you'll forgive us, but Mrs. Knight and I will have to be making a move."

She was bewildered. She did not know whether to be alarmed or indignant. "He can't be far away, can he?" Hesketh's disappearance now preoccupied her to the exclusion of everything else. McKendrick and her daughter-in-law were on the point of departure, and this to her only meant that they would not be able to take part in any search. She begged them to come back into the house until the heat of the day had passed. But McKendrick had already taken his seat in the car. Mrs. Black looked so lost that Helen felt sorry for her. They kissed affectionately.

"I'm sure he'll turn up," said Helen, rather as though Hesketh were a pet cat who had strayed. The tone made her mother-in-law look at her curiously, and Helen received the statement from the heat-flushed face as clearly as if it had been uttered: "Yes, that's what he is, isn't he? A lost pet." But when Mrs. Black actually spoke it was to say: "You're much too good for that boy of mine. Oh, how could he be such a fool?" She waved after them but even before the car had reached the corner she was looking about her once more, as though expecting Hesketh to emerge from the shrubbery in one of her neighbours' gardens.

McKendrick drove fast and well. In no time they had crossed the Severn bridge and were sliding through the city traffic. There was still an unusually large number of troops about, and their presence gave an air of crisis to the city. The heat stagnated in the narrow streets. As they passed the cathedral the chimes fell heavily from the tower as though the atmosphere were too thin to hold them. Soldiers sprawling about on the green began to stand up as N.C.O.'s went about shouting orders. Helen had never been so glad to leave a city behind her. If she had stayed only one hour longer the destruction which threatened it would have caught her, too. Even now if she were to look back on its roofs and towers, disaster could catch up with her. She was in flight. She would never come there again, whatever happened. Never! Never!

To her surprise McKendrick brought the car to a standstill once they had reached open country.

"What are your plans?" he demanded with brusqueness of a man who is too self-conscious to be courteous.

"See a lawyer, I suppose."

McKendrick continued to look straight ahead. "No, you can't do that. I can't have one of my officers being bothered with divorce-court proceedings at a time like this."

Helen said nothing. McKendrick had offered her a lift with the object of gaining an opportunity to lecture. Behind his obvious impatience there had been this wish to monopolize her attention for a while. She was too surprised to speak, but all the time her anger was growing.

"I must beg you not to start divorce proceedings, at least not for a while," he said.

"That's my affair."

"It certainly is." For all his gaucherie McKendrick did not allow himself to get flustered.

"What do you mean?"

"That it's your affair. It's everybody's affair. This is not *only* your affair, though. It's public business. Without a word of exaggeration, the country is now in such a position that the presence of a trained man at the right place at the right moment might make all the difference. You don't think I've driven a hundred and twenty miles this morning for the fun of it?"

"Perhaps I'm losing my sense of humour." She was so blinded with anger that she could not see how to get out of the car. The handle of the door seemed to have disappeared. McKendrick put a restraining hand on her forearm.

"Please listen to me," he said.

"I should never have come with you if I'd suspected this. Well, I suppose I've got to walk back to Worcester." She had no sooner spoken than she realized how absurd she was. This was the way you spoke to a man who gave you a lift and then made advances.

"It's a matter of national importance," McKendrick said with a solemnity that Helen had to respect, "that I get your husband into the air within a fortnight. Provided he's fit, that is. And perhaps even provided he's not fit."

"Well, I can't help you. Whether or not I start divorce proceedings won't make the slightest difference. And if it did—"

McKendrick waited.

"Even if it did I shouldn't listen to you. Why is everyone against me? Mrs. Black, Hesketh—they're both on Oliver's side. He's done wrong, not me. I'd divorce him if it meant the fall of the British Empire, which it certainly doesn't, anyway."

"If you put it like that, there's not much more to be said." Yet he made no move to drive off. And Helen, sitting somewhat stiffly, remained in her seat. The road was empty. Because they were on a hill they could see for a couple of miles, perhaps, across fields and woods to where the heat-haze shut down.

"You haven't caught me in a patriotic mood, Mr. McKendrick."

"Believe me, I don't blame you. Cigarette?"

"I don't smoke.

Plainly McKendrick had not given up hope of seeing Oliver. His impatience to be on the road again was a blind. And in spite of her passionate resentment of McKendrick's point of view she wanted to say: "Yes, yes, let's go and look for him." Her yearning to see Oliver and hear from his own lips an explanation for his behaviour was too strong to be resisted. The sun shone directly on to her closed eyes, and the red wings of blood across her sight were shutting down on pride, anger, self-pity. Her yearning was so strong that when she opened her eyes and a vivid blue tree struck between her and the sky she could not be sure McKendrick had not heard her confess it.

"Do you know this woman your husband is with?"

"No."

"It just isn't like him," McKendrick protested. "Anybody else but Knight. I just wouldn't believe it."

"Shall we go?" She meant to Reading.

"You wouldn't be game to go out to that cottage and have a scout round?"

"No," she said, in spite of the excitement which took hold of her. "It wouldn't do any good. Even if they were there we shouldn't do any good."

McKendrick appeared not to have heard. "The

sleuths could run your husband down in a couple of days but when they brought him in what use would he be to me? A pilot who is resentful or unhappy in some way is just a damn nuisance. He'd kill himself. They always do. At some crucial moment they say to themselves: 'Oh, what does it matter?' Everything is exaggerated in the air: speed, human reactions. On the ground a chap may be morose and the next day he shakes out of it; in the air he kills himself. He decides to kill himself in a split second."

"I want to have nothing to do with this."

"You'd rather have your husband picked up and court-martialled?"

"At least it would probably keep him out of the air. If he goes up again how long would he have to live? Two months?"

McKendrick drove on for some miles. They passed through a couple of villages, and on either hand were farms and orchards; but strangely they saw no other traffic. They had the afternoon to themselves. Unexpectedly McKendrick turned right at a sign-post which said: *Malvern 8 miles*. This was not the route to London, and Helen, realizing that McKendrick had never for one moment abandoned his intention of visiting the cottage, made no protest. They crossed the river once more and passed a village with a green pepper-pot dome on its ruined church. The little church gave a foreign flavour to the landscape, and although Helen had been abroad on holidays she felt farther from home than she had ever been.

"How do you know where to make for?"

"I've a rough idea. Mrs. Black gave me directions. I know the district fairly well."

"She did, did she?" Helen's excitement grew. Her doubts had gone. Once Oliver and she saw one another, all misunderstandings would be resolved. One look and they would be in each other's arms. Oh, faster, faster, for God's sake, drive faster, we must arrive before it is too late!

Their first view of the Malverns was from a point some five miles away, when the neat outline of the hills emerged from the haze. For a while they followed a road running parallel with the hills; then unhesitatingly McKendrick turned left and drove straight for them. Details could now be picked out; a grey house on a spur, a patch of woodland, a quarry. McKendrick turned right. He drove as though he knew the district intimately. They were making a cross-country journey of some complexity but he never appeared to be in doubt. Their route was so confusing that had it not been for the landmark of the hills Helen would not have known where she was.

"Wouldn't you rather see Oliver alone?" she asked when they came to a stop before joining a main road.

McKendrick lit another cigarette. "Sure you won't have one? . . . No, I want you to be there."

"Why? He obviously doesn't want to see me."

"I wouldn't be too sure about that," he said cryptically.

Half an hour later they were at the very spot where she had waited for Hesketh a few hours earlier. In this valley there was no haze and the trees and cottages cast heavy shadows. The air sparkled over the river. A one-carriage train pulled out of the station and as it crossed the embankment it had the sharp, simple definition of a child's drawing; but for the mass of vapour the train was two-dimensional. They could see green fields through its windows. They could in fact quite easily count the number of passengers. One in particular caught Helen's attention. He had stood up to lower the window before settling down opposite another passenger—whether his companion was a man or a woman it was hard to say. And then the train had disappeared under a bridge.

"That's Oliver," Helen said wonderingly to herself. She was quite certain. Although it had been impossible to pick out any details, the stance, the way the head nodded from side to side on the shoulders, the abruptness of movement, were familiar.

"Where do we go from here? Up that hill, isn't it?" said McKendrick.

She nodded without speaking. Her calmness surprised her. If at that moment they had met Oliver walking along the road she would have greeted him with no embarrassment. "Hallo, so there you are!" she would have said, and it would have seemed quite normal for him to kiss her. She would have wanted no explanation.

"I suppose this is it," she said when they arrived at a cottage lying back from the road behind trees bearing clusters of small green plums no bigger than grapes. The place appeared deserted. She opened the gate and walked up the path. She did not knock at the door but tried the handle and found that it was locked. She peered in through one of the windows and saw a settee covered with a white dust-sheet. The back door was locked, too.

"I suppose this is the right place?" she said to Mc-Kendrick who had followed her round the house.

"Must be." They were high. From the chicken-run they could see for about a mile down the road, and there was no other cottage. The only sound was the hum of bees.

"Did you see that?" she asked.

"See what?"

"I thought I saw somebody among that gorse." For a fleeting moment she had seen a head moving against the gold about fifty yards away. She had the impression that a man with a well-cropped head had looked in their direction and immediately dodged out of sight.

"Wait here," said McKendrick. He put a hand on the stone wall and vaulted over. He walked away into the radiance, looking this way and that. When a bird rose from the ground at his feet he started and gazed back. He was already too far away for her to speak to him. Then he had disappeared from sight and she was quite alone.

When Oliver's father was alive the family used this cottage as a week-end retreat; and Mrs. Knight had lived there during her widowhood. Helen knew all this because Oliver had frequently spoken of the place. She had never been there before but she knew it to be a spot where much of the happiness of his childhood had centred. Here it was, too, that he had met Jane. So much Helen had learned from Hesketh.

She was not resentful, as she had thought she might be. She made a complete circuit of the cottage, peering hungrily in at the windows, yearning after she knew not what. The doors were locked and the windows were firmly fastened; it was impossible to enter without smashing a pane of glass. She walked round a corner and saw McKendrick climbing back over the wall, the toes of his shoes yellow with pollen.

"Not a sign of anyone," he said. He came up to her, and unexpectedly put his arms on her shoulders. "You look a little sorry for yourself."

"Don't you think I've got a right?"

"Not really." He dropped his hands and looked away. "It would be easy enough for a dozen men to hide in that wilderness. But I don't see why I should look for them, not really. Do you?"

"You've given it up as a bad job?"

"H'm! Is it possible to get in?" He nodded at the cottage. "Locked, eh? Whoever it was you saw over there—you don't think it was your husband?"

"I'm quite sure it wasn't."

McKendrick tried the doors and windows. "No, this isn't in my line, playing the snoop. I can't do it. Would never have done it anyway if I didn't have such a regard for your husband. But he must be mad, mad as you make 'em." McKendrick consulted his watch. "I suppose it was a pretty forlorn hope anyway."

They drove slowly down the hill. McKendrick stopped and asked a youth herding some cows through a gateway if anybody had been staying in the cottage at the top of the hill recently; but the boy said he had seen no one. He never went up as far as the cottage. His home was on the other side of the village.

"I never realized before," said McKendrick, "what a damn fool you can feel merely asking a few questions. That lad thought it was highly suspicious."

Helen was thinking: "I can't possibly tell him I thought I saw Oliver in the train. He would ask me why I didn't tell him at the time. But I couldn't be sure, could I? I couldn't swear it was Oliver, any more than I could swear it was Hesketh among the gorse."

The sun was so hot. The heat seemed to come between her and any kind of certainty.

Long after the sound of the car had died in the quiet of the afternoon, Hesketh lay motionless among the gorse; eyes closed, face to the sky, head pillowed on the coat Jane and Oliver had silently surrendered. McKendrick had come very near to finding him; concealed by a single hillock of bramble and gorse Hesketh had listened for minutes (it seemed) to the hum of insects, the beating of his own heart, and McKendrick's breathing. Hesketh had been so braced for the meeting that now, as he lay between sleep and waking, he could not be sure that it had failed to take place. "They're gone! I warned them! I sent them away!" Had he experienced the joy of crying those words aloud? He could not be sure, even, that McKendrick was still not standing a couple of yards away and the joy yet to come.

VI

Two nights in succession Knight had the same dream. He was back at school once more, preparing for an examination. But for some reason he had not studied one of the most important subjects. The examination lay a fortnight ahead and he did not even know what the forgotten subject was; no one on the teaching staff could tell him. And even if he were told he could not possibly cover the ground in a fortnight. The outcome of the examination was of the greatest possible importance. His career depended on it. The headmaster opened his mouth to speak but instead of words a blackness emerged which blotted out his face.

177

Knight understood that the headmaster was refusing to accept responsibility; he believed that senior pupils should prepare for examinations by themselves, because in this way they learned to think. And Knight accepted this point of view. He had overlooked this vital paper and there was no one to blame but himself. On both nights the dream woke him. The second night the dream carried over into full consciousness and he lay in bed thinking: "I must have more time. Surely they will allow me more time!"

There was no sound from Jane's bed; or, rather, she made no sound that could be heard above the murmur of the sea outside. By this time Knight was wide awake. He wrapped himself in a blanket from the foot of the bed—the morning air was cold—and walked to the window. The sky was stainless. Between the promenade and the edge of the sea was a fifty-yard stretch of wet sand. But for the gulls there was no sign of life. To the left the promenade rail followed the line of the bay; to the right it led the eye to the wooden chalet of the cliff railway—and so the eye continued, following the ramp to the lawns at the top of the cliff. It was impossible to look at the scene without sharing some of its sanity.

"Is that you, Oliver?"

He laughed, and went over to her bed where he knelt for the warm hand to come out and fondle his hair. "Who else do you think it would be?"

Jane was as wide awake as he. "What's the matter?"

"I can't sleep. It's morning, anyway. I had a

dream." He was reluctant to describe the dream but when she insisted he said: "Oh, all right."

"Let's go out, now, straight away," she said when he had finished. "Let's get dressed and go out."

"Where are we going, Jane?"

"Let's get dressed and go out before breakfast," she said.

Until the bombing of the *Dundas* the nature of his flight had been obvious; he was running away from the Germans. His objectives, too, were clear. He wanted to see his wife and he wanted to rejoin his unit. But the moment they lifted him out of the water on to the hospital ship he was aware of one objective only: that of reaching Helen. It had obsessed him. Yet here he was with Jane. Why? While Jane dressed he stood gazing out of the window. Two sea-gulls rose from the sand, fighting over some titbit. Eagerly he followed their flight out to sea because he thought there might be meaning in it. But the meaning eluded him. In the sea the nature of his flight had first become mysterious and now here he was, back at the shore once more, trying to read symbols.

He washed in the hand-basin, and dressed hurriedly. Jane was ready and waiting, sitting on the edge of the bed with a questioning smile on her face that arrested him in the act of putting on his jacket.

"Well," he said, "what have we got to be afraid of?" She shrugged. It was so early there was no movement in the hotel. Although they had not made plans there was never any doubt of their intentions. Knight opened the door and Jane walked quickly ahead as though to keep an appointment. By the time he had caught her up she was already at the front door and what was more had found how to unlock it. He followed her into the sunlight with the realization that they were embarking on another stage of their flight, and that every step he took was carrying him farther away from what he most desired. Possibly the same was true of Jane. For they were not ordinary lovers. In spite of his confession to Black he could not have said to her: "I love you." He could not conceive of her saying it to him.

A breeze blew off the sea, and over and above the pounding of the surf they could hear a high, harp-like strumming as though winds were racing into one another high in the atmosphere. Halfway up the climb to the cliff-top they stopped and gazed at the spinning sea. By their whiteness the drifting gulls set off the grey-green wallowing of water; over the sands of the bay there was a fume of mist which extended, lower than the roofs, along the streets of the town; as fast as the breeze carried the mist out to the suburbs it seethed up from the wet sands. The slate roofs flashed; they might have been the upturned keels of boats dragged from the water. Far out, the horizon was a firm line.

"If we went on walking where should we get to?"

"I don't know," said Knight. "Swansea?"

They passed the ornate shed which housed the terminus of the cliff railway, they passed a miniature-golf-course and the last of the red bungalows. Still they had met no one, and the farther they walked the less likelihood there was of an encounter. The cliff-top turf was scattered with thrift. "More time for what?" Knight was asking himself, because he was remembering his dream.

"What's that?" said Jane. "Look! Down there! At the edge of the water."

The land curled round. They were walking due south with the bay, the town, and the rising sun on their left hand. Jane was pointing down into a cove where because of the sheltering cliff the water was calm and the colour of lavender leaves. Knight looked.

"I can't see anything."

"It's an animal."

A creature there certainly was, of some sort, almost the same colour as the grey rocks among which it moved.

"It's a bird. Must be a gull."

"Why doesn't it fly like the other gulls? It's a different colour, too."

"Looking for worms, I expect."

There was an easy descent to the cove, and a few moments later they were stepping over the long pools which the retreating tide had left between the ribs of sand. Some twenty yards out from the foot of the cliff the rocks began.

"You'll never catch it," Knight shouted; for by this time they could see the creature quite clearly: a common gull unable to flutter its wings because of the oil gumming its feathers together. But it could run. Its head popped in and out. When it was not running, comical as all birds, it was trying to look in all directions at once. Another gull floated sedately as a duck in the calm water a stone's throw out.

"Stay here!" said Knight. He said she would break her ankle if she went racing over the rocks like that.

"The poor thing. Couldn't we catch it and clean it? It will die."

"Stay here until I come back."

The rocks were of such a size that within a few paces he was out of sight. Now what? The gull had disappeared in this direction but although Knight scrambled about for what he guessed was a good five minutes, there was no sign of the bird.

"Hi!" he shouted for Jane. Immediately her answering cry came back. "Stay where you are," he shouted. "I'm coming."

He could not return without the gull. "Pray God I find it," he said aloud. He had heard about sea-birds fouling themselves in oil and he was filled with hatred of the ships that discharged their filth in this way. Monstrous! He tried to check the upsurge of anger and compassion but the feelings were too powerful. He looked about with tears in his eyes. Absurd to get worked up about such a trifle! It was out of proportion. Hundreds of gulls, thousands, no doubt, died in this way every year; yet here he was behaving like a silly girl. At first the tenderness frightened him because it seemed to link up with his dream; unless he found the gull within a certain time he would never find it. Then fear turned to exultation, and he jumped from rock to rock, saying: "Helen, Helen, Helen," and the thought of his wife became so vivid he scarcely knew whether he was looking for her or for a gull at the edge of the sea.

In this way he came across a man lying among the rocks with his head turned away from the sun. The sight was so unexpected that Knight stopped dead. Even now it could only be about six o'clock—not an hour when one lay down for a sleep in a sheltered spot. The man must have been there some time. They had not seen him from the top of the cliff. Knight turned to see whether by any chance Jane had followed him; then, because it struck him that the man was familiarly clad in flying-kit, he stepped across the rocks and saw how one of the heavy boots was missing and the bones of the foot were revealed in all their white delicacy. The still-helmeted head was thrust firmly, face downward, into a cleavage of the rock.

"Not Coastal Command," Knight thought, "not with those boots." He was R.A.F. The probability was that Knight knew him; he had only to free the body, turn it over, and search for the identity tabs—round his neck, perhaps, or on his wrist—to find a name he had at the very least heard of. No sooner did the thought enter his head than he put it from him. Calmly he considered what best to do. The dead pilot had not immediately stirred any feelings. Out of the corner of his eye Knight suddenly detected a movement. Turning his head he saw the gull, almost within grasping distance, lying on a patch of seaweed with one of its legs stretched out. The plumage looked as though it had been daubed with black treacle. The bird was looking at him without fear, and—it struck Knight—without self-pity. If he had wanted, he could have captured the gull without difficulty. Instead he turned and went slowly back to Jane.

"Let's go in for a swim," she suggested. She had forgotten the gull.

"We haven't got costumes."

"There won't be anybody about for hours yet."

Not taking her suggestion seriously he crouched over a pool where a brown spider-crab was sulkily stirring. Already the shallow water was warm to his fingers. Heat gathered in the shelter of the rocks. The sun reduced the water in the cove to transparency; only out in the main bay where the wind drove the waves shoreward did the sea have positive colour, positive white and positive iron.

"Jane!" he rose to his feet shouting. His cry echoed back from the cliffs. She had undressed behind the rocks and was already so far out in the cove that the water lapped about her naked thighs. She did not look back but he could hear her calling for him to come in. Where she flawed the surface there was brilliance but her own form poised between him and the sun was black. With a flash of white she plunged.

Knight looked round. She was right, of course. The hour was too early for anyone else to be stirring. He undressed rapidly. By the time he reached the water Jane was already halfway to the troubled water outside the cove and swimming strongly. He shouted for her to come back.

The rocks cut at his feet. He could not plunge into the water as he would have liked but was forced to pick his way with agonizing slowness. The water rose only up to his knees but his whole body was numbed. Then he was on sand, rushing into greater depth with an occasional paralysing wave splashing his stomach. He plunged. Momentarily he was silly with shock. The familiar brine, the familiar chill, the familiar pressure of water upwards—they struck a shell from his mind, the *Dundas* lurched under his feet once more, he was swimming in the sea off Dieppe again, and it was Helen, not Jane, who called for him to come.

The exercise exhilarated. He had no history; he was merely a man swimming before breakfast in a summer sea. Until he remembered Jane his memory was innocent. He trod water trying to lift himself but shoreward there were only the cliffs rising and falling; and seaward, parallel bands of crystal. After some minutes he found that Jane was swimming easily at his side. She had waited for him.

The nearest land was a cluster of rocks where the cove joined the main bay; beyond the rocks the sea looked like a running hedge of grey and white.

Knight was so close that he could put a hand on her shoulder.

"Let's make for those rocks," he called. Jane did not answer. Water poured from her mouth and she bored stubbornly seaward. "Jane, it's dangerous." She was a stronger swimmer than he. She did not speak but took him by the hand. Already the waves were strong enough to lift them like corks. They bored through the crests and came out gasping in the troughs. By pulling on her arm he tried to guide her towards the rocks. At first she resisted. He swore at her.

The only time she spoke was to call his name. Her legs and arms were about him, dragging him down. Knight was taken by surprise; they were already so far beneath the surface that the light was a steady, green radiance and he saw her face, with hair and bubbles streaming upwards, like a stone angel. Knight's panic left him, and he was no longer afraid. He took her by the throat, saw the mouth open in pitiful astonishment, gripped tighter, and struck out vigorously with his legs. The golden morning and the bitter sea-air was all about him, He was free. Vomit rose to his mouth. He spat, drank in air, and floated, momentarily exhausted, on his back.

Jane, however, was not to be seen. Knight plunged and fought to keep below the surface while he looked about him, breathing out slowly. He followed the green bubbles into the air and plunged once more. This time he saw Jane, her back arched like a cat, and drifting away from him. By snatching at her hair and kicking wildly he found it possible to surface and draw her after him, floating on her back. Thank God there was no current! Thank God, too, she was unconscious and unable to resist! What he knew about life-saving was negligible but once he had her floating on her back he tried to support her head and shoulders with his own body, clasping her body with his legs, and back-stroking for the rocks. It worked. He closed his eyes because of the sun-dazzle and struck wildly, wastefully, exhaustingly at the heavy water. Time and again he thought he would lose his leg-grip. But when he suddenly released his hold, and supporting her with one arm, trod water so that he could take new bearings, he found it possible to stand on a sandy bottom. Currents sweeping across the mouth of the cove had made a bar; from that moment on there was no difficulty.

He laid Jane belly-down on the shore and water poured out of her mouth. The wild idea came to him of holding her up by her legs so that the water would run out of her like a bottle; but now he remembered the little he had been taught of artificial respiration. Five minutes later she was sitting up, there was colour in her cheeks, and Knight was lying face downward at her side sick with exhaustion. Hours later—or so it seemed—he was able to talk.

"So you tried to kill us, eh?"

He stood up when she made no reply. He should have felt anger, compassion, relief—some emotion big enough to measure up against the eloquence of her stony silence. But he was too tired. Sleep was what he wanted.

"Can you walk?" She stood up and he took her arm. "If we don't get dressed we'll be run in for indecent exposure." She walked ahead and Knight noticed the sand across her shoulders and buttocks; the fine powdering of white in patches across her back which was the brine drying out in the sun and wind. The situation became unreal to him. He caught himself wanting to make fatuous remarks about the weather.

When Jane came back from behind her rock, fully dressed, Knight was just putting on his jacket.

"My hair is in a terrible mess." They were the first words she had spoken since coming out of the water. Knight pulled out a packet of cigarettes and they sat smoking and looking about them like holiday-makers. From a point somewhere farther round the coast a fog-siren boomed out like some stranded, complaining sea-beast. Yet the morning seemed as clear as it had ever been. Knight suggested that they were testing the apparatus. The tide was out so far they could see a sandbank in the middle of the bay.

"Life's a habit like any other habit," Knight said. "I find it very hard to break myself of it. Another thing, there's a dead man over there." He nodded in the direction where the drowned airman lay. Aware of his cruelty he turned his head and looked into her face. The statement appeared to make no impression on Jane. The round brown eyes looked back into his without so much as a question. Perhaps she thought he was joking. Knight explained the circumstances in greater detail.

This time she was shocked. "Let's go away from this dreadful place."

He ought to feel pity for her but he could not; it was as though the sea-gull had used up all the pity of which he was capable. "We can't go away from this dreadful place; we're here until we die."

"No, for ever," she said unexpectedly, "but I can't accept it. I can't accept it. I ought to be able to accept it, but I can't, Oliver."

Even now the defiance was not broken; he could see it in the angle at which she held her head. But she was frightened, too.

"I don't know what you're talking about." He stood up. "Let's go and report that type over there on the rocks."

At the top of the cliff they found that the wind had dropped and a sea mist was shutting out all but a hundred yards of visibility to the south and west. A car passed them on the coast road. Early morning walkers were out with dogs. Knight wanted to speak to Jane tenderly but whenever he spoke he found he was uttering words of denial. He had after his own fashion understood her words uncommonly well: that night he would dream his dream again and awake asking for more time.

Hesketh walked out of the station and made his way down to the front where he breakfasted at a table under a large striped umbrella. He carried no luggage and in his light-brown jacket and shirt open at the neck might easily have been mistaken for a holiday-maker.

"What's going on, on the pier?" he asked the waitress.

"Don't ask me, they're getting ready for the invasion, or something. Demolition or something. They're taking it down."

The green-domed pavilion was already isolated. The central portion of the pier had been dismantled and only the supporting uprights remained. Hesketh could see soldiers walking round the pavilion and he observed to the waitress that they would be completely cut off at high tide. No doubt they had mounted guns on the seaward side. Yet children were taking donkey rides on the sands and their parents were lolling in deck-chairs with newspapers over their faces.

"Just when the 'oliday season's beginning, too," said the waitress. "It's too bad, isn't it, when you come to think of it?"

"Do you know this address?" asked Hesketh. He showed her the first sheet of a letter.

"Take a No. 12 bus from the clock tower and ask the conductor to put you off. It's up on the hill behind the station."

When half an hour later the bus deposited Hesketh at the end of the road where his father lived, he found that he could see all over the town. To the left a convoy of army lorries was approaching along the coast road; only to the southwest was vision obscured by a sea mist, and from this direction came the boom of a remote warning siren. As always happened just before meeting his father, Hesketh wanted to abandon the visit; he had a fluttering in the belly, and a sour taste in the mouth. "At all costs," he told himself, "I mustn't let him quarrel with me."

"You're to go right up," said the woman in the hall as soon as Hesketh had explained his business. "Your father's expecting you. It's the top floor, two flights. How proud you must be. Such a very active man; but seventy is young these days, isn't it? You'll find him decorating his room."

Hesketh looked at his father's landlady sadly. She wore a blue mob-cap, carried a broom, and was a gawky, red-faced, hoydenish fifty with an air of conspiratorial gaiety. "It's not a bit of good," he wanted to tell her. "He'll never marry you. All my father's landladies fall in love with him, but he never marries them." Hesketh assumed that the woman was a widow. His father always lodged with widows.

On the top landing there was so much furniture that Hesketh had to climb over it in order to get to his father's door. The door itself stood open and Hesketh could see a step-ladder, pails, tins of paint, brushes, and rolls of wallpaper. Mr. Hesketh was stripping the old paper off a wall and sneezing.

"Hallo, Dad," Hesketh said quietly.

The white-coated figure turned and he saw the big-nosed, red, vaguely Wellingtonian face and heard the familiar cockney voice. "Well, come on in, my boy," Mr. Hesketh said testily. "Don't stand there! 'Ere, look at this!" He put out a hand and tore a huge strip of beflowered paper off the wall. "See 'ow easy it comes off? If you ask me this room's damp, or it's the salt in the air, one o' the two. 'Ere take this!" He thrust a piece of sandpaper into his son's hand. "You might as well start rubbing the window frame down."

"I've come to talk, not to work."

"We can talk and work at the same time, can't we? . . . No, not like that! 'Aven't you ever rubbed any paint-work down before? Let me show you. What it really wants is a blowlamp, it all wants coming off, but damn it all, I'm not in the decorating trade, I only want the place to look tidy. What 'ave you come to see me for?" He darted the question swiftly. "Not," he went on amiably, "that I should question the presence of a loving son." Hesketh stepped back and his father shouted at him: "Mind that bucket of paste!"

"I'm looking for Jane."

"Oh!" said Mr. Hesketh, his eyes on the floor, but cocking an ear.

"I'm looking for Jane and Oliver. Have they been here yet?"

"Why should they?"

"I thought they might."

Mr. Hesketh went as far out on to the landing as the accumulation of furniture permitted, and peered down the stairs. He returned, shutting the door behind him.

"She's got ears like a Red Indian."

"They haven't come, then?"

"Perhaps they have and perhaps they 'aven't," said Mr. Hesketh.

"Five days ago Oliver came to Luton. They went off to Worcester together. The Air Force is after Oliver."

"And they're not in Worcester now?" Mr. Hesketh said drily.

"No."

Unexpectedly Mr. Hesketh said: "Poor kids!" and glowered through the window at the railway station and sidings which were spread out below.

"You don't say 'poor' me."

"I've always been sorry for you, my boy," said Mr. Hesketh, and his son flushed.

Mr. Hesketh went back to work. The wallpaper had a pattern of trellis-work, red roses and blue trumpet-flowers; as it was stripped off, many other patterns were revealed beneath. Hesketh partly opened a roll of the new paper to see what colour his father had chosen: to his surprise he saw trellis-work—but instead of flowers there were canaries, robins, and magpies.

"Unusual, ain't it?" said Mr. Hesketh. "If I gave you a bit of jagged glass instead of sandpaper I reckon you'd get that paint off better, what d'you say?"

"You don't seem very interested in my news."

"Interested? Of course I'm interested. But what's it got to do with me?" Having teased his son sufficiently Mr. Hesketh now cross-examined him carefully. "It makes you look a bit of a fool, doesn't it, my boy?" he said at last.

"All that matters to me is Jane's happiness and well-being."

Mr. Hesketh repeated these words, barking with angry, contemptuous laughter. "You ought to read the newspapers. Don't you ever read the newspapers? There's a war on, you know. We're all going to be bombed to bloody 'ell, then we're going to be invaded, then we're going to be deported to work in the salt mines; and what d'you say to that? 'All that matters to me is Jane's happiness and well-being!' You're mad! For Christ's sake get out of my sight and don't come back till you've got a uniform on!"

"I shall go when they call me up."

"At a time like this all you've got to say is: 'All that matters to me—' "

"You know perfectly well what I mean. I'm responsible for Jane and I feel I can do something to help her. I'm not responsible for the war and there's precious little I can—"

"You can join the Home Guard."

"All right! I'll join the Home Guard. That can wait until tomorrow but this other matter is more urgent. Let's take one thing at a time!"

Mr. Hesketh handed his son a pair of shears and gave instructions for cutting the margin of the new wallpaper.

"If you think this place is going to be bombed why are you decorating it?"

"Oh, they wouldn't bomb *this* house," said Mr. Hesketh. He implied that they would not dare to.

"They're bound to have a go at the station."

"Well, a man's got to do something, hasn't he?" Mr. Hesketh exploded.

"That's what I've been trying to tell you."

Hesketh trimmed a roll of paper while his father finished stripping the room. By this time it was eleven o'clock and Mr. Hesketh suggested they followed his usual practice of going into town for a coffee. The bus took them down into the sea mist which now covered the town; visibility was cut down to about twenty yards, though overhead the grey had a brilliance that showed how thin the blanket was.

"A morning like this there could be a couple o' thousand Jerries on the beach and nobody the wiser," said Mr. Hesketh.

"Did they come and see you last night?"

"Who? Jerries?" Mr. Hesketh began to laugh. "I fought 'em off with a screwdriver, my boy. Loved every minute of it. My generation's very bloodthirsty; too old for the 1914 lot. But we're going to 'ave a go this time. I expect you noticed all the nasty stains on the stairs."

"I mean Jane and Oliver."

The waitress brought their coffee. Hesketh had breakfasted at this same restaurant in sunshine; now in the steamy atmosphere the striped umbrellas looked out of place.

"Yes," said Mr. Hesketh some minutes later, "they came to see me."

"I know this is a hell of a joke as far as you're concerned—"

"How did they know where to find me?"

"I told them. In any case, Jane knew your address."

"So you sent them to me. Yes, my boy, you're quite right: I do think it's a hell of a joke. A fellow runs off with your wife. All right, we accept that. It's happened to a lot of better men than you. But they're a bit uncertain where to go, you see. They don't like their little love-nest. So, being a nice sort of chap, you chases after 'em and makes one or two suggestions. 'Go and see my dad,' you say. 'He's an old fool. He'll fix you up.' Is that how it was, Martin?"

The mist enclosed them like a room, and Mr. Hesketh's gritty voice rang out the more loudly.

"There now, you've broken your cup."

It was true. Hesketh held the cup in one hand and the handle in the other. Listening to his father he had without realizing what he was doing snapped the handle off.

"I don't want to quarrel with you."

"But we're not quarrelling, my boy. Just 'aving a 'eart to 'eart, father to son talk, aren't we? I'd like to knock some sense into that bloody fat head of yours."

"What did you say to them?"

"What did you expect me to say, tell me that?"

Hesketh did not answer. He had urged them to come to his father because in his desperation he could think of nowhere else for them to go. He could still see their eyes. At first they had looked at him as though he were a stranger. They had looked at one another more than at him. It was the kind of courtesy one receives from people to whom one's presence is irrelevant but mildly comical. Only when he mentioned McKendrick and urged them to go while the going was good had they looked puzzled. They could not understand his motives. Their eyes became small and frightened.

"For what Oliver's done, he'll have to answer to his own wife. With Jane it's different. She's lonely. She will never have another child. I should think you've got to be a woman to understand that kind of loneliness. I can't bear that she should be alone in that way. So far as I'm concerned she may do anything, anything, to get out. First of all I thought I would do them some harm. But I heard Jane laughing, you understand? They didn't know I was there. I heard her laughing."

"If I had a husband like you I think I should 'ave a bloody good laugh, too."

"I tried getting her to go to church but she said it meant nothing to her any more."

Mr. Hesketh did not care for this kind of talk. "I said I'd look in on them sometime this morning. You can take the girl back home and give her a good hiding, if that's the way you feel. But if you want my advice, I'd get rid of her. People aren't like cups. You can't mend 'em when they get their handles knocked off. I don't like calling my daughter-in-law a bitch—"

Hesketh jerked his cup, and the tepid coffee shot over his father's face. A milky drop collected at the point of the nose; wrinkles and recesses became channels and lakes. Even as Hesketh noticed how the jutting upper-lip protected the chin he was aware of his father's astonishment turning to anger; the face darkened, the head came forward. But the storm did not break. Mr. Hesketh glanced round to see whether anyone was watching; the mist was so dense even the façade of the restaurant was invisible. No one else was taking coffee on the terrace that morning. Tables and umbrellas floated around them. Mr. Hesketh leaned back in his chair, and gazing at a point immediately overhead, began to laugh. He mopped his face with a red spotted handkerchief—the kind of handkerchief, Hesketh was irritated to notice, favoured by stage navvies. It was his father's way of boasting his humble origin.

Mr. Hesketh put half a crown on the table. "Let's go for a little walk, my boy," he said abruptly. "I expect you know the last time an enemy force managed to land in this country it was at a spot not very far from here. Wish it was the French we was fighting this time, too."

"Tell me where Jane is staying, and I'll clear off."

"My dear boy, I couldn't bear to part company with you so soon. It would be very nice if you and me was the first to engage the enemy."

He led the way down on to the beach. After some minutes of ploughing through softer sand they came to where the beach was hard, and here a boy was throwing a stick for a barking terrier. Even this did not satisfy Mr. Hesketh. He walked on until they could see the waves breaking into a dark swath of seaweed. Now they were quite alone. They could see nothing but water, sand, and seaweed. It seemed natural that they should look at one another.

Hesketh tensed before he realized the cause. His father was smiling at him and grunting, "I've—never —allowed—any—cheek—" Anticipating the blows, Hesketh leaned forward, and catching his father by the wrists, exerted all his strength to keep them at his father's thighs. The struggle was silent. He kept his head low and held it so that it lightly touched his father's belly. When he released his grip he gave a jerk which sent his father staggering backwards.

"You're quite strong, Martin."

"I get exercise."

But this time when he approached, Hesketh made no move to defend himself. He stared in the direction of the sea. He felt the knuckles of a clenched fist resting against his cheek. As though by way of experiment Mr.

Hesketh had placed it there and was now awaiting developments.

"What are you trembling for, Martin? You didn't really think I'd strike you, did you?" He patted his son's cheek affectionately. "I think we'll pop back into town now. We ought to catch 'em just about. What the devil was the name of that hotel?" He was in an excellent humour. As they paced over the seaweed he held his son by the elbow, squeezing it, and chuckling to himself.

"That's it," said Mr. Hesketh. "Golden Sands Private Hotel."

They stood looking across the road at the hotel which stood out from the others in the terrace because it was the only one to be camouflaged. The contours of buff and green made the building look smaller than its neighbours, though they were all of a size. A man in a white hat was sitting in a deck-chair just inside the open front door.

"Right! Now clear off, will you!" said Hesketh.

"What's that?"

"I said: Clear off!"

Mr. Hesketh looked at his son slyly. "I 'ope you're not going to be an embarrassment to 'em."

"Oh, for God's sake go away."

"Having given 'em a helping hand so far it wouldn't be right to stand about goggling at 'em. Remember what I say, Martin, my boy. No idle curiosity! Remember your dignity. And keep that filthy temper of yours under control." He walked away laughing.

Hesketh entered a small garden and sat where a shrub partially screened him from the hotel windows and yet allowed him to command a view of the front door. He was prepared to wait all day if necessary. After he had been sitting in the garden some time he realized that it was set aside in memory of the men of the town killed in the 1914 war. There was a granite column bearing many names, and surmounted by a bronze eagle with spread wings.

One moment Jane was sunk in a profound sleep, the next she was wide awake. She gazed at the ceiling. If she had been awakened by a noise it was not repeated. She turned her head sharply and looked at Oliver's bed: it was empty. Her body tingled with energy. What had happened? A light which was at once grey and brilliant poured through the window. Walking across to it she looked out. The tide was coming in fast. She saw the line of foam shining just beyond the point where the mist would normally have shut down on visibility. The little public garden with its war memorial, away to the right, smoked. A woman was calling to a child with a bucket and spade: "Don't run ahead so, Juliet." A boy on roller-skates went gravely along the pavement. Two soldiers leaned on the railings and stared seaward, their heads close together.

Jane sat at the dressing-table and brushed her hair. After lunch Oliver had suggested they needed a rest. They had lain on their respective beds without speaking. Their feelings were neutral as the colour of the day itself; but unpredictably the sun had now burst

through—for her at least. An altogether strange vitality had taken charge. She applied her lipstick carefully and walked out on to the landing. Where was
Oliver? Perhaps there was good news of some kind.

"Mrs. Hesketh," said a voice from the dining-room
when she arrived in the hall, "your husband's gone
out. I was to tell you he'd not be long. Didn't want to
wake you, he said." The Golden Sands Private Hotel
was in reality a boarding-house. In the dining-room a
woman Jane knew to be about her own age but who
looked much older was tidying up after lunch and setting the tables for high tea. The air reeked with the
smell of cooking. The woman came out, shaking her
grey locks and screwing up one watering eye. Mr. and
Mrs. Birch owned the establishment, and this was their
daughter.

"He's not my husband," said Jane.

Miss Birch removed the cigarette from her mouth
and stubbed it out in a saucer. "Oh, I don't know
about that!" She grimaced. A plate stood on the
table by the telephone, and she picked it up, holding
it at an angle so that the light could fall on it and reveal whether it was clean or not. She was blushing and
could not meet Jane's eyes. "He went out about half
an hour ago."

A large room, known as the lounge, led off the hall.
The only occupants were an elderly couple who sat
asleep—obviously permanent residents—and looking
from them to the mist outside, Jane felt another pulse
of joy. For a moment she had thought Miss Birch was
referring to Martin. The correction had come auto-

matically to her lips. "What a fool I am," she thought. "Now they will certainly ask us to go. What an idiotic thing to blurt out!" Yet somehow it did not seem to matter. An upright piano stood in one corner of the room, and Jane opened it and struck a chord before remembering the elderly couple. She turned to apologize. They were sitting in exactly the same position but their eyes were open looking into space with a fixity which pretended they had never been asleep. An apology would have been tactless. Rather than wait for the attack to be launched Jane went into the hall and here, as she expected, Mrs. Birch was waiting for her.

"My dear, I must ask for your ration books. If you'd ask your husband to sign the book, too. The police are extra sharp these days."

"He's not my husband," said Jane, quite amazed with herself.

Mrs. Birch was a big, mannish woman who walked with a stick, and now it lay across her parted knees. She turned her head sharply to the right as though listening to a whisper from behind and Jane saw how her forehead and nose made a line that would have been straight but for the smallest of indentations at the brow. It was like the head on a coin.

"But you're sharing a room!"

"Yes."

"But you are married. You've got a ring."

"Yes, I'm married."

Mrs. Birch put her stick to the ground and levered herself to her feet.

"Well, put yourself in my position. You're not a

girl. You know what you're doing. I'll not let you sign the book. You won't get a bill out of me. You'll get no divorce evidence out of this house. We've never seen you before. I was at Weymouth for seven years. Did you know that?"

"No."

"I ran the Golden Sands at Weymouth for seven years, and nothing like this ever happened. When we came here we changed the name. We've been here twenty-four years. Would you like a cup of tea? My daughter always makes a pot for her father and me this time of day."

Mrs. Birch led the way slowly along the dark passage without speaking. Her husband came forward to assist her up the step into the kitchen. After giving Jane a furtive look he at once turned to a table on which he appeared to be assembling a radio set. He was a small, tame-looking man with a pipe and slippers, and all the time that Jane was present he never once raised his head from the confusion of equipment with which he tinkered. Miss Birch smoked a cigarette, poured out tea and from time to time gave startlingly loud sighs and yawns.

"This morning," said Jane, "we got up early and went swimming. I tried to drown us both."

"Do you take sugar?" said Mrs. Birch. "Nancy, for heaven's sake wake up and pass the sugar."

"I don't take sugar," said Jane. "Thank you."

"We can talk quite freely in here. There's no risk of being overheard. In the hall you never know who's going to pop up. But you'll have to go, you know. You understand that, don't you, my dear? We can't have adultery going on here, can we, Charles? Business is business. Nancy, darling, don't tell me we've had the last of the cream biscuits. That's better! I thought there were a few left. Well, this is a nice how-d'you-do! Put yourself in my place!"

"I shall tell them everything," Jane was thinking. For the first time in months she was taking the initiative. The situation was entirely of her own making. She would force these people to listen to her confession. She was so excited that she had difficulty in drinking her tea, and when she put the cup back on the table it was only half empty.

"This hotel is my property. Dad over there is on a naval pension, such as it is. I've always been mistress of my own household. The business is registered in my name. . . . What did you want to drown yourself for?"

Mr. Birch and his daughter were nonentities. Mrs. Birch was only pretending to be a fool. She talked nonsense but her grey eyes were on Jane all the time and she missed nothing.

"I've been unhappy."

Mrs. Birch cleared her throat contemptuously. "And if you *had* drowned yourselves, just think of the bother that would have got me into. You never thought of that, I suppose. If there's anything I hate it's identifying people for the coroner."

When Oliver came back they would gather their few belongings together and leave the hotel. In half an hour's time she would probably say good-bye to the

Birches, and it was most unlikely that she would ever see any of them again. She had to seize the opportunity.

"We were running away."

"From your husband and his wife—if he's got a wife? You mustn't mind my speaking bluntly. I've always called a spade a spade. Anyway it was wrong of you to come here like that. You've done me an injury and I'm punishing you. But I don't want you to think I'm old-fashioned and stuffy. How old are you, my dear? You see, I'm old enough to be your grandmother."

"I don't think we're running away from my husband."

"The police, then?" The woman was unshockable.

Jane found that she was laughing; but the gaiety was pure, it rose from the heart. There was no defiance in it. She was braving no mere summer lightning; there was no wind in the storm, there was no sea breaking at her feet. She was buffeted by a different gale.

"I think," she said, "we're running away from God."

Mrs. Birch expressed her disappointment by telling Nancy to give her father another cup of tea.

"That's a funny thing to say."

It scarcely seemed to matter whether Mrs. Birch listened or not, or, if she listened, whether she understood. The bonds had been broken. If Jane could speak in this moment of liberty (there was no knowing how long it would last) the confession would permit her

return to that state of grace before the child was conceived; in comparison with the present it *was* a time of
grace. Perhaps it was the mention of God that embarrassed Mrs. Birch. She would not permit Jane to
say another word where it could be listened to by her
husband and daughter. She took Jane out into what
she called the garden; in reality the surrounding buildings would have shut out the light on even the sunniest
of days, the grass plot had the merest sprinkle of green,
and the shrubs were the hiding-places for cats. Mrs.
Birch picked up a white cat and fondled it. She pursed
her lips and chirruped. The creature looked at Jane
with green, complacent eyes.

"Nothing mattered. I couldn't bear to think that
anything mattered. When they told me that the baby
was dead they were terribly shocked because I said it
didn't matter. What else could I say? I've always been
a religious sort of person in a priggish, respectable sort
of way. The only way I could make sense after the
baby went was to think I was fighting God. I hated
Him so much I wouldn't let Him hurt me. Nothing
mattered. I tried to live as though nothing mattered."

A black cat stood on the garden wall arching its
back and spitting at the white cat which Mrs. Birch
still held in her arms. Now it struggled free and darted
under a shrub. Mrs. Birch shook her stick at the strange
black cat shouting: "Be off with you! Go on! You ugly
brute!" Wisps of sea mist stole across the upper storeys
of neighbouring buildings. The effect was dreamlike.
The whole town was drifting through cloud. "Give me
a stone," said Mrs. Birch, and Jane handed her a small

pebble. Before she could throw it the black cat had gone.

She was bored by Jane's talk; her curiosity stretched after more ordinary facts: Where was Jane's husband? Had she a father and mother? How long had she known this man? Above all, what was his name and where did he come from?

Jane could see nothing vulgar in this curiosity. It did not occur to her that Mrs. Birch led a dull life and was determined to extract as much titillation out of her guests as possible. Jane was too grateful to Mrs. Birch for such thoughts to enter her head.

"When we ran away from Martin we thought he would—oh, may God forgive us!—kill himself. It seemed right for him to kill himself. I thought a sacrifice was wanted. A sacrifice would make everything clean again."

"You're not in the Salvation Army, are you?" said Mrs. Birch.

They were standing where an apple tree spread its branches against the wall; as yet the apples were no bigger than nutmegs, and Jane took one in her hand, thinking of Eve and the Garden of Eden. "I knew a girl in the Salvation Army. She used to sing hymns here on the beach with the rest of them, but she went on the stage, she did. There were a lot of stories told about her."

Jane picked up one of Mrs. Birch's hands and to the woman's surprise and embarrassment, kissed it.

"You're a very silly girl, aren't you?" Mrs. Birch meant this. Jane was beginning to disgust her. "I should think the sooner your young man gets called up, the better for everybody concerned."

"He's a pilot in the Air Force. He flies fighter-planes. Last week he came back from France and his ship was bombed. All he wants is to go back to his wife."

"You know," said Mrs. Birch kindly, "you talk as though you weren't all there."

"Do I?"

"You're quite sure that everything you've been telling me isn't just a pack of lies?"

"Lies?"

"You've not been having me on? One thing I'll say in your favour. You're not sly. You don't look sly. But you've not been pulling my leg, have you?"

"No."

Jane wanted to find out whether Oliver had returned, but when they entered the kitchen once more Mrs. Birch would not allow her to go upstairs. She would not allow Jane to collect her things from the bedroom even when Nancy came back and said: "No, he's not in. He went out, you know. He said he wouldn't be long."

"Nancy will bring your belongings downstairs. I'll not have you setting foot in that room again. It's not proper. Now you sit there while I make out your bill."

"He ought to be back by now. I'll go and see if he's in the lounge."

But for the elderly couple, the lounge was deserted, and Jane went to the front door and looked through the film of mist at the sea. For the first time since they had left Luton she did not know where Oliver was; her ignorance gave her a sense of freedom. Perhaps he had gone to see Martin's father. She crossed the road, entered the public garden and looked up at the bronze eagle before passing through a gate and continuing her walk along the promenade. A clock struck three. Because the tide was in, the children could not play on the beach, and there were dozens of them coming and going with their parents on the broad pavement—very young children, below school age most of them, but there were others who showed by their pallor that they were recovering from illness. Jane found herself looking into the children's faces as though for someone she knew.

At the end of the promenade she climbed steps and found herself on a seawall which stretched away into the mist with the narrow shingle and breaking waves on one side and what appeared to be a waste of sand and pebbles on the other. After walking for about fifty yards she turned and looked back at the town; the mist shut it out. What was there to fear? The mist poured over the wall at such a rate that the wall appeared to be moving out to sea; yet the mist was not hostile—the atmosphere was domestic, a laundry atmosphere, a cooking atmosphere. The danger of losing herself simply did not exist; in order to fall off the wall she would first have to climb over the railings, and this she had no intention of doing. Perhaps uneasiness came from the regular beat of the sea on the shingle and the answering rasp as the wave withdrew;

the rhythm of the sea was so much slower than the beating of her heart. A single, solemn stroke from a bell floated in from the sea; some seconds later she heard the bell again. Common sense told her the tolling came from a buoy; yet most bells rang from towers. When she remembered that she had told Mrs. Birch they were running away from God she was shocked by her audacity. If she turned she would find that someone was watching her—but no, there was no one in sight. Yet the feeling remained. She was under observation. Down there, perhaps, on the narrow strip of shingle a man was standing.

Jane began to walk back towards the town. Twice she stopped and looked sharply behind her. By this time she was not afraid; her emotion was too strong to admit ordinary fear. The vitality possessing her since waking that afternoon had found strange expression: an exuberant dread. Some trick of the wind had kept the bell-buoy silent but now it rang out again, with startling loudness. Jane cried out. A gull dropped from the air into the sea, and she watched it riding the waves; the bird opened and closed its yellow beak, giving cries that mimicked her own. She ached for human company.

Back in the town she entered an amusement arcade where youths were smoking and working the machines. A loudspeaker roared out some popular tune. The air was tainted with tobacco smoke and the smell of burnt rubber. A man in shirt-sleeves leaned over his counter and invited her, in a tired voice, to shoot a packet of cigarettes off a shelf, but she walked on and found a village idiot rolling his head and eyes inside a glass case; momentarily she had thought him real. At the far end of the arcade a girl was sitting at a desk. She too was tired.

"Sixpence to see the Hall of Mirrors, lady."

Jane had no money with her—her handbag was in the hotel bedroom unless Nancy had brought it downstairs with the rest of her belongings by this time. Nevertheless Jane did not hesitate. She smiled at the girl and walked through the door into a vestibule where she was confronted by a mirror which made her look immensely tall and thin. A loudspeaker was shouting with laughter.

"Hey, lady!" said the girl, who had come out from behind her desk. Jane walked into the main hall and found perhaps a dozen distorting mirrors. She looked at herself in each of them. She walked slowly and did not smile. Here she was all head; there her head was the size of a pin. A melancholy, childlike wonder looked back from every mirror that did not distort her features beyond recognition.

"Excuse me, lady!" said the girl across the width of the room.

Jane found another door and walked through, thinking it might be the exit. Instead she found herself in a smaller room. Here all the mirrors reflected truly but there were so many of them and they were so placed that wherever she moved she could never see less than a dozen reflections of herself. She was in the presence of a crowd. In some of the mirrors she could see the back of her head, in others her profile. She took a step for-

ward and the crowd of Janes advanced to meet her, or
retired, or turned away. Wanting to get out she looked
for the door and could not find it. The dark-haired,
wide-eyed women closed in on her mercilessly.

"No," she said. "Leave me alone."

The girl from the cash desk walked up to her.

"Say—are you all right?"

At first Jane could not answer.

"You look a bit seasick to me."

"I'm perfectly all right, thank you."

Jane walked like one shocked back to the open air
and looked round at a world peopled by other living
creatures than herself.

At half-past three in the afternoon the tide was high.
Having scrambled down the cliff path, the Inspector,
two constables, the ambulance-driver and his assistant,
leaning on a folded stretcher like a punter on his pole,
Knight, and a small boy who had turned up from nowhere, all stood on the rim of shingle looking across
the cove to where the mist shut down. The mouth of
the cove was obscured. The rocks where Knight had
found the drowned airman that morning were under
water.

"Go on, sonny," said the Inspector. "Time you went
home for your tea." He detailed a constable to take
the boy to the cliff-top. Up there a crowd was gathering round the parked ambulance. "We don't want
anybody else down here," said the Inspector. "You'd
better stay put up there for a while, Sims. Don't let
anybody come down." The cliff was only about forty

feet high at that point and they could hear people asking each other what had happened. Faces appeared,
staring down.

"I'm going to catch prawns when the tide turns,"
said the boy, showing his net. The police uniforms did
not impress him. Neither was he curious to know why
these men had suddenly descended on his solitude.
The thought of prawns made him stubborn, and
eventually Sims had to take him firmly by the arm. By
that time a new-comer had arrived. The Inspector
noted the cropped, foreign-looking skull and the heavy
boots. Knight anticipated his order by saying quietly:
"I know this man."

"Oliver, for God's sake tell me what's happened.
Where's Jane?"

"Jane's all right. She was fast alseep in the hotel
when I left her."

The Inspector took off his flat cap and scratched his
head. A wave broke over his boots and he stepped
back hurriedly. He appeared to be angered out of all
proportion.

"Well, where is he?" he said to Knight.

One way they could walk about forty paces, no
more; the other way they could walk perhaps thirty.
Beyond, the waves washed the foot of the cliffs. Gulls
fell screaming out of the air and banked away at the
sight of the men strung out now along the edge of the
water searching. After listening to Knight intently
the Inspector said: "Damn it all, man! You say you
found this chap at six o'clock this morning! Why
didn't you report it before?"

Knight held himself stiffly and looked back into the Inspector's face. "You're quite right. I'm sorry."

"Eight or nine hours gone by. Possibly he's been carried out to sea again by now. I don't know. Damn it all, this is a serious matter. If we ever find the poor devil I should think the coroner will have quite a speech to make to you."

The men who had been searching along the narrow strip of shore now returned and said they had found nothing.

"He was just about where that gull's riding. There are rocks under there. I got the impression he was pretty firmly wedged. When the tide goes down I reckon he'll still be there. If not, he's probably ashore farther round the bay."

"Who are you looking for?" said Hesketh.

Knight walked with the Inspector along the bank of shingle. As they went the Inspector shot questions at him. Was he on holiday? Was he on leave from the armed forces? As though to emphasize his displeasure he even asked a question to which he already knew the answer. What was Knight's name? To all these questions truthful answers were given. As soon as the Inspector understood that Knight was an R.A.F. officer his manner changed appreciably. He was politer but no less bewildered.

"Why didn't you report the matter immediately?" he asked for the third time. "What have you been doing all the morning?"

"If you think it's necessary I'll make a statement at the police-station afterwards," said Knight, and sat

down to remove his shoes and stockings. There were
people on the cliff-top above; by this time the nature
of the search had become so obvious that all were
silent.

"What makes it so bloody annoying," said the Inspector, "is that if you'd waited another two or three
hours before reporting I shouldn't have had to waste
all that time hanging about. The tide would have been
well out by then." It was an attempt at humour and it
sounded savage.

But Knight could not wait for the tide to fall. Having wasted so much time he could waste no more. The
shingle cut his feet so he moved out to the sand and
prepared to wade or swim round the margin of the
cove until he reached the point where he calculated
the body might have grounded. It was a crazy idea.
By walking along the top of the cliff he could have
reached his destination more quickly; but he wanted
to demonstrate zeal—not to the inspector but to himself. The Inspector ordered him to come back. The
next wave rose to his thighs but he pressed on. There
was certainly no danger. The tide was on the turn and
the water was running slack, swilling round the cove
like liquid in an idly tilted cup. He could even see, a
hundred yards away, the rocks where Jane and he had
come ashore that morning. The mist was lifting. The
sea gleamed like pewter. Hearing splashing, he turned
and saw that Hesketh, fully clothed, was wading towards him. He pressed on the more quickly and Hesketh followed, calling: "Come back, you fool."

Knight could feel the sand spraying up between his

toes. The face of the cliff had crumbled, and at this point the waves washed the debris into smooth and shining amber. A rusty bicycle-frame, a felt hat, driftwood, and ice-cream cartons—all these in turn caught Knight's eye. He climbed on to a rock and waited for Hesketh to come up with him.

"Mind you don't get your feet wet, my dear," he said as Hesketh unwarily stepped into a hole where the water rose to his waist. "This has nothing to do with you. Why don't you mind your own business?"

"But it might be extremely dangerous to—"

"There's no danger at all. I'm going to follow the shore round to where I think this chap might be; then I'm going back to the hotel to get changed. You can see both Jane and myself there if you want to. Only don't follow me now. This has nothing to do with you."

About five yards of water separated them. Hesketh stood astride on a seaweed-fringed rock, his trousers clinging to his legs and water dripping from his boots; he shivered, dog-like, and Knight saw him as a kind of dog: he was in pursuit, he was possibly dangerous— "God knows!" Knight thought, "he has the right to be dangerous!"—yet at the moment he was fawning. Hesketh's light, almost feminine voice added to the mystery. Nothing could have been more mysterious than Hesketh's sudden appearance at the cottage— with no anger, it seemed—with none of the conventional feelings of the outraged husband, but only a concern that Knight and Jane should get away before McKendrick caught up with them.

"Please be sensible, Oliver."

Knight slipped off his rock and went floundering on through the shallow water. He knew that he was acting like a fool but desperation would allow him to behave in no other way. He tried to concentrate on the job in hand. No sooner did he see his vision of the drowned airman—than it occurred to him how unendurable it would be if Hesketh were to make the find. Hesketh was a civilian. He did not understand the tact of a soldier in the presence of the dead; he would slobber, be sentimental. Worst of all, he might be shocked.

Because Hesketh had not moved from his rock, Knight turned and shouted: "Stay there! I'll be back in a minute."

This was the signal for Hesketh to jump into the water and wade after him. On all sides, now, there was brilliance. The mist was lifting. In deep water there was a fly-like, darting sparkle. Knight waited for Hesketh to come up with him, and spoke in a high, strained voice: "If you go back and wait I'll be with you in five minutes." His self-control broke, and he began swearing. Hesketh's face revealed nothing but concern. "Don't you understand," Knight said wildly, "what Jane and I have done to you?"

The Inspector with a group of people round him was standing on the cliff-top at a point above them, shouting, but his words were masked by the surf. The wind had veered. Out at sea a deep-toned bell could be heard. Hesketh's face was a blank.

"All right, Oliver, I'll go back and wait if you like. I only wanted to help."

He splashed back to the shore, and Knight stared after him. In that moment he knew that there was no chance of finding the airman; he had waited too long, the day was wasted, all his zeal was in vain—and indeed it was absurd. He was behaving foolishly. But pride made him continue the search for another half an hour. By this time the tide had fallen sufficiently for him to return by jumping from one patch of sand to another, from rock to rock. The afternoon had become warm. His legs were brown to the knees with wet sand. On the cliff the wind-screen of the ambulance flashed in the sun. A motor-boat had appeared in the cove and a man in a blue jersey was examining the shore through glasses. When Knight returned to Hesketh he felt worn out by jealousy—a jealousy that involved the dead airman and Jane equally; for both of them he had had to compete with Hesketh. Yet now that the airman had gone, Jane, too, seemed remote.

"Well?" said Knight wearily.

Hesketh had removed his boots and socks and laid them in the thin sunshine to dry. Now he put them on again, wet as they were. He drew on the socks with deliberation. It might have been two or three minutes before he finally laced his boots and stood up. The movement seemed to release a marine reek of seaweed and brine. He tossed a pebble from his right hand to his left. All this time Knight's eyes had not left his face.

"Let's go back to the town, Oliver."

"I'm not leaving this beach until I find that type, if I stay here all night."

"How's Jane?"

Knight shrugged. He did not know how to answer such an absurd question.

"Have you quarrelled, Oliver?"

"What makes you think we might have quarrelled?"

"You've no right to leave her alone all this time." Hesketh was flushed with indignation. "You left the hotel at half past two. I know. I saw you."

"Listen," said Knight deliberately. "Jane and I have been sleeping together. Do you understand that? She has left you—do you understand? We are adulterers, and you, d'you know what you are? Listen! You're a cuckold. You don't seem to understand what we've done. You ask how she is. For Christ's sake! You don't ask how I am. I'm very well, thank you. I'll tell you something else. This morning we went swimming. Yes, out there! In this very bay. She tried to drown us both. But I pulled her out. We're both very well, thank you! Do—you—understand?" He stood so close to Hesketh, looking into his pale eyes, that he could speak little above a whisper.

"Helen thought I didn't understand, too. But I do!"

"Helen?"

"She came to Luton. I don't know how she knew you were there. Then we both went to Worcester. Where she is now, I just don't know. Perhaps she's still at Worcester. Perhaps she's gone home. I do understand, Oliver, far better than you think." Knight turned and marched to the edge of the sea where he squatted abruptly, and examined the hair-like ripples which at the moment of return to the parent wave were absorbed by the sand. There was an optical illusion.

The sea, on an inclined plane, was pouring its waves downhill at him. Helen, he thought, Helen was his wife. A wife should be with her husband. Why was she not here? Hesketh stood between him and the sun and a shadow fell across his outstretched hand. He was reaching for a shell. At once he drew his hand back.

"Let's go back to the hotel, Oliver."

The two men walked up and down the beach, for the most part in silence. Once Knight told Hesketh that if he was so worried about Jane why didn't he clear off back to the hotel. She was his wife, wasn't she? He, Knight, was not worried about her. Occasionally he exchanged words with the Inspector. Their shadows were eight feet long across the sands before the spot where the airman had lain was sufficiently uncovered for it to be established that he was no longer there. And still Knight would not give up. Time and again he returned to the rocks where the airman had lain, and taking tide and wind into account, tried to work out where he should have been carried. The ambulance had gone, even the Inspector had gone; only one constable remained, not searching—it had been generally agreed that a further search was a waste of time—but pacing solemnly up and down the wet sand, and glancing occasionally in Knight's direction in a way that suggested he was there to keep a check on Knight's movements. The crowd on the cliff-top had dispersed; many of them had come down to the sands, and children were at play. All shadows ran towards the water. Several times Hesketh came up to Knight and urged him to come back to the town. Knight did not answer.

Hesketh sat on a rock watching his every movement.

The constable came up to Knight, stamping sand off his boots. "There's nothing doing, is there?"

"Then what are you hanging about for?"

"My orders are to stay here until you go."

"Then you'll be here all night."

Hesketh came up and said: "It's six o'clock. Jane will be wondering where you've got to."

"I'm staying here till I find him," said Knight doggedly.

"Find who?"

Knight turned on him. He was about to answer Hesketh angrily when the expression of profound concern on Hesketh's face checked him. There was now only enough mist in the air to mellow the evening light. The laughter of children echoed round the three men, and Hesketh's question: "Find who?" Find who?" was borne up by the sound like a stick on water. Knight was struck by Hesketh's dignity; the question had been put without rancour. Hesketh made an odd, deprecatory gesture with his right hand, almost as though he was withdrawing the question. His cropped head glistened. But there was too much abnegation in his manner to think he looked like a convict. He had taken an oath of service. He was medieval. He was a monk. He was a celibate. He was certainly not a fool.

"I'd like a few more minutes," said Knight. He carried Hesketh's question with him to the edge of the sea, and watched a child gravely fill a bucket. The dead airman was real. He had rested hereabouts and he, Knight, had found him. There was no deception.

A stranger had come, a stranger had gone. If he was not found today he would be found tomorrow; if he was not found here he would be found farther round the coast. Then why get worked up? Why was the thought of another making the discovery so unbearable?

"Let's go!" He returned to Hesketh and spoke abruptly. He nodded when the constable reminded him to call at the police-station as soon as possible. All three walked to the foot of the cliff and the scatter of people looked at them curiously.

"Currents play funny tricks on this coast," said the constable. "There's a regular whirlpool off the Point, you know. Wouldn't surprise me if this chap turned up under the prom in the morning."

"He's wrong, you know," said Knight when he and Hesketh were halfway back to the town. They had deliberately outpaced the constable. "Nobody'll see that fellow again, mark my words."

"You had no right to leave Jane by herself."

Knight stopped and laughed harshly. "She's your wife, not mine."

"You could have thought of that before." Hesketh spoke quietly. Knight considered how they must strike any one of the dozens of strolling people they met. Damp, flopping trousers might indicate they had been fishing off a groyne and fallen in. Yes, they might have passed for hopelessly incompetent anglers but for the policeman following closely behind. They were bedraggled like fugitives rather than sportsmen. People were bound to eye them with curiosity rather than amusement.

"You're quite right," said Knight. He had made a similar confession to the Inspector. "What are you going to do about it?"

"Do? What can I do?"

"Cite me in divorce proceedings; push me off the cliff; forgive me. I mean, forgive us."

"I'm not concerned with you, Oliver."

"Then why didn't you pester Jane instead of me? You must have known she was in the hotel."

"I can't see her without you. Surely you understand that?"

"No," said Knight after a pause. "I don't."

Hesketh asked many questions about Jane as they descended the road to the town. Did she eat well? Was she sleeping soundly? And so on. Most difficult of all: Was she happy? Knight answered this with an impatient shake of the head. He meant to indicate the futility of such a question, but Hesketh thought he was saying no. He stopped in dismay and said: "But she *must* be happy. You must make her happy."

"I wasn't joking when I said she tried to drown us this morning."

More questions followed. They were put with clinical precision and Knight found himself answering them as though he, like Hesketh, was interested only in her restoration to health, and that he himself was a mere instrument to that end.

"Excuse me, sir," said the constable who had now overtaken them. "The Inspector particularly asked me. He particularly wondered if you'd be good enough to go to the station and make a statement."

"I've no particular objection. In fact, I particularly said I would."

The constable flushed at the mockery in Knight's voice but made no comment. A stiff breeze blew in from the sea, dispersing the last of the mist. The shops were closing and girls came out into the streets laughing, leaning into the wind, tying kerchiefs over their heads. At the bus stops queues looked questioningly at the three men as, with Knight in the lead, they followed their shadows along the pavement.

"Wait here," said Knight outside the police-station.

"You don't have to make a statement, Oliver. You're wasting time."

"Time?" said Knight. The word made him pause. He hesitated with the constable poised at his elbow. Time! Surely there was a remark that the word inevitably demanded? At that moment Knight felt there was ample time for any duty he had to carry out; but he realized something vital had been overlooked, and the uncertainty caused him to speak to Hesketh with more consideration. "I won't be long."

As it happened he spent no more than five minutes in the police-station. The Inspector had gone home, and the sergeant-in-charge went through the routine quickly. He was a sharp, foxy man who took it into his head to play down the importance of what had happened. Drowned airmen were washed up every day, he seemed to imply; but he was nettled when Knight took his lack of interest as a matter of course and prepared to go. Probably acting under instruction, the sergeant asked how Knight had spent the morning.

Why had he delayed so many hours before reporting his discovery? Mr. Knight would understand that funny things went on in the world. Incidents were sometimes reported which had not in fact taken place; a girl would imagine she had been attacked in a dark lane, for example.

"Have you got in touch with the Air Ministry about me?"

The sergeant hesitated. "We sent them a wire, if that's what you mean."

Knight turned sharply and walked out of the dark room where he had been interviewed, crossed the stone-flagged hall, and stood blinking in the sunshine at the top of the steps. The sergeant was already at his side.

"What about your statement?"

"I'll come back in the morning. I'll speak to the Inspector."

"Well, I can't stop you. You're behaving in a damn funny way."

"That's right," said Knight. "I'll come and speak to the Inspector in the morning." To Hesketh who was waiting patiently in the street he remarked: "You were quite right. It was a waste of time. Let's go and look for Jane." He had to raise his voice because at that moment a drum-and-bugle band swung out of a neighbouring yard. They were a detachment of Sea Scouts, about twenty in all, and each youth was either drumming or bugling; the sun flashed on their instruments. At their head strode a youth in a leopard-skin jerkin, brandishing a mace. Faces appeared at windows. Small boys came running. The procession moved off towards the front, in the direction Knight and Hesketh would have to take. The march rhythm was inescapable. It was impossible to hurry ahead because they had to slip past or through so many groups of onlookers. They could not trust themselves to side streets in an unknown town. They could not afford to wait until the Sea Scouts had gone.

Together with the band, a crowd of children, and two barking dogs, they emerged on to the sea front where the breeze flattened the hair on Knight's head. Empty deck-chairs billowed. Flags stood out like trembling boards. To Knight it seemed that the wings of the poised bronze eagle quivered against the yellowing sky.

"Let's wait until the crowd's passed."

Above drum and bugle they could hear the whining of a crane on the pier. Demolition work was proceeding at high pressure. An iron girder rose in the air and twisted sluggishly. In the window of a café an elderly man in a grey flannel suit sat eating ice cream. A youth in a blazer made a joke to the girl on his arm. There was a scene of war; there was a scene of holiday; they were set side by side inconsequentially and the result was a strange, dreamlike evening.

Hesketh took Knight by the arm. "Jane's over there! See her? She's sitting in that little garden. What's she doing, sitting there like that?"

Jane did not notice their approach until the two men were upon her. Knight saw how at the sight of her husband she coloured and turned her head sidewards; her hair, stiff and untidy, stood out in a way that made her face seem smaller. She wore no stockings and he was struck by the whiteness of her legs.

"Allow me to introduce you. Mr. Martin Hesketh, an old friend of mine; Mrs. Hesketh, an even older friend."

"Jane, darling, I haven't come to make a scene."

"Now cut that out, Mr. Hesketh," said Knight abruptly. "Don't disgust us with your nobility. Come to the point, and then I think one of the two of us had better clear off."

There had been a shift of wind, and the air was cool, almost autumnal. Hesketh continued to gaze eagerly, almost pathetically, into his wife's face. Knight watched them both.

"Oh, your clothes are wet!" Jane tried to touch Knight's trousers but he moved away. "And yours, Martin. Your clothes are wet. You're soaked. What have you been doing?" There was real maternal solicitude in her voice. The two men drew nearer. Hesketh spoke easily, even a little gaily. Knight dropped his pose of bitterness and irony. An unpredictable friendliness had sprung up.

"No," said Jane, when she understood what they had been doing, "you shouldn't have done that. You shouldn't have got yourselves wet."

"The tide took him out."

"I didn't see anyone there this morning. I don't believe there was anyone." Jane stood up and the two men with one voice asked her if she was feeling the cold. "You were there all the afternoon just looking?" she asked Knight.

"I wouldn't spend all that time looking for somebody who didn't exist."

They walked slowly along the front with heads close together, so that they could hear each other's remarks over the drumming and bugling of the Sea Scouts' band. The procession was returning, the din growing louder. Jane pointed away to the southwest where clouds, raggedly overlapped, were releasing light in steel lances.

"We're going to have a storm."

"Let's go back to the hotel," said Knight.

"We've been turned out."

Even this remark did not appear to demand explanation. Knight accepted the situation as he would have to accept the storm which Jane said was coming. "I suppose I'd better go and get our things," was all he said. "We must find somewhere to spend the night."

"I'm frightened," said Jane.

"Don't be frightened," said Hesketh.

"There's no need to be frightened," said Knight. There was the same note of tenderness in both the men's voices.

"You're alive, Oliver. You're not in the sea. You don't have to go on looking for yourself like that."

Knight was excited by her words; he argued with her out of pride. Yet pride was not enough to conceal that he was on the verge of a discovery.

"I'm frightened. Don't leave me, Oliver! Don't go

off looking for yourself in the sea like that. There was nobody on the beach this morning. I must have you and keep you." In spite of all the arguments Knight could bring to bear Jane continued to insist he had imagined the dead airman, and Hesketh who walked by their side with bent head was silent with amazed despair. Out at sea there was a succession of heavy concussions as though naval guns were firing. Now that they were all three together once more they appeared to have no thought of separating. Jane walking between Hesketh and Knight had an arm of each.

For the third night running Knight was awakened by his dream. Not until he rose from the bed did he realize that he was fully dressed, even to his shoes. Curtains bellied out over the drumming window, and when he went to close it he saw a flare of lightning over the black sea; summer lightning, thunderless. He was still so dizzy with drink that he could not think clearly. He did not know where he was. Surely Jane and he had been turned out of the hotel. Yet there was the bronze eagle on the war memorial. An occasional wave broke on the edge of the promenade and spilled across the road. But for the storm the scene was unchanged. He was standing in the same room where he had dreamed the night before. In the intervals between the lightning the night was intensely black. Even so he closed his eyes in the attempt to be rational. "The dream," he thought: "What does it mean? What examination? More time for what?" As a boy he had never worried about examinations. Even at Cranwell where he studied the sciences and mathematics for which he had no aptitude he had always performed creditably. Possibly he had worried more than he realized.

"Oliver!"

At the sound of Jane's voice he turned. For some reason he had assumed he was alone in the room. His head ached. "I'm drunk," he thought. Then he remembered how the previous evening he had insisted on taking Jane and Hesketh to a pub and buying drinks for them. He himself had wanted to get drunk as quickly as possible. He remembered getting angry with Hesketh because the fellow stuck to beer. Jane had drunk nothing, nothing at all. He stumbled, swearing gently, towards Jane's bed.

"Where's Martin?"

"I don't know, Oliver."

"He's a despic—despicable cuckold!"

"What are you smoking for?"

He smoked little and it was certainly unlike him to smoke in the middle of the night; momentarily the room flared up under the match and he saw Jane in her nightdress sitting up in bed. "There's a storm brewing. You said there was going to be a storm. I got up to shut the window."

"Don't talk so loud. People will hear us."

"Where's Martin?" He did not wait for an answer. "What are we doing here?"

"There was nowhere else to go. We walked about until very late, talking. You had a lot to drink. We went to Martin's father but he wouldn't let us in. We came back here and walked in. There was no one to stop us. They were all in bed. Martin got in through a window and opened the door."

"He had no right. I don't remember anything of all this. You should have stopped him. What the hell does he mean putting his wife into a bedroom with another man?"

Knight struck another match and peered round the room to see whether Hesketh was asleep on the floor. Even now the dream clung about him. "I must have more time," he insisted to himself. Nothing—not even Jane's presence or Hesketh's absence—had so much meaning as his dream.

"What are you getting up for?" Jane was standing in the middle of the room dressed only in her night-gown; he remembered how it had been their first purchase on arriving in the town so very long ago. By putting out a hand he could have touched her. "Go back to bed, for heaven's sake, girl."

The front of the hotel was receiving the full force of the southwester and although the glass door which gave on to the balcony was firmly closed, the curtain stirred in the draught streaming through the keyhole and the cracks. Out at sea the silent lightning was lowered and as quickly withdrawn; but in that moment Knight saw her figure, naked under the thin gown, in sharp outline. She drew back the curtain and began fumbling with the catch of the door.

"Jane, for God's sake—"

"But can't I watch the lightning if I want to? You come too!"

Before he could reach her the door burst open and the cold, salty sea-wind exploded into the room. A picture rose and rattled on the wall; a small carpet bounded away like a dog. Knight's intention was to drag Jane back into the room but when he reached her side and she whispered into his ear: "Look! Look at the night!" he gripped the iron railing with his left hand and supported her with his right.

After the first shock the wind seemed more friendly; although it might be cold it was not chill. The clouds were torn apart, and the moon looked down. The night was a dusky pearl. Without the help of the intermittent lightning they could see right away across the white-caps to the horizon. But for all that it was a wild night. An occasional wave burst on the edge of the promenade, and the wind whipped off spray which even at that height they could feel on their faces. Then the flood of water, gorgeous with moonlight, came swilling half-way across the road, and for that moment they might have been afloat and slowly forging out to sea.

When Knight put an arm round her with the idea of drawing her into shelter he found her strangely warm. She enjoyed the night as her natural element.

"Oh, let me go, Jane. Release me!" he found himself pleading.

"Ah!" She sighed as the white incandescence flared out of the sky. To the right the cliffs stood up in monumental black but Jane's attention was never distracted from the play of the moon, wind, and water. She was fascinated. Her hair, quite ashy in the moonlight, was blown back from her brow; her face and slender throat glistened, and Knight was put in mind of the figurehead of a ship. Where was the voyage taking her? Where lay the harbour?

He picked her up and carried her back into the room where he dropped her on the bed. When he had secured the door he returned to her side and said: "You don't have to behave like a damn fool, you know."

"You're drunk."

"I always want to be drunk."

"No," she said, and he flung himself upon her, kissing her on the warm neck and above the breasts. If he were to forget his dream it would not be in the stormy night but in the fight of his body against hers. For the first time since they had left Luton together she resisted him, and to his ears her breathing was louder than the gale outside. When she said: "No, no, no," he was not angry; only apprehensive that her words meant there was even less time at his disposal than he had thought. Her body was hills, plains, rivers—a whole continent to be traversed, and the discovery made, the fabled gold-mine reached before the summons came from the jealous king. Gold-mine? Why should he think of gold? He was looking for a drowned airman. Jane's cry, faint and far-away though it was, startled him as the cry of the crazed vixen had startled him three or four nights ago. So recently? Then perhaps there was more time left than he had feared. He licked his lips and tasted salt. The briny spray, blown by the wind? Or tears? Or blood?

Jane tried to sit up but he pushed her back. She

spoke with suprising composure, begging his forgiveness for what she had done that morning.

"In the sea," she said, "when we went swimming." Only then did he understand. "It was wrong," she said, and then after a pause: "He would not have forgiven me. It's wicked. It's unforgivably wicked. Oh God! Go away and leave me, Oliver. Go back to Helen before it's too late."

"That's all I want. I want Helen." He spoke between his teeth. "You bitch! Let me go! I want to go to Helen." Although he held Jane in his arms he could sense that she was escaping. She was dissolving, like a wraith, under his grip. "I didn't mean to say that, Jane." He was shocked by what he had called her. "Please forgive me for calling you—" He could not repeat the word. "Listen to me, Jane!" Unless he did something immediately she would have left him for ever. He saw her spirit moving out into the stormy moonlight. This, unless he could arrest her, would be a final abandonment. In desperation he assured her it would have been better had they died together in the sea that morning. If Jane were to leave him he could never find the way alone.

When the door opened, the window overlooking the sea burst open too. Knight had failed to secure it properly. The wind boiled like a river through the room until the new-comer, whoever he was, had closed the door. Because of black-out regulations it was impossible to switch on the light. Knight stood up.

"Who's that?"

"It's me, Martin. I heard Jane cry out."

Knight went to the window and took some care to shut it firmly. He had to stub his toe against the wooden frame before he could get the bottom bolt to slide into its socket. Hesketh's presence bewildered him. Had he been waiting all this time in the corridor outside?

"Jane!" said Hesketh softly. There was no reply and Knight could hear him walking across to the bed. A minute passed in which there was no sound but the hammering of the storm against the window. A single flash of lightning—intense but noiseless—revealed that Hesketh was on his knees by the bed. The illumination was too brief to reveal what he was doing. Hesketh's voice, when it came, sounded surprisingly matter-of-fact.

"Go away quickly now, Oliver. You must get out of the hotel without being heard. I want them to find just the two of us together."

VII

I want them to find just the two of us together."
The words puzzled Knight. To begin with he took them to indicate that Hesketh was thinking of the proprieties: If a man and a woman were found together in a hotel bedroom the fact that they were married went a long way towards being an explanation; and an explanation would certainly be necessary. Jane had been turned out of the hotel once.

As the night passed Hesketh's words sounded increasingly sinister. No train ran to Cardiff until four o'clock, and Knight dozed in a corner of the waiting-room. All the seats were occupied by sleeping soldiers, and occasionally a snort, or a snore, or even the clink of a bottle, would jerk him back to consciousness. "*Find the two of us together.*" Knight stared at the popping gas-mantle. In the hotel bedroom there had been the ring of sanity in the words. They had been an order for release. "*Go to your wife and leave me with mine.*" Here, in the dim waiting-room where khaki-clad limbs were draped grotesquely across the horsehair-padded seats, and the gale still thundered at the sealed window, the words carried a threat. Perhaps he ought to go back to the hotel. Yet when next he woke his thoughts were entirely of Helen.

The local train was only half full, and Knight secured a compartment to himself. At the first stop he was joined by a sailor with all his kit who stretched out on the opposite seat and immediately fell asleep. Outside Cardiff the train jerked to a standstill and air-raid sirens wailed in the distance. A heavy-footed man walked down the track, whistling. Without moving his head Knight could look through the window at the end of the compartment and see a barrage balloon silvering in the first light of morning. "Now that they are together again," he thought, "everything will be all right." There was the sound of steam escaping from the engine. The morning lacked all movement. For a while, the engine falling silent, it lacked all sound. In that moment the happenings of the past few days appeared to Knight a mysterious ritual. The flight itself, the scream of the vixen in the moonlight, the distressed gull, the dead airman, the ordeal in which Jane and he had nearly drowned, his own dream, and

Jane's confronting of the storm on the balcony—all these seemed the movements of a ceremony for the composure of troubled spirits. And it had ended here and now in this moment of silence. Silence? He became aware of the wind. It blew with such force that he could feel the carriage very slightly rocking.

The sailor woke, yawning and stretching. He glanced out of the window and offered Knight a cigarette. The tang of the tobacco at once carried Knight to that moment in the hotel bedroom when he closed the window against the gale and Jane asked him why he was smoking. He stubbed the cigarette against the sole of his shoe and stood up, to look across an expanse of waste land with a smoking refuse-dump, to the derricks, cranes, and oil storage-tanks of some dockyard. At Cardiff, he thought, he could take the next train back. When he opened the window he could hear the remote atmospheric strumming he and Jane had heard yesterday morning, as they left the town on that absurdly early walk. If he caught the next train back from Cardiff he could be with her again before noon.

Three hours later he was standing on the platform of Reading station. The express had been crowded. He had stood in the corridor wedged between suitcases and kit-bags, and now that at last he had freedom of movement he swung his arms, he lifted now one leg, now the other, he braced his shoulders back, trying to work the stiffness out of his body. He drank a cup of tea and ate a stale bun in the buffet. There had been a shower of rain, and outside the station the roadway was steaming in a hot sun. "She's a hundred miles away," he thought, watching the troops carry their gear to the waiting lorries. Even relaxed in a barber's chair while the man shaved him and tried to marshal the conversation so that he might satisfy his curiosity about the customer who had turned up in such a stained and crumpled suit, Knight was thinking of Jane: the lightning had revealed her foreshortened face, lying like a mask of porcelain beneath Hesketh's scrutiny. "*The two of us together.*" Was there a threat in the words?

"Feel better now?" said the barber. He stood wiping his hands on a towel and grinning.

"I'm all right," said Knight quickly. "What makes you think I'm not?"

"Yes," said the barber in his thick, confidential voice, "you look a lot better for that, chum. Haircut?"

At the corner of the street was a telephone kiosk. Knight opened the door with the intention of telephoning Helen but the face that looked back at him from the small mirror made him pause with the instrument in his hand. "Hallo," he said to his reflection, "you look as though you need building up." The face had shocked him so much that he said the words out loud. The eyes were dark; he could see the veins in the hanging lids. The lines running from his nostrils to the corners of his mouth were powerfully marked. On the lobe of one ear was a fleck of soap the barber had missed. "Sleep, that's what I want." He framed the thought silently but deliberately. Outside the kiosk

he realized that he dared not telephone Helen in case
she should forbid him to come up to the house.

More time was wasted in looking for a taxi. When
he found one—and he had to walk back to the rank
outside the station—the driver lowered his newspaper
and looked him over, saying: "You'll find it cheaper
by bus, mate."

Knight gave him a pound note and told him where
to drive to. At the best of times it was a twenty-minute
run; that morning they were held up by an army convoy just outside the biscuit factory, and as Knight
shifted impatiently in his seat he could smell the biscuits coming out of the ovens. Until that moment he
had not realized how hungry he was. The nutty sweet-
ness that hung in the sunny air added a totally unexpected torment to the moments of waiting. Helen
would give him biscuits! Helen would give him food!
He had a momentarily clear vision of biscuits on a
white plate being offered by a pair of hands he knew
to be those of his wife. And now he was not merely
impatient. The yearning for food seemed to have set
off the yearning for Helen. By the time the taxi was
climbing the avenue of lime trees to the house the twin
passions had become a single, unanalysable craving.
He tried to remember what Helen looked like, and
failed. He was on fire.

Yet he dismissed the taxi when they were still a
couple of hundred yards from the house. The road ran
round three sides of a common before returning to the
red, eighteenth-century terrace where Helen's parents
lived. Knight prepared to set off along the footpath

that wound between banks of bramble and bracken but the driver called him back. Knight had forgotten his change.

"S'pose you've not just broke out of jail or a lunatic asylum or something, mate?"

"Do I look as though I have?"

When, some minutes later, Knight glanced back, he saw the taxi at the spot where he had left it, and the driver staring after him. A bearded man stood honing a scythe at the end of a swath of grass, and the blade flashed regularly in the sun. "Time," thought Knight, "surely they will allow me more time"; and he broke into a trot. A white dog rose from its sleep among the long grass and came barking after him. The bearded man shouted, and the dog returned obediently to his feet. A clock stuck the hour. Knight began counting the strokes but when he had counted up to five he stopped abruptly and listened to the beating of his heart instead. Knowing the right time would not tell him whether he was too late. Only Helen could tell him that.

Instead of the customary knocker the door of the house had an iron ring that hung from the jaws of an unidentifiable beast. Even now Knight caught himself wondering what it might be. Bear? Lion? It was, supposedly, a sanctuary ring from a church in the neighbourhood long since demolished. Knight had forgotten its existence until that moment. It checked him. Immediately beneath it was a white-headed bellpush. The ring was there only for ornament, but Knight, steadying himself, was on the point of taking it not in one hand but in two when the door swung abruptly open and a shortish man in a white linen hat stood on the threshold looking him angrily up and down, saying: "Well? Well? Well? Well?" Knight had not thought of meeting Holloway.

"Well?" said the man. "Well?"

They looked into each other's eyes.

"Where's Helen?" said Knight.

"Oliver, son." The man's fierceness suddenly melted. Lines of self-pity appeared on his face, and the large spaniel-eyes moistened. He removed his linen hat and began using it as a handkerchief to wipe his face. "What the blazes is happening? Nobody tells me what's happening. You know I'd do anything for Helen. Anything. Do you know what? I'm supposed to kick you out. Helen's mother says—oh, God, son, where've you been?"

Knight stepped past him into the hall.

"You an' me's got to have it out, you know." The man began whispering, and his North-country accent sounded the more strongly. "I'm Helen's father, you know. What sort of a way is this to—"

The hall ran right through to the back of the house. The garden door stood open and at the far end of the lawn he could see Helen herself, standing like a statue, looking towards the house. To Knight's excited mind she appeared to shine in the sun.

In his haste Knight knocked over a small table. The sudden movement startled Holloway, and he began shouting, launching into another fit of shallow anger. The same sun shone in the garden that shone anywhere else that morning but to Knight it seemed brighter. He paused. Brilliance came back from the wet lawn. With his eyes shut he called her name, and when he opened them again his tears broke the day into dazzling crystals.

She was walking away from him. He saw that her back was turned, and that she was making for the orchard. The turn-ups of his trousers, wet from the grasses of the common, flapped against his ankles.

"Helen, sweetheart," he said. By putting out a hand he could have touched her hair. "Helen, won't you look at me?"

The pause was so long that the sweat became cold on his face.

"Don't send me away, Helen."

She turned abruptly, and Knight caught her left forearm with his two hands. His grip was gentle, and she could have removed her arm had she wished.

"Sanctuary," he said.

Only then did he dare to look into her eyes. Her lashes glittered. She reached up to his hair with her right hand, drew his head down to hers, and kissed him on the lips.

A number of people stood around. Helen's mother fingered the ribbon of black velvet at her throat while she turned her head uncertainly from side to side, her *pince-nez* flashing in the sun. Holloway's eyes did not leave his daughter's face. Behind these two, with his legs planted unnaturally wide apart, was a man in khaki. Catching Knight's eye he turned away as though embarrassed, and removed his cap. A completely bald skull, pink as crab, showed up against the dark tree behind.

"Come on!" Helen muttered. Ducking her head as though running through rain she made for the house, and Knight followed automatically. Not once did she look round. Her white dress flashed in the darkness of the hall. She was moving so quickly that Knight knew she had gone into the drawing-room only by catching a last glimpse of this whiteness disappearing through the door.

"Well?" she said. Now that they were alone, Helen stood erect, looking into his eyes. She had taken in the details of his haggard face without compassion. "Well?" she said.

Knight kept his distance, staring. The face he had vainly tried to recall blossomed suddenly before him—blossomed and faded as he looked. He saw that she was ill with grief. The blue eyes were set in an accusing darkness, the cheeks had lost their fullness. In his joy at the way she had received him back this changed face was all that remained to show they had ever been parted. He did not feel the history between the wedding night and now. The lines on her face scared him; and then they made him impatient. He looked at her with the eyes of imagination, and re-created the beauty he had known. Incredibly, he had arrived! He was in the presence, almost bewildered to find it human! Helen was in the room! He was looking at her! He could love her without fear!

"Well?" she said again.

He stepped forward to take her in his arms but she caught his two wrists and pushed them away.

"Strange as it might seem," she said with the familiar note of irony, "I'd like to know where you've been."

"Not now, Helen. It can keep."

"Now! This minute!" she insisted.

"I've not seen you for six months. Your letters—I couldn't read them properly I love you so much. Don't you understand? How can men be away from their wives? I'd have gone out of my mind if I hadn't sort of—pushed you away from me. It's wrong to love anyone as much as I love you. I'd play tricks. I had to. I used to say to myself: 'Now for this afternoon I won't think of her.' But it wouldn't work. So I had to say: 'I'll not think of her for—well, for an hour, half an hour.' Helen, once I got very scared. I was flying, and it came into my head to fly home."

"You don't love me, Oliver." She spoke impatiently, and he saw derision in her eyes.

"Let's go out of the house and have today together. Just one day! I beg you! A day we don't ask questions. Can't we just be with each other? I meant what I said when I used the word 'sanctuary.' " He broke off and looked at her steadily. "Please forgive me, Helen." With a shock it occurred to him that the kiss in the garden had been given more for the benefit of her parents than out of welcome. He had rejoiced too soon. Helen was not his wife; she was a stranger. "What do you mean, I don't love you?"

She laughed. When she spoke there was genuine

amusement in her voice. "I'm not tricking you into making pretty speeches. I don't want to hear them. All I want are a few simple facts, and I mean to have them."

"Helen, darling." There was a chair between them which Knight pushed aside. "I will tell you everything that's happened during the past week; and I'll try to explain it so far as I'm capable of explaining it. But not now. Can't you see I'm—I'm—"

"Where's Jane?"

The name sounded quite unfamiliar when Helen spoke it. Momentarily he saw Jane through his wife's eyes and did not recognize her.

"You know that she's ill?"

"So her husband told me. Where is she?"

Where was she? The clock on the other side of the common struck the half-hour. Knight stiffened in protest. It was unfair. Time was running out.

"Why do you think I have come home to you, Helen?"

"I'm doing the questioning. You've not brought her with you, have you? She's not outside waiting to come in, is she?"

He could hold out only a little longer. Sitting down, he closed his eyes and tried to concentrate on the happenings of the night before.

"No, she's not waiting to come in," he said at last. From the window he saw the wind running east over the long grasses of the common. Blade, bush, and flower set eastward in oceanic movement, breaking in long flurries of yellow gorse. The bearded man was still at work with his scythe.

"Then where is she?" said Helen.

The white beard fluttered in a sea breeze. The old man rocked from side to side. He might have been on a boat.

"Helen, you've got my clothes? There's that uniform, isn't there? The one I had when I first came out of Cranwell?"

She took him to their room, showed him the uniform hanging in the wardrobe, and left him. He made no attempt to detain her. In the bathroom he stood with his head on one side listening to the murmur of voices on the lawn. A radio tinkled. A plane drummed overhead; the wind broke in the trees like water across a reef. His uniform reeked of camphor. He dressed quickly, and stood gazing at himself in a mirror with one hand resting lightly on his wings. Since the marching-out parade at Cranwell when he first wore the uniform he had stoutened; the cloth was as tight as a drum across his chest, and when he lifted his elbows the rest of his tunic rose with them. He undid the top button and prowled about the bedroom.

"Helen!" He called her name several times. He went out on to the landing, and called there. But no reply came.

After taking a particularly deep breath he thought he could hear a slight tearing sound, as though the tunic was giving along one of the seams. He tried to undo the buttons but appeared to have no control over his fingers. "Helen! Helen!" He went on calling from the bedroom. "For God's sake come and take this tunic off. It's strangling me!" He caught a glimpse of himself, red-faced, in the mirror. Why could he not get free of the damn thing? One of the metal prongs of the belt-fasteners dug painfully into the tip of a finger. He swore. The tunic seemed to have a malign personality of its own. The struggle with button and fastener was at its height when the door opened and Helen walked in.

"This tunic. It's too tight. I can't breathe in it."

Helen deftly undid the buttons, and helped him out of it, making some remark about asking a tailor whether alterations could be made. She stood with the tunic on one arm as though waiting for him to make some further comment. Obviously she had been crying; it was also obvious she was unashamed of the fact because she had made no attempt at concealment. Knight sat on the edge of the bed saying: "God forgive me!" over and over again while Helen looked on.

"I'm still waiting for you to tell me what you've been doing since you came home from France," she said.

"Please, please, let me think!"

"Think?" She stiffened with anger. "There's nothing to think about. Except excuses. Oliver, for God's sake!" She wanted to remove her wedding ring and fling it in his face, but the ring was too tight for the gesture to be possible, and sobbing she shook her left hand towards him. The ring flashed in a shaft of sunlight. Knight caught the hand, and in spite of her struggling, succeeded in kissing it.

"Somehow," he said, "I've got to show you this would never have happened if I had loved you just a little bit less. It must be wrong to love anybody as much as I love you. Listen to me, just a moment, Helen. I came home on a boat, and it was bombed. As it went down I could have walked to you on the water. But if I'd seen you waiting on the dock I should have been tempted to run the other way. There's something bad about all this. You're so—fair! Look, the back of your hand is like silver. I don't know why loving you should frighten me so much. When I'm away from you you're like a light so bright I can't look at you. It is difficult to come near you. Now I am here and I can see you I don't know why I should be like that when I'm away. It seemed easier to die than to come to you. Was there a storm here last night?"

"A storm?"

"It was a very wild night. We were in a hotel looking out over the sea. Jane went out on to the balcony. I thought she was going to jump into the road, and made her come back into the room. Hesketh was there. He told me to come away so that just the two of them would be found together—those were his words—and I walked about in the wind, knowing that something had happened, something had been broken, and I could come home."

They stood looking at one another, and Knight still held her hand. A curious, hesitant pride looked out of his face, and Helen knew it was pride for her.

Without understanding his words she had been moved by them. Her anger had gone, leaving helplessness in its place.

"Do you want a divorce?" she said.

"A divorce? I quite understand that—well, that you might want to divorce me. You've got every reason for wanting to see the last of me. If you want a divorce I shan't fight it. Is that what you want?"

"Is that what *you* want?"

"No."

"What about Mrs. Hesketh?"

"Jane? She must have gone. I told you something broke. She died in the night, and Hesketh said to go away, he wanted them to be found together."

"Died!"

"Yes, I told you. It all broke."

He looked up and saw Helen's white face poised in the air. The declaration, now it had come, was scarcely less unexpected to him than it had been to her, and he turned away so that she would not see his face.

"But it's incredible. Was she taken ill?"

He stood at the window. The bearded man had now propped his scythe up to hone it once more, and Knight watched until the stone was put away in its bag, and the man had rocked steadily away behind a mound of gorse. Only then could Knight find it possible to speak.

"When I arrived, Helen, why did you kiss me?"

She did not answer. He turned and repeated the question. She had not moved from the position in which he had left her. The tips of her fingers rested on the back of a chair, and she was looking straight ahead. He repeated the question.

"I don't know, Oliver," she said.

The miracle had not come about. He had run too late for sanctuary.

"I'm not worth it, Helen." He picked up the jacket from the chair in front of her, bent hurriedly, and brushed the backs of her fingers with his lips, muttered: "God bless!" and walked out of the room.

The two men, one in police clothes, the other in mufti, climbed out of the car, and stood momentarily dazed by the heat. The red terrace stood between them and the wind. Tar bubbled in the road. Over the radiator, air and vapour trembled in silence.

"This is it," said the man in plain clothes.

At the open front door they hesitated. The policeman removed his flat cap, and using it as a fan, flicked air over his face. The detective-inspector put an index-finger on the bell-push, and stood with sweat running into his eyes while the brisk ring faded. When Mrs. Holloway appeared at the door he was examining a curiously marked pelargonium.

"This *is* nice," he said to her. "A new one on me. Pillar-box red and white, all in the one petal. Are you Mrs. Holloway?"

"Come inside at once, both of you!" she ordered. The rimless *pince-nez* flashed once, twice, like a semaphore. Once she had the two men in her drawing-room she turned on them even more fiercely. "How dare you come without an appointment? It might have been inconvenient. What's your name, may I ask?" she said to the man in plain clothes.

"Everett. Detective-Inspector Everett."

"I see no necessity for bringing a uniformed constable with you, Mr. Everett. What do you want?"

"Well, if I may say so, ma'am, our visit doesn't seem to have taken you by surprise; not so much as all that, anyway. Mind if we sit down?" He wiped his face with a handkerchief. "This is a matter of routine, you understand."

"Edgar!" She raised her voice, calling for her husband. "I don't know, Mr. Everett, by what authority you're here. I'm sure the Air Ministry wouldn't have wished it. My son-in-law has given particularly distinguished service. A week ago he was picked up out of the sea, he's been taking a rest, and he'll be returning to duty in due course. She jerked the sentences out. The black velvet ribbon quivered at her throat. "A week ago! Only a week ago! He was in hospital before that."

"He's not here now, by any chance, is he, Mrs. Holloway?"

"I don't think you can see my daughter, either. She's indisposed."

Holloway came slowly into the room, looking about him as though for a mislaid pipe. He was so embarrassed that he might have wandered out again had not his wife spoken sharply.

"Edgar, these men are policemen, though what

they want with us I've not the slightest idea. Have you a search-warrant, Mr. Everett?"

"All right, Tim," said Everett in a tired voice, "better go and wait in the car, there's a good chap."

Mrs. Holloway raised her little chin.

"No, don't you let him, Edgar. We can't have a policeman outside the house for all the neighbours to look at. They'll think you've been embezzling the company's funds."

"Sit down again, Tim."

"My son-in-law is not a deserter. It's preposterous. Mr. Knight is a Regular officer, and if everyone had served the country half so well we shouldn't have Hitler on the other side of the Channel at this very moment. I shall speak to the Air Ministry myself. Edgar, you'll speak to the Air Ministry."

The settee twanged musically under the detective-inspector's weight, and he tried to move as little as possible for fear of breaking a spring. "I wish you hadn't mentioned search-warrants, Mrs. Holloway."

"For heaven's sake come to the point, man," Holloway shouted at him. "Coming into anybody's house like this! We've got other things to do. We're busy people!"

Everett was unmoved. "I wish you hadn't mentioned search-warrants. This is a friendly visit, to ask you to help us. You mustn't jump to the wrong conclusions. This is a routine visit. I know perfectly well that you haven't seen your son-in-law since he came back from France. I also know that for the past few days he's been travelling about the country with a young woman who is not his wife."

"Well, dammit!" said Holloway, "we're men of the world!"

"Mr. Everett, what's that got to do with you?" Mrs. Holloway flushed with indignation. "What you say may be true, it may not be true. The young woman, as you call her, is an old friend of the family. She's a much older woman than my son-in-law. She was kind to him when he was a child."

"Did you know the lady, Mrs. Holloway?"

"Well—" Holloway began, but his wife interrupted him.

"Of course we know her. I told you she's a friend of the family. But this is no business of yours. Now you must tell us what you want."

Everett shot a glance at the constable at his side, raising an eyebrow.

"Well, you'll be very sorry to hear, then," he said to the Holloways, "that this woman was found dead this morning in a seaside hotel."

Listening from the next room, Knight half turned and then stopped. He dared not make a step for fear of falling. His body was numb from the waist down, as though some nerve-centre had been sought out and struck by a merciless enemy. "Then it is true," he thought. She appeared to him with singular clarity as he had seen her in the air-raid shelter at Luton, leaning forward to hold the hand of a child, and shining with a quite unexpected beauty. He relived the happenings of that night with intensity. They were out under the stars again, and Jane was asking the boy whether he had ever seen the sea. The boy ran away, as he had run away before. On the other side of the door the voice said: "He always does that." "Let's go home, darling," Hesketh said again. "Yes, let's go home," she said, and Knight saw her sleeping with a spot of light glistening on the closed lid of her left eye. He spoke her name aloud.

For the first time he noticed that he was not alone in the room. The bald-headed man had come in from the garden. He must have heard what the detective-inspector said, because the house was so quiet that even now they could hear the creaking of springs from the drawing-room. The major—in spite of his baldness he could not have been much more than thirty—looked at Knight curiously.

Knight went over to him and said in a low voice: "Did you hear what he said? He said she was—" This was an appeal. He wanted the major to deny that the detective-inspector had said anything of the sort; failing that, the major must help him meet the grief by—well, by advice; to explain, in a word, what it was to die. Knight walked into the garden, ashamed that anyone, even the bald-headed major who now appeared a very old acquaintance, should witness his grief. The major followed him.

"Don't you remember me?"

"Yes, your name is Frost. You were the D.A.P.M. at Dieppe, and you put me on the *Dundas*."

The two men walked the length of the garden, ducked under an apple tree, and passing through a door in the wall, found themselves in a lane. On the other side of the lane was woodland.

"What are you doing in this part of the world, Major?"

"Oh, I just happened by. Cigarette?"

The two men penetrated the woodland for some distance, came on a felled tree, and sat there smoking. Here and there patches of still-wet foliage were discovered by the sun and set flashing like green mirrors.

"I was curious to know whether you'd survived that bombing," said Frost. "We met under strange circumstances, you'll remember. I've a pal in the Air Ministry, so I thought I'd call. When I was there I happened to run into your C.O. Fellow named McKendrick."

Knight nodded. He was aware of an unpleasantness he could not identify. When he had stubbed out the butt of his cigarette he realized there was a rankness in the air.

"So you ran into old Mac. That still doesn't explain how you got here."

"Oh, McKendrick told me a long story. My home's at Wycombe. How far's that? Only a few miles. I thought I'd pop over."

Knight recognized the smell, and stood up abruptly.
"Fox! Smell it?"

"No, I don't smell anything," said Frost.

They poked about, looking for any tracks the animal might have left—Knight with determination, Frost obviously not caring. Under the trees the heat was more oppressive than in the full sun. Where the wood cleared, willow-herb seeded round the lip of an ancient gravel-pit; at first sight the silks were vapour drawn up from the pool that lay there.

Knight found a patch of grass just in the shadow, and stretched himself out, lying on his side and cushioning his head on his crooked right arm. "Forty winks," he murmured. Almost immediately he was asleep. For the first time Frost was aware of the tumult of the wood pigeons and the noisy shouting of a cuckoo. He hitched up his trousers, and squatted, holding a fern in one hand with which to brush away the flies from Knight's face.

"Knight," he said softly after some time had passed. "Wakey, wakey, son! We've got to get on." He touched Knight's left ear with the frond. "Wake up, son! The flies are eating you!" Knight did not stir. Frost straightened up, lit a cigarette, and walked away to a seat on a tree-stump where he sat watching the sleeping man, and thinking of that curiously similar moment at Dieppe eight or nine days before. When finally he stirred Knight gently with his toe he had smoked all the cigarettes in his possession, and the shade had passed on. Knight blinked in the sun. "Wakey, wakey!" said Frost. "You've had the best part of an hour."

Knight sat us stiffly and rubbed the back of his neck.

"I needed that."

When their eyes met, Dieppe was in both their minds. There was a similar sense of catastrophe in the air, and they spoke to one another with the same gentleness. A rabbit bobbed up, caught sight of them, and made off leisurely across the chequered grass, flashing its scut.

"You wouldn't see that if there was any fox about," said Frost. "You must have imagined that fox. I didn't smell anything."

He gave Knight a hand to help him rise.

"Where do I get something to eat? I'm hungry. I've not eaten since last night."

"I heard that policeman talking. I heard something about a girl being found dead. Did you have anything to do with that?"

Knight nodded. He did not question Frost's right to ask. He knew nothing about the man that was to any purpose, but was perfectly ready to surrender to him.

"How did it happen?" said Frost.

"I wanted to get to my wife."

"No, I mean tell me just what happened."

The two men talked. They walked for a while and then they sat for a while. Frost produced a piece of chocolate which Knight ate. He also chewed leaves and spat them out again. They saw squirrels and rabbits; but for wild creatures, no one came near them until the afternoon was well advanced, when, finding themselves near a road, they walked to the nearest village, and caught a bus into Reading.

"Here's your boat," said Frost. "This time I'll come with you."

Worried by the sun, Detective-Inspector Everett pressed the buzzer for a constable to come in and lower the slatted blind. The tobacco smoke rose now in alternate bars of blue and white. Knight, with a meal inside him, had one idea in his head; he wanted Everett to send for a typist so that he could dictate and sign a statement but so far no opportunity had arisen to make this request. Except for asking to stay with Knight the major had not opened his mouth since they arrived. Everett sat fumbling with a pencil, and frowning; he behaved like a busy man who had been interruped in the middle of important work and resented it. Knight felt that at any moment he and Frost might be ordered out of the station.

The telephone rang, and Everett picked up the receiver, and in a way that showed this was what he had been waiting for. After identifying himself he said little but "yes" and "no" and he made notes on a pad with a pencil. He said "Good-bye" and was about to put the receiver down when he realized his caller was still speaking. "Righto!" he said, "I'll tell him."

For perhaps half a minute the three men listened to the traffic in the street. The blind had mitigated the fierce glare of the sun but it seemed to have cut off the free circulation of air. There were beads of sweat on Everett's face. He pressed the buzzer for a second time. The same constable returned and switched on an electric fan.

"Seems you're known to my colleagues down there, Mr. Knight. That was Rackett Bay on the phone. Among other things my colleague asks me to tell you they've recovered an airman from the sea."

Knight stood up eagerly. He was about to speak

when he checked himself, nodded, and sat down once more. The subject was not for present company. The police had never doubted the existence of the airman. Only Jane had doubted; and, after Jane, himself.

"I'm afraid you'll have to attend the inquest, Mr. Knight. Though I realize it will be painful for you."

Knight thought the man was playing with him, and kept his mouth shut.

"And that's tomorrow afternoon. Travel down in the morning. It's a formality, of course, but a necessary one."

"What do you mean—a formality?"

Everett stood up impatiently, brushing cigarette-ash off his jacket.

"Well, heavens above, man. You know the sort of thing. There's no doubt what the coroner will find, but it's got to be tied up nice and properly, that's all."

Unexpectedly, Frost stirred and spoke.

"And what will that verdict be?"

"Murder and suicide."

"Suicide?"

"Yes. The fellow—what's his name?—Hesketh wrote a confession. He made a very nice full statement. He had the empty bottle in his hand. Christ, you don't mean to say you didn't know?"

Everett stared at Knight with a band of sunlight, like a mask, across his eyes. The tip of his tongue appeared, and they saw the white teeth pressing down on it.

"Surely you knew Hesketh was dead, too? Strike me, but I'm making a mess of this. It's the heat." He dropped his hand on the buzzer but before the constable could appear he had drawn the blind up himself and the room contracted under the brilliance.

"We know now, don't we?" said Frost.

The constable looked from Knight to Everett, wondering why he had been summoned. Perhaps the catch which secured the blind had given way; the last time he had entered the room was to shut out some of the glare.

"That's all right, Jeff," said Everett. "Let's have a bit of light and air. Bring us in some tea, will you, there's a good fellow."

"What do we know?" Knight asked Frost.

"Flying-Officer Knight is naturally anxious to get back to his unit," said Frost. "It's probably in everybody's interest that he should get back as quickly as possible. He's a fighter-pilot."

"Who are you?" said Everett.

Frost identified himself but if he thought Everett would be impressed by the knowledge that he was an officer of the Military Police he was in for a disappointment.

"You know as well as I do, Major, that we'd have Horatio off his bridge if we wanted him for a civil offence; or for that matter if he had the sort of important evidence to give that Mr. Knight has."

"Horatio?"

"Certainly. You must have read your Macaulay, Major Frost, even if you haven't come across him in Polybius. You're not, by any chance, thinking of placing Mr. Knight under arrest, are you?"

"It had crossed my mind."

"Where that would get us I don't quite know. Maybe I'd better look it up in a book."

"Perhaps the Etruscans won't give you time."

Everett grunted.

"Obviously Knight thinks they'll give us plenty of time or he wouldn't have gone missing for a week. It is a week, isn't it?"

"Hesketh didn't kill Jane," said Knight. "I killed her."

To Knight it seemed crazy that they should all sit there sipping hot tea after such a declaration; but even he drank. The unsugared liquid scalded his throat. Sweat started out on his face. He lowered the cup and looked about the room with swimming eyes. Everett leaned forward across his desk, watching intently. Frost stood with legs planted well apart. Above the whine of the electric fan and the snarl of the traffic they could hear the remote drumming of an airplane; the sound came in on another wave-length, so to speak, calling in a quiet but insistent voice.

"The police are not interest in metaphysics," said Frost.

"This one is," said Everett.

"Knight, if you use language like that you are running the risk of being misunderstood. You may be in some way responsible for these deaths, I don't know; that's a matter for your own conscience. It's of no interest to the police mind, like mine."

"Major, has it occurred to you that I represent the civil authority, and you represent the military authority? I'd have turned you out of the room before now if it wasn't for that. Now will you keep quiet and let me conduct the interrogation in my own way? Knight, I must warn you that anything you say may be used in evidence against you. Did you kill Mrs. Hesketh?"

Knight could see that Everett was not going to press the question immediately. He was looking at Frost. The two men were embarrassed by the expression on his face; and Knight, standing up with the wind from the electric fan beating on him like a benediction, saw that they were both wondering about his sanity. Perhaps they were right. Perhaps he was mad. Only a madman would have killed Jane. But if he was mad then sanity was a kind of deceit.

"He said: 'Go away. I want them to find the two of us together.' "

"Who said that?"

"Hesketh."

Knight marvelled at Hesketh's stature. Jane had gone ahead into the storm, and Hesketh with noble dignity had sat down to write to those they were both leaving behind. They had escaped across the frontier, and there was the message to prove there had been no connivance by any of the natives. "No more victims," Hesketh had said to the authorities; "no one within your borders had any share in this." To Knight the message was forgiveness on such a scale that he trembled at the thought of rejecting it.

"I'm sorry."

Everett repeated his question. "I asked you whether

Mrs. Hesketh was still alive when he said: 'I want them to find us together.' "

Knight shook his head. It was the vital question, and the time when he could have answered had passed. If he had walked to the bed when Hesketh bent over it, he would have known. If he had turned from the door when Hesketh had asked him to leave the hotel without being heard, if he had ignored Hesketh, if he had pushed the man aside, if the more time that he had cried out for in his dream could be turned back in its course; only then could he have answered Everett's question.

Knight turned and made for the door.

"I must see my wife."

He assumed that either Everett or Frost would try to stop him; but neither of them moved, and when he opened the door he saw why. A constable was standing in the corridor.

"Everett." Knight returned to him. "Listen. I came to see you of my own free will. I'd overheard what you said at my wife's place. But I didn't know until I entered this room that Hesketh was dead. When we parted we were on good terms, and his wife was lying on the bed. I swear that we parted on good terms. You could never prove a charge against me. I need say nothing. And, by God, I shall say nothing unless you tell that man to stand out of my way."

Everett stood up and the electric fan fluttered his hair.

"What's in your mind?"

"I'm going to see my wife. You can have my word for it that I'll be present at the inquest."

Everett came round in front of his desk and exchanged glances with Frost.

"What d'you want to see your wife for?"

"What—!" Knight laughed abruptly, stepped into the corridor, and walked slowly to the head of the stairs. No one pursued him. He looked back, and seeing that the constable was gazing after him in bewilderment, assumed that Everett had signalled for him not to interfere.

Once in the street, Knight began to hurry. At the corner he looked back and saw that the thickset man in plain clothes who had been standing by the sergeant's desk was following on the opposite pavement. Everett had certainly telephoned his instructions the moment Knight had left that upstairs room; and now here the man was, head uncovered, grey-suited, and middle-aged, pacing along and not caring whether Knight observed him or not.

The previous night, holding Jane in his arms, he had thought of gold. Then, it had seemed, the fabled mine lay on the other side of an untravelled continent; now the mine had been reached and plundered. He was weighed down with gold. But the farther he went the lighter his burden became; unless he could reach Helen quickly the ore would have changed to dross, and the tormenting journey—travellers falling by the way, birds circling under the hostile sun—be all in vain. An aircraftman saluted him and Knight nodded back; he had no hat, and it bothered him that he could not acknowledge the salute properly. He walked through a department store but when he emerged into the street on the other side the man in the grey suit was still on his heels.

When Knight rang up from a kiosk he took it as a sign of grace that Helen should answer the telephone herself. But at the sound of her voice his nerve failed him, and he stood listening to her impatient "Hallo! Are you there?" for some moments before he could find the words to ask whether she would meet him in the town. "I'm by the bridge, by the boats. Could you come quickly, Helen?"

Now it was his turn to ask if she was still there. The wire crackled. Her voice had betrayed no surprise, no feeling of any kind. "She'll never forgive me," he thought. Catching sight through the kiosk windows of the man in grey he pictured himself as Helen must think of him—unreliable, selfish, faithless—and wondered at his own optimism: Why the hell should she forgive him?

"Yes," she said. "I'll come in the car."

Knight was so shaken that when he stepped outside the kiosk he walked straight over to the plain-clothes man, and asked him if he could row a boat. "Because if you can't you're going to have a tough time of it. We're going on the river." The plain-clothes man looked away and said: "I'm sorry, sir. You must have made a mistake. I don't know what you're talking about."

The swans floated in a wide arc round the moored

boats, and as Knight spoke to the waterman he gazed at the birds, wondering at their beauty. The past and the present were knitting together, the wound was healing. Like the two ducks he had seen on the French village pond, the swans became images of peace in a world at war. If he turned his head the nuns would drive up in their car once more, and seating themselves on the green grass for a picnic, exorcise devils by the beauty of black gowns and starched white wings about pale faces.

"Well!" said Helen. It was ten minutes later. "Here I am."

He started and turned.

"I'll give you five minutes," she said. "I've an appointment to keep."

"Five minutes!" Curiously enough she was wearing a dress with a large white collar. "You look like a nun." But they might not have been nuns; they might have been disguised German soldiers.

"Oliver, I've not come for any chit-chat. I wish I were a nun. I wish I'd never thought of being anything else but a nun. Why is that man watching us?"

"He's sort of tagging along."

The westering sun lent a pink to her face, masking the signs of care. The warm flush made him catch his breath. These were the eyes he had seen in dreams. "All magnets do not attract," he thought; some repel, as Helen had repelled, thrusting him out into the darkness. Even as he looked at her fairness he could feel her transforming love into a powerful negative force.

Not hate. It remained love but of an intensity so great he could not bear it.

"If we went on the river we'd get away from that chap for a bit."

She looked at her watch. "There's no time."

"Surely we've all the time in the world?"

"I might as well say that just before you telephoned, Major Frost rang up and told me to expect you. He told me about Hesketh, and the rest."

"I'm glad I haven't got to tell you."

She spoke quietly. "I suppose you're satisfied now. I suppose you're satisfied with all the damage you've done."

They walked along the towpath, their eyes for the most part on the water and the swans. Her voice rose. She spoke so vehemently that other walkers, out for the early evening air, turned and stared. To begin with she had hoped to forgive him by putting his conduct down to the effect of bombing; she had tried, with all her heart, to think of him as a sick man. But he was not sick. He was bad. If Frost had not persuaded her, she would have refused to see him. Her father and mother did not appear to understand; to hear them talk anyone would think a war excused any kind of cruelty and deception.

"You'd rather say all this than listen to an explanation?"

"Is there an explanation?"

"At least we might try to settle on just how much I'm bad. We might discuss the proportions of good and bad."

"I hate the way you mock at everything! Can't you be serious even now?"

"We might decide how much I'm guilty."

"Guilty!"

Two of the swans had followed them downstream in the hope, possibly, of some titbit. As Knight lifted his eyes one of the birds half rose out of the water, shaking its wings, but it settled back once more. Both birds were on the move, turning into the current. They stretched their wings in the pink sunlight. Moving in a wide arc across the water they gathered speed, extending their necks stiffly, and then ran over the miniature waves with their webbed feet, before, becoming airborne, they creaked off diagonally to the opposite bank. Knight looked at Helen. Their eyes met and she flushed before turning away.

She had accused him of mockery, but he could not have been more serious. He saw Jane and Martin breaking, like the two swans, into the air. But already he had no clear conception of the nature of their taking flight. On oath he could have declared that his ignorance was not innocence but he could swear to nothing more. Why, when they had entered the hotel after an evening of drinking together, had Martin not remained in the bedroom with Jane and himself? The events of the previous night were mysterious. The mystery was not dark; rather it had a brilliance that dazzled. The eye, blinded by too much light, caught glimpses of a hand frozen in one imploring gesture by the lightning-flash; by a human figure poised momentarily before the storm, by a wing lifting, and a feathered body turning over the water. It was a time for wonder rather than pity. With those last written words Hesketh had driven him out of the police-station in search of Helen once more. The words did not mean what the jury would make them mean: "I am guilty." They meant: "Be happy and free, love your wife, but love her, love her, love."

The five minutes which Helen had said were all she could spare him had long since passed, and they stood quietly watching the boats on the river. Smoke drifted from the chimneys of the town and deepened the evening light to a ruddy glare. Swallows flickered under the railway bridge. On the opposite bank a man threw what looked like a biscuit-tin into the water, and when the splash reached them after some moments it sounded like the snapping of a twig.

"What else did Frost tell you on the telephone?"

A change had come over Helen. She was as anxious, now, as Knight himself to protract the meeting. He remained quite passive under her scrutiny. The man in grey, farther down the towpath, had lit a cigarette. The moment he realized they were watching him, he checked his hand in the act of throwing the match into the river. Before he turned away they saw him place the used match in the match-box.

"Oliver, we could cut across the field and get back to where I've parked the car by the main road."

"Yes," he agreed. "I suppose we could."

"We could get clean away."

"We?"

"Yes, we could—"

The suggestion was impracticable—they would be picked up within half an hour; but that was beside the point. The gesture carried an unmistakable meaning, and although Knight did not lift his head or for some time give any indication that he had recognized that meaning he could feel his body responding; it was the same feeling he had experienced when Everett told him the airman had been picked up from the sea—but it was more violent. His heart moved. When the first violent throb had died away he put a hand out to Helen. He faced her. The blue eyes, he saw, were as wild as his own. Momentarily her strength failed; she looked away. But his cry of pain brought the eyes back again. He found himself silently calling on God to give him strength enough to meet those eyes; he called noiselessly on angels for support. Then, as suddenly as it had begun, the ordeal was over. For the second time Jane made her strange remark, that they were running away from God; Hesketh himself parted the curtain of fire, and Knight finding himself on the other side, saw the face of a woman who was in all blessed certainty his wife. They clung to each other, shivering.

"Did you know what I meant by sanctuary?" he asked.

At last she said, "I think so."

Some minutes later Knight called to the man in grey and said they would all walk back to the town, together.

A NOTE ON THE TYPE
IN WHICH THIS BOOK IS SET

This book is set in Monotype BASKERVILLE, *a facsimile cutting from type cast from the original matrices of a face designed by John Baskerville. The original face was the forerunner of the "modern" group of type faces.*

John Baskerville (1706–75), of Birmingham, England, a writing-master, with a special renown for cutting inscriptions in stone, began experimenting about 1750 with punch-cutting and making typographical material. It was not until 1757 that he published his first work, a Virgil in royal quarto, with great-primer letters. This was followed by his famous editions of Milton, the Bible, the Book of Common Prayer, and several Latin classic authors. His types, at first criticized as unnecessarily slender, delicate, and feminine, in time were recognized as both distinct and elegant, and his types as well as his printing were greatly admired. Four years after his death Baskerville's widow sold all his punches and matrices to the Société Littéraire-typographique, which used some of the types for the sumptuous Kehl edition of Voltaire's works in seventy volumes.

Composed, printed, and bound by Kingsport Press, Inc., Kingsport, Tennessee.